On The
Cusp

On The Cusp

An International Murder Mystery

Erik Erickson

REGENT PRESS
Berkeley, California

[paperback]
ISBN 13: 978-1-58790-690-9
ISBN 10: 1-58790-690-2

[e-book]
ISBN 13: 978-1-58790-691-6
ISBN 10: 1-58790-691-0

Manufactured in the United States of America
REGENT PRESS
www.regentpress.net
regentpress@mindspring.com

You can be on the cusp of something.
Appreciate the cusp, not the something.
Appreciate the moment now.

Ernest Holmes

PROLOGUE
1975

I CANNOT SEE the killer's face. I've never seen it, but the voice is always the same. I have heard it all too often. It is deep and resonant and always reminds me of a villain's voice in an opera. But this voice is terrifying, unlike the opera, which I've always enjoyed. This has an evil sound. It scares me beyond my imagination, and from the first time I heard it I knew it represented a fatal threat.

This time I know that my luck has finally run out. Providence is no longer on my side. This is the end of the line, and I feel a balance of terror and relief. There have been no mistakes and there will be no escapes.

He has me tied to a chair in a large room. Two old Victorian sofas face each other in front of a stone fireplace. An ornately carved coffee table separates the sofas. Four embroidered wing chairs fill in the corners of the grouping. The three windows opposite the fireplace are concealed by heavy draperies. I suspect it's morning but no natural light comes through. I wonder if Vanessa is out looking for me. What I can see of the room radiates age and wealth.

I might be somewhere on the Upper West Side because the room has that feeling to it, although I know I could be anywhere in the city, or anywhere on earth. The Dakota keeps flashing through my mind, but I know I'm no Lennon, and I wish whoever it is had killed me quickly outside. My perceptions are seriously blurred by overindulgence, but I do know that I was on my feet and having a grand time. My new acquaintances were spending freely, and everything was coming my way. Somewhere around closing time forever became now. It began in the back of the limousine, where my new friends were not my friends at all.

Under normal circumstances I would find the throbbing injury combined with my horrible hangover to be overwhelming. This is hardly normal because my pain is on the periphery. Even the blood dripping down my neck does not concern me. I was obviously hit on the back of my head, and now here I am, tied to a chair.

The man across the room wearing a ski mask is in one of the wing chairs near the fireplace, dressed in black, except for his sparkling white running shoes. Black sweats, tight black shirt, black socks. Even the ski mask is black. My ninja nightmare has returned with a grim reaper and sickle. This is clearly a death march, minus the movement.

The visuals could not be any worse, but it is the voice that makes me shudder. I do not hear it often, but when I do, it is calm and composed.

"This won't take long," the ski mask says. I cringe. "You won't feel a thing. Don't fight it. It's simple and painless." The masked man walks over behind me.

"Why?" I ask, buying time, playing my desperation. "That's all I want to know. For god's sake. Why? I'm begging you."

"It doesn't matter." The voice is colder than ever.

"It matters to me."

"Nothing matters for you."

"Then," I tell Dr. Peterson, "a gloved hand comes across my face and I wake up screaming. It never changes! It's been happening for months. I can't sleep. It's the nightmare that won't go away. I've had bad dreams, but they don't return like this every night! This is a total mind fuck."

"It will go away," Dr. Peterson says softly.

"You said that the last time." I feel like shouting. I think I might know my psychiatrist better than Peterson knows himself.

"You've placed yourself under a lot of stress, Andreas," Dr. Peterson says wholeheartedly. "This is a natural consequence."

"What's fucking natural? The same exact scenario?

The same voice? I've told you about what's happened while I'm awake. Someone is trying to kill me. These dreams are halfway toward being true. It adds up to being a real scary story. Will you believe me when I'm murdered? Please investigate my death thoroughly after that happens."

"Give it time," Peterson says kindly. "Trust me on this one."

"You're starting to sound like a lawyer." I think this is an insightful insult. Peterson looks offended, which makes me feel a little better. My intended humor has never worked well with Dr. Peterson.

"Sleeping dreams rarely come true, Andreas."

"Rarely? Rarely is not never."

Peterson smiles before assuming a more serious demeanor. "You're stressed out. You're worrying too much, drinking too much, doing too many drugs, and lying about it all too often."

I have heard Dr. Peterson say stuff like this before. It used to carry more weight. I recognize that his statements are psychological standards, calming tactics that pay dividends, emotionally for his patients, economically for himself. Everyone involved thinks it is money well spent, particularly Peterson. The psychiatrist is universally well liked and respected. He always seems peaceful and positive, both within himself and in public forums. The wise, competent doctor with a dry, self-deprecating sense of humor.

"Andreas, I have another patient waiting," Peterson says with a twinkle. "You're overwrought. But you're doing fine. Calm down. You're okay."

"That's easy for you to say. You've obviously never had dreams like this. Or recent experiences like mine."

"Definitely not." Peterson flashes his wry smile. "But you've given me my opening. You've heard me say this before, and I know you don't want to hear it again. Your intake and lifestyle contribute to irrational thought processes. Both waking and sleeping. You eat poorly and don't get enough rest. Any of these things can create unconscious delusions. Clean up your act now, Andreas."

9

"Dr. Peterson," I begin with a grimace, "I've never argued with your advice. But I'm afraid you missed it this time. What if someone is really trying to kill me?"

"It's always good to see you." Peterson's presence is powerful and benevolent. "We've practically grown up together. You'll always be a favorite. I mean this most seriously, Andreas. Call me anytime, day or night."

"It can't get much worse, can it?" I know I'm bargaining.

"Oh yes it can," Peterson laughs. "Things can always get worse."

"How much are these sessions with you costing?" I ask.

1

NEW YORK
AND BEYOND

HERE HAVE BEEN other times when I thought I should make a move. It might be the speed and smoke that makes me feel this way right now, but I doubt it. I have found that I reach surprisingly sound conclusions after using drugs. My chess game always improves, and it makes me a better lover. This time is different. It's worse by far, a bad predicament, puzzling, with no predetermined path. Recurrent nightmares that I wake up from right before being killed have convinced me that the time has come. And then there are two seeming botched attempts on my life while I'm wide awake. I have always been able to change course without necessarily changing locations. Now radical action is required. I have to get out of New York City.

"You're turning into the most paranoid guy I know," Vanessa tells me.

"I have reason to be."

"I'm not so sure. Especially as to your two 'close encounters,'" she replies, shaking her head softly.

"That's what everyone says. I can't believe it! You weren't there, either time. Why would I just make this up?"

"Just two unfortunate accidents." Vanessa looks me in

the eye. "Number one: You're still alive. Number two: Who could possibly want you dead? And number three: If anyone did, they would have got you by now."

"It's gratifying to know I'll get the last laugh. Giggling from six feet under. Saying I told you so. It's my favorite phrase, but it will be small satisfaction from that level."

"Clean up your life and you'll live forever." Vanessa looks at me and smiles her pretty smile. "How's the teaching going?"

"It's the same. It's okay."

Teaching is not what I had originally thought it would be. The students are apathetic, confused, or violent. Most are regrettably younger versions of their parents. When the bell rings, I become an authoritarian figure immediately. I only let up when they demonstrate complete obedience. Because of the large class sizes it is difficult to be an ideal teacher in the New York City public school system. I can do the job well, but not when someone I do not know is trying to kill me. Besides, the flow of conversation in the faculty lounge invariably leaves me depressed. The chairman of the English department has dementia, which no one acknowledges. The main reason most teachers stick it out is the paid summer vacation. They find it difficult to break old childhood habits. And tenure is forever, which cuts both ways. I know teachers who are still working who should not be still breathing. They wallow with their fellow conservatives. Ronald Reagan is their man, and they think his wife is a sex symbol. On close inspection, I decide the librarian has the best job in the system. I cannot understand why she is always so cranky. It must be all the sex thrillers she screens before allowing anything on her sacred shelves. I suspect she knows that it is ridiculous to censor anything, because like drugs, or any illegal substance, it can always be found somewhere, usually nearby. Plus I know that these kids can tell personal stories that would make us all shudder.

Despite doing nothing productive, and answering to no one's call, my popularity has risen within the school administration since I announced my departure. They are all so happy to see me go that they can't help liking me for it. Everyone pats me on the back and tells me how fortunate I am. I sense a lot of hypocrisy mixed with the goodwill, but I don't give a shit because they want what they cannot have, and everything is not enough for them.

"No responsibilities and able to travel," the vice principal exclaims. "I wish I were your age again."

"You were never my age." We both know only a few years separate us, but the evaluation is correct.

"Where are you going first?" they all ask. "How long will you be gone?"

I do not know the answers to these questions but amuse myself by giving different replies to different people.

"I think I'll go straight to Nepal and smoke hashish for a few months," I tell the campus cop, who is not amused. I have always thought humor is one of the major differences between common citizens and official authority. Cops are never mirthful. Generally, they can only laugh at sadistic jokes, and they never acknowledge simple innocence. Teachers who can't handle the classroom trenches become administrators. They do it because they're terrible teachers, and it is the easiest, most lucrative job in the system. Many of my fellow faculty members are extraordinary teachers, but the workload and pay drive them away, and only the worst remain.

For the first time in my life I do not know where I will be in the fall. I will spend the summer in the city but be somewhere else in September. I applied for a teaching job in Australia but received a rejection. Since the Aussies don't want me, I have decided I did not want to go down under anyway. The description of the continent's locale always conjures up images of a macabre mortician explaining the eventual placement of the body, and maybe the soul. My uneasiness has increased because I feel something terrible is gathering around me. Australia is not going to be part of it. Going down under in any regard is not in my plan, but I would sure like to know what the fuck is going on here, and who wants me dead.

I decide to take a walk around town and consider my options. There is nothing I like more than a pleasant stroll on a beautiful spring day in Manhattan. The exercise always makes me feel less slothful and guilty. It is Saturday morning and I have no immediate responsibilities. The papers are graded and the school year is almost over. I decide to buy some drugs and liven things up a little. I realize that it is no longer considered trendy to put manufactured chemicals into your body, but I rationalize. These fads come and go, and after all, it's the weekend.

I leave my apartment in Chelsea and walk down to Washington Square Park. My usual reliable connection is hanging out around the arch. I cannot understand how this guy gets by in his profitable business without legal repercussions. Cops are always walking about. I have a good relationship with my dealer based on a controlled substance. We chat briefly about the pleasant weather before a small quantity changes hands. I have been using variations of the product since my college days. My fondness first developed during late night study sessions. My appreciation for the high has never diminished, and my present dealer offers such a consistently superior quality derivative that I think he must be an honorary member of some special pharmaceutical society.

"You look a little tense today, my friend," the dealer observes.

"You would be too if someone was trying to kill you."

"Ain't that the truth," the dealer says as he walks away.

At this hour the sun is still shining on MacDougal Street, and I retire to the Caffe Reggio for a cappuccino on the sidewalk. I have a few hits off a joint while I sip my drink, then go inside to use their phone and call Vanessa. She is at a rehearsal. We agree to meet for lunch at a cafe across from Lincoln Center, and I'm hoping she has the afternoon off so we can shoot back to my place for some private afternoon delights.

I have time to kill, so I decide to cruise around my favorite haunts. The nicotine and caffeine mix well with all the other drugs in my system. I feel relaxed and positive during my short saunter down MacDougal to Bleeker Street. Even the obnoxious tourists and aggressive male hustlers don't bother me today. Everything is going my way. I am meeting a beautiful woman uptown for lunch. It doesn't get any better than this in New York.

I stop at a small bar for an Irish coffee and run into Will Kraft, the horrible German language teacher from my school. Kraft is delighted to see me, and I am so high I don't really mind seeing him either. Even assholes are tolerable when I feel this way. The good ones are really good and the bad ones are tolerable.

All Kraft can talk about is his upcoming summer trip to Germany. His package tour is two people short of a complete group and he pleads his case incessantly.

"Come on. You guys will love it," Kraft says. "And it will help me at least break even. It's only for a couple of weeks. I know we would all have a great time."

I know damn well we would not all have a great time. I can't stand Kraft and Kraft resents me. I have rebuffed all of Kraft's previous attempts at friendship because I suspect the German teacher is a closet Nazi. He brags about always voting Republican, and the thought of touring around Europe with this fascist makes my skin crawl.

"I don't think so, Will. Vanessa is too busy."

"Think it over, Andreas."

"I already have."

I down my Irish coffee and head uptown. I walk fast and nearly collide with slower moving pedestrians. I have spent too much of my life darting around this type of foot traffic, and I always find it amusing. It is a nonstop, brisk pace all the way to Nat Sherman's tobacco shop. I invariably love to see him behind the counter, because Nat is living proof that tobacco and smoke are good for you. People inhaling have obviously been good for Nat. He always looks good in a wealthy sort of way. It is reassuring to see him still selling, smoking, and breathing. There are no vegetarians hanging around this establishment. Nonsmoking health freaks are not welcome here. The patrons' yellowish skin and deep wrinkles attest to the fact that these are men who love their tobacco. They all look happy. I think of Nat whenever I start to feel guilty about not exercising more and still inhaling so often. And I am also happy to see that Nat has never looked better. I exit back onto Fifth Avenue and light up a raspberry-colored cigarette. I am secure with the knowledge that at least *he* is not going to kill me. When I realize I'm running late for my rendezvous with Vanessa, I hail a cab and have the driver drop me at Columbus Circle. From there I jog the last few blocks and work up a slight sweat. I tell Vanessa that I walked the whole way from downtown. She laughs and gives me a hug.

"Don't bullshit me," she says as I sit across from her at the rail. "You're high as a kite."

"I ran into that asshole Kraft. He bought me a shot and insisted I share a joint. Sorry I'm late."

"Will you ever learn? Why can't you recognize reality?"

"I'm under a lot of pressure."

"You're bringing it on yourself." Vanessa is disgusted. I can sense it.

She peruses the menu while I excuse myself and go downstairs to the men's room. My psyche wants another blow, and I am in no mood to compromise. When I return to the table I am feeling terrific. It is one of those moments that makes me feel that everything is in perfect harmony. Lunching with my wonderful woman makes it exquisite. This is the life I hope never ends. I admit to taking advantage of everything that has ever been given to me, but I don't think I deserve the death penalty.

Vanessa shocks me out of my stupor. "Sometimes I think you're out of your mind."

"Your perceptions frighten me," I say with my quirky grin.

"So what are you going to do now that you've quit? Living off your parents is no longer an option. Or is it?"

I am briefly taken aback because I do not think I have quit anything yet. She can see that I am confused. I detect it, gather myself, and shrug.

"I'm not talking about all your bad habits," Vanessa sneers. "I'm talking about your job."

"It's the same story. I still don't know what I'm going to be doing. I only hope I'm still breathing."

"That's ambitious!" Vanessa says. "Inhaling unhealthy powder is your problem."

"I'm too happy to argue with you right now. I love you too much."

"What about the arrest? Have you got a lawyer yet?"

"No lawyers for me. I hate lawyers. My father being the only exception. But he's corporate. I haven't told him. Anyway, the arrest just might be the thing to push me out of my rut. Kick back at the folks' condo for awhile and think it over. They don't extradite people from Florida for drunk driving."

"They should," she says. "You are such a fucking idiot. How can you be this stupid?"

"I love how you are always so supportive."

"If you don't make some decisions soon you might end up thinking it over in jail."

When she mentions jail, the bottom falls out of my pleasant reveries. My night in jail was enough to last me a lifetime. I felt lucky when I got out, only because I wasn't raped and no one tried to kill me, although I worried about both of those possibilities the entire time. I learned then and there that jail is a place to avoid. It can turn innocent people into monsters. I still play the "Come From The Shadows" album. Joan Baez said it best. "Raze the prisons to the ground." The sharpness of the moment gets the best of me, and I try to pivot back to humor.

"Notwithstanding my physical limitations, I think we make a very handsome pair." I say this with a turned up nose and a shoulder swagger, my best Mussolini impression, and like the original, lacking in subtlety or class. It gets a laugh.

"I think you're crazy."

"Your insights always frighten me." I flash the look that always serves me well.

Her large blue eyes look directly into mine. I look away, toward Lincoln Center, and then back at her.

"If I do end up moving to Florida, do you promise to visit me?" I am looking for another laugh. "Maybe you could move down and we could hang out on the beach."

Vanessa shakes her head scornfully. "This whole thing is ridiculous. I can't believe anyone would change their life over one DUI. Just pay your dues and forget it."

"I need a change anyway. I've got to get away."

"The great escape to Florida does not become you. Everyone there is over twice your age. Plus I can't see you riding around in a golf cart and napping on the patio."

"Speaking of naps, what say we slip back to my place for an afternoon of debauchery? I promise no legal repercussions, just lawful sex."

"I'd love to," she winks, "but I've got to get back to rehearsal."

She gives me a kiss and glides across the busy intersection. I admire her fluid movements and perfect posture as I watch her disappear. It reminds me of my own slouch and I throw back my shoulders. The quick movement runs counter to its intended effect. A sharp pain shoots across my collarbone. The drugs throw me into a temporary panic. I think I have either torn a major muscle, am having a heart attack, or been hit by a stray bullet. This is New York. All three could be happening at the same time.

"My god!" I lean forward and start to groan.

"Are you all right, sir?" a gorgeous passing server asks me.

"Probably." I flinch. "But if I collapse face down on the table, call 911 and tell them I deserve to die. Vouch for me."

It is a great relief when the pain subsides and my arm movements return to normal. I wonder what the hell it was and worry about the big one that will surely come only too soon. I leave the restaurant and walk to the bar where I first met Vanessa a year ago, just after she had arrived from Alberta. Her mother knew my aunt Margaret, my favorite aunt, who called and suggested I contact the young Canadian.

"You're the perfect young man to show her around the city," Margaret told me. "She is an innocent young woman a long way from home. I know her mother well. She comes from a very good family and I know she could use a friend."

"Aunt Margaret, I remember the last time you arranged a date for me. She wasn't pleasant."

"I still don't believe those stories of yours." Margaret laughs. "Although I always love hearing them. This girl is a ballet dancer. I've never met her but I hear she is quite lovely. Do me a favor and show her around."

It turned out to be the best advice I ever listened to. It was the dancer image that initiated my first call. I reasoned that the chances were high that she would at least have a toned body. On top of that, she sounded sweet when I talked to her on the phone. When she stepped into the bar I knew I had not made a mistake: The tall, long-legged Canadian was striking. I made a mental note to drop to my knees and kiss Margaret's feet at the next family reunion. From that day on I have not dated or even thought about anyone else. Vanessa is still too superb to be true, the kindest person I have ever known, and that is the reason she seems to get more attractive every day.

I walk into Central Park, where it starts to sprinkle as I circle around the Lake. I decide to cut through the Ramble and seek refuge in the Natural History Museum.

"Hey guy! Could you give me a hand please?" It is a very plaintive voice coming from a small knoll about twenty feet to my right. I keep on walking. "Hey! Please come over here for a second. I need help."

The man behind the voice is standing next to a bicycle. He is looking over his left shoulder and is slightly stooped over the bike. He sounds anxious and looks harmless.

"What do you need?" I ask.

"I have to show you."

I walk over to get a closer look and see the bicyclist has his erect penis in his hand.

"Will you watch me masturbate?"

"No. Not today. I've got better things to do."

"I'll give you fifty bucks if you let me suck you."

"Please put your dick back in your pants. No sale." I am hoping to avoid a scene. It confirms my already held belief that you never know what you are going to get in New York. "Don't ruin the day for anyone else. Make sure it's always mutual. Trust me. I know. I'm a teacher."

I leave the park and have a quick drink at the Donegal Inn. It will help keep me in good spirits. It is dark, noisy and smoky inside on a sunny Saturday afternoon when I enter the Irish pub. This crowd is seriously committed to sports and alcohol. Many of them are already over-prepared with drink. I quickly consume a pint of Guinness and a shot of Jamesons before exiting back toward the park.

My last few weeks of teaching are the most enjoyable of my short career. I turn my classes over to my student teacher, Natalie, an idealistic twenty-three-year-old. She is very smart and I like her, but I wonder how long she'll last. I spend most of my time playing Frisbee on the playground with the students.

When the school year finally ends, my frivolous spending climbs astronomically. Jazz clubs, trendy cafes, and French champagne take their toll on my meager finances. Worst of all, I have not formulated any plans, because I am riddled with doubt and indecision. All my friends anticipate my departure. I feel I would be letting them down by not going somewhere, but that is the least of my worries.

Am I allowing myself to be frightened out of town without reason? I have been aware of random street crime all my life, because this is where I grew up. The two recent events made me more than uneasy. I escaped both times, but if I had not functioned well, and been in good shape, I'm convinced I would be dead. I still bolt upright in bed when I dream about those close calls. I am sure I was the target. Of course all my friends disagree with me. Vanessa is increasingly skeptical of my conspiracy theories. I can't honestly say I blame her, because even I know it doesn't make any sense.

"I feel for where you're coming from," she says. "But you must admit, it's wildly absurd. Stuff like this doesn't happen to people like you. Who would ever want you dead?"

"I'll admit it sounds crazy," I sigh. "All I can say is you had to be there."

"I'm glad I wasn't. Who wants to be pushed in front of a train?"

"If the shove had been one second earlier I'd be dead. The platform was crowded. The shove was very hard. Luckily I was able to push off the side of the incoming train. Then that crazed car attacked me three weeks later. On my own fucking street, for Christ sake! In Chelsea! At three in the morning! I can tell you think I've lost my marbles. Why would you ever want to hang around with a loser like me?"

"Because nobody makes me laugh as much as you do."

Despite my indecision about the future, it looks better than it ever has, but only when the fear goes away. This is the first time I feel as if my life has not been charted out for me. Prep school at Dalton, right up the street from where we live. NYU with honors. I can say from experience that being the only child of a wealthy New York lawyer, and having a wonderful psychologist mother, does not necessarily make life as easy as people might think. Great parents do not necessarily make everything simple. But handsome always helps with first impressions, and I learned how to play the life game early on, because both my parents are inordinately kind and gentle. I liked to make them laugh, and they always encouraged my humor, because they were a consistently amusing couple themselves. The only time I ever disappointed my father was when I announced that I wanted to be a teacher. It was initially uncomfortable for both of us, but he eventually accepted my decision not to follow in his footsteps because of help from my mother, and we put that brief rough patch behind us. I feel sorry for my mother because I think she always wanted a daughter, but health problems prevented that from ever happening.

Everyone knows I consume copious amounts of drugs and alcohol, but recently much of my enjoyment has been generated by all the Canadians I've met. Vanessa seems to know every interesting Canadian in New York.

"You Americans are so self-centered," Vanessa says. "You take credit for all the good and deny the bad. Look at Viet Nam. You guys ruined the entire region. And then you pat yourselves on the back for getting rid of some puppets who don't do exactly what you say. Canadians have the whole world's best interests at heart. We have a better society."

"Even your good friend Peter Wilson?"

"You are such an asshole," she says with a laugh. "But at least you're predictable. I knew you were going to bring Peter up. I'm complimented. You're cute when you're jealous."

"Jealous fuck! I just don't like psychotics, Canadian or otherwise. The fact that he is desperate to get into your pants has nothing to do with it."

"We've been through all this before. You know how I feel about Peter. I don't think he is what you say he is."

I shake my head. "There is something seriously wrong with that guy."

"I've known him all my life. Remember? Our fathers roomed together in college. And he always speaks very highly of you."

"Of course he does." I'm becoming caustic. "Smooth Dr. Wilson is never going to get caught trying to blatantly poison your perspective. He's too smart and subtle, and he knows you too well. There are two irrefutable facts about Peter. Number one: he's in love with you. Who could blame him? Number two: he hates my guts."

"Wrong on both counts. At one time he may have been infatuated with me. But he no longer is. He's a rich, successful doctor for heaven sakes. And a very eligible bachelor. I've heard you admire his women friends many times. He may have resented you a little at first, but that passed. He always tells me how much he respects you and the job you do."

"Sure he does. Most doctors I know are condescending creeps. They're only in it for the money. Peter is a giant step beyond. For one thing, he's the only doctor I know who dabbles in the arms trade. I have a friend who knows weapons dealers. Your good doctor dispenses death with his extracurricular prescriptions. He's a major league dealer."

"You're just wrong," Vanessa says. "I can't believe it. He would have to be one of the world's greatest pretenders."

"He is."

"I think you're emotionally exaggerating your dislike."

"I kind of hope I am. But I know I'm not. That guy is out of his mind."

I wake up late the next morning thinking I might die before I get killed. Yes indeed, it's true, once again I have the worst hangover of my life. Even a cold shower doesn't make me feel any better. I am flooded with guilt and vow sobriety while I trudge downstairs to check my mail. My friend Cris has written me from California, and it is the best news I've had in months, maybe ever. Cris tells me he has finished his thesis and is about to get back on the road, going to Bali but taking his time getting there. He says he and his girlfriend Kerry are going to travel the long way around. They have freighter reservations and expect to be in New York by late August. The ship is scheduled to sail for Morocco in early September. I telephone Cris immediately.

"Is there any chance you might like to come along?" Cris asks over the phone.

I am ecstatic. "I thought you'd never ask."

"I thought you were still teaching."

"I regained my sanity and find myself unemployed."

Cris gives me the name of the shipping agent. The next day I am waiting at the agent's door before they open. The agency represents foreign shipping lines, including the Yugoslavian line that Cris has booked.

"I'm sorry," the desk clerk says. "We're booked up for the next six months. These ships are relatively small and don't carry many passengers."

I sense her indifference and am overcome with alarm. I have to get on that boat. My expectations have not been this high in a long time. My focused madman murderer theory still haunts me, but this is no time to be shy. It might be another "Titanic" but I do not care. I deserve an equal opportunity to go down with the ship like everyone else. It's much better than being an "accident" victim in New York.

"Accidentally on purpose," I say softly.

"What?" The clerk asks.

"I know this is going to be hard to believe." My life is on the line. Board the boat or bust. "I have an inoperable brain tumor," I begin. "I'm dying of cancer. The doctors give me six months. A year max. I've quit my job. My best friend since childhood wants me to accompany him on this voyage. Please, I beg you. Do a dying man a favor."

The clerk gives me a long hard look. I try to look as pitiful as I can. Vanessa thinks I should be an actor. The clerk disappears into another office. Five minutes later she returns. When I hear what she has to say, I have an inkling of what it must feel like to win the lottery.

"If you are willing to travel a level below the other passengers, on the sailor's deck, we can book your passage."

It is settled at last. I finally have a plan. I am off to Morocco in early September. It could not get any better than this, a freighter to North Africa exceeds my wildest dreams. I am off like Allen Ginsberg and Paul Bowles. Suddenly my world has been thrown upside down and I see myself on top. I am going to Africa on a boat. Now I remember how I felt as a kid before Christmas.

"So where are we going after Morocco?" I ask Cris the next time I call. It's hard not to cackle.

"I know where I'm going. You'll have to make your own choices. I'm headed across the Sahara to Senegal. This is going to be my around the world organic drug trip. I plan to visit every country that has ever been famous for its mind-altering natural substances. 'Yes please' is my motto."

"You're the travel agent of my dreams!" I can't believe what I'm hearing.

"Hey!" Cris exclaims. "This is going to be the trip of a lifetime. Around the world! I'll hit all the old hippie watering holes. It's the perfect time to go. I've got a great itinerary, but I'll save the details until we get together."

It is the last day of August when Cris and Kerry fly into New York. We're old friends and greet each other like brothers. There is a special bond between us; in addition to sharing experiences, we played soccer and lacrosse together. We've both had our share of love affairs over the years. Sex, drugs, and rock and roll basically define much of our reality.

I have noticed over time that Cris is attracted to particular physical characteristics, and Kerry fits his bill: she has a classic California look, straight from The Beach Boys, with short blonde hair and blue eyes. She is pert, pretty, and precocious. Her ready smile reveals dimples that light up the room. I hope I am going to like her this much forever, but I know this look can be trouble, because I have succumbed to it before myself. Kerry is three years younger than Cris, though she looks younger still. She is articulate and very excited about the upcoming journey.

"I think Cris is a genius," she says. "First of all he has the good sense to take me with him. We're all going to have nothing but fun. I've never even been to Europe. Now I'm going to Africa instead. On a boat! This is insane."

I am glad to see them both. It has been a difficult wait. No one else I know wants to hear about my phantom killer story anymore, and they're also sick of my bragging about my recent stroke of luck with the boat. I know my boasting has been unbearable, but my life is at stake, and it's great to see Cris, who is taking me away to safety, and away from my jealous, resentful New York crowd.

The normally cheerful Vanessa has been moody. She is afraid my departure will mean the end of our relationship. When I try to convince her otherwise, she often reacts angrily.

"I'm sick of listening to your travel plans. Can't you understand I don't think it's funny? And that I'm going to miss you horribly?"

"How could you possibly miss such an egotistical asshole?" I joke.

"That's a question I'm having an increasingly difficult time answering. Keep it up and I might quit trying," she replies. Our deteriorating relationship is a big concern. I know I want to run away. That is my constant certainty, but I am afraid of losing her when I do. I argue that other great love affairs have flourished from afar, but I am hard pressed to name any of them. Plus the thought of leaving Vanessa in the clutches of the big city makes me nervous.

"I can't understand why you don't shelve your career for awhile." This tack leads nowhere. I have tried it before. "Come along. This is the chance of a lifetime."

"I'm living my chance of a lifetime right now! Why can't you ever understand that? As a young girl I dreamed of dancing here. I worked my ass off for two years in Winnipeg and now it's happening. And you're asking me to give it all up for nothing?"

"Nothing? You call the rest of the world nothing? Believe it or not, there is life beyond New York. Long after your precious Baryshnikov is dead and gone, they will still talk about Marco Polo."

"Get off your high horse!" She raises her voice. "And you aren't exactly striking out to conquer new worlds. I don't see the three of you looking much further than drugs and self-indulgence. All you think about are yourselves and your selfish trip."

"Selfish? You think trying to stay alive is selfish?"

"You've had a couple of close calls. Big deal. You escaped and you'll be accident-free for decades to come."

"They weren't accidents."

"You're a broken record. Your massive fucking ego is beginning to play tricks on itself. Or trying to play tricks on me. Maybe both. I'm afraid your false fears are manufactured justifications for leaving me behind."

"Not so."

She is tired of two extra people hanging around our apartment every day. Cris and Kerry party late but always come back to our place for sleep. Vanessa has decided she can do without their smiling faces and ritualized grooming habits. She will never again feel guilty about the time she spends in the bathroom. Cris and Kerry monopolize every plumbing fixture. Their routine must be maintained at all costs. Flossing and brushing are paramount. They forget that others may have to use the same facilities. Vanessa is convinced that they think their bodies deserve more attention, but she has to admit that the two sets of gleaming California teeth are perfect.

"I guess it's because they're so happy all the time," Vanessa sighs. "I try not to blame them. And don't misunderstand me, I like both of them. I just don't want to live with them. I want them to leave. But when they do I know you'll be going with them. They are carrying you away."

"Hardly," I say. "I'm doing this of my own free will. And I wish more than anything else you were coming with me."

"I wish you were staying here and helping me out."

"I can't. I wouldn't be good for anything. Believe me."

I am the only one of our group of three who has a difficult time waiting for the ship. Cris and Kerry are enjoying New York to the hilt.

"I think the Stock Exchange is great," Kerry says as we walk through the Financial District. "That spectacle on the trading floor was quite a show. They buy and they sell, but they don't do any real job well."

"Speaking of people who don't do jobs well," Cris says, "I talked to the shipping agent this morning. She doesn't think the ship is going to stop in New York."

"What do you mean, not stop in New York?" My heart skips a beat.

"Apparently, there's not enough freight here. They think they might dock in Mobile instead."

"Where in hell does that leave us?" I ask.

"Stuck outside of Mobile with those Moroccan blues again," Cris sings. "We'll probably have to head south if we want to get on that boat."

My final night with Vanessa is horrible. She cannot stop trembling and crying. We make love all night, and she finally weeps herself to sleep. Four hours later three vagabonds are on the sidewalk waiting for a taxi to Hertz.

We head south. Kerry complains as we cruise along in the rented car. "I've always hated Southerners," she says. "Their voices make them sound like the idiots they are. Look at their voting habits. Jimmy Carter is an aberration. The only decent governor Georgia's ever had. Most of the white people think George Wallace and Strom Thurmond would be an ideal ticket. They'd elect Hitler if he was on the ballot."

"What about New Orleans?" Cris says. "It's more fun than San Francisco."

"Cris," she says, "I studied political science. I wrote a paper on southern voting patterns. I've never been to New Orleans. And quit contradicting me."

"I'm working on it. But your generalizations keep giving me more material."

"I'm always right."

The amphetamine we have ingested makes me feel better, and I know our souls and psyches are saturated as we speed down the interstate. I am relieved that Cris is behind the wheel, and that the cooler with the beer in it is on the back seat next to me. After a few hours, time is something I no longer understand. The brew slides down easily as we roll along. I have noticed that the interstate has given way to a winding two lane road. There are few towns, lots of trees, and spectacular views. I am not sure where this transition took place, or when, but I am sure it is a clear indication that I should slow down and take better stock of my situation. A mental compromise is reached. Instead of applying the brakes, I will coast for a while and make a full assessment later.

"By the way," I say, "where are we?"

"I decided to get off the freeway and take the scenic route." Cris answers with a broad smile. "We're on the Blue Ridge Parkway. Probably somewhere in Virginia."

Cris notices the tank is low and we pull off to find gas. It is several miles to the nearest small town.

"Oh my god! Look at that." Kerry directs our attention to the billboard on the outskirts of town.

"The Ku Klux Klan Welcomes You to North Carolina," the sign reads.

"Jesus Christ, Cris." Kerry exclaims. "Should we get back on the interstate so we can drive above this shit? Don't forget, this is the state that sent Jesse Helms to the Senate. These people are collectively brain damaged. We're talking Cro-Magnon."

"I must admit Cris," I say, watching a pickup roar past us on the right hand side, "this doesn't look good."

"I've never been to North Carolina before." Cris grits his teeth. "But one thing is for sure. There are certain elements in this area that do not encourage minority tourism. I can see that clearly. The billboard is disturbing. I hate to say it, but right now I'm glad I'm white."

"You're in the Whiteness Protection Program," I chime in from the back seat. "Thankfully, we all are."

At eight o'clock we drive up to a convenience store in Boone, North Carolina, where we buy more beer and ask the clerk where we can buy whisky. Cris is beginning to grind his teeth and thinks it might help take the edge off. Plus we all agree it might put us on the same level as the local populace. The pockmarked clerk gives us a vacant stare and begins to scratch his ear.

"Why do all of these people look like their parents were siblings?" Kerry asks under her breath. "I feel like I've inadvertently walked onto the set of a horror movie. Everyone I see has already mutated. It's not a pleasant sight."

"Hey dudes, what's goin' on?"

The strange voice with the strong twang comes from a young man standing behind us in line. I think he is obviously the local stock car driver Richard Petty look-alike winner, although Petty cannot possibly have this many tattoos hidden beneath his driver's uniform. But this kid does have the same facial features, the same sunglasses, the same haircut, and the same concentrated smile.

"We're looking for some hard liquor," Cris tells him.

"You won't find any around here. But I do know where you can get as much as you want for free."

"Where's that?" Cris asks.

"Just down the road in Blowing Rock. It's furniture market time. And if you act like you're part of it, everything's free. Including all the booze you can drink."

"What's a furniture market?"

"It's like a convention, dude. One of the local furniture makers rents this entire old hotel. He picks up the tab for all the out-of-town buyers. It's an alcohol party."

"Sounds like fun," Cris says. "Where is it?"

"Follow me, dudes."

The young racer roars off toward Blowing Rock in his Toyota pickup. I think it's the same truck that passed us on the right earlier in the evening. The road is narrow and Cris has a difficult time staying with him. Kerry is not convinced we should be following at all. She has strong reservations about our new friend, and nighttime in rural North Carolina does not appeal to her.

"What if they do this on a regular basis?" she asks Cris. "Send one of the local retarded yahoos into town looking for a blonde tourist with great tits, and the two morons she's traveling with drive right into the trap. And it's instant *Deliverance* for all of us. You guys aren't going to like having to bend over and grab your ankles. Well…Cris might enjoy it. If they're gentle."

"No trade secrets, my dear. Besides, this is going to be a great hit, a cultural experience. Part of being on the road. So far North Carolina is the most foreign place we've been."

"Ever, in my case." Kerry is along for the ride.

Fifteen minutes later we are inside a Victorian hotel, a beautifully preserved structure with immaculately furnished and appointed interior public rooms. Our guide was correct. It looks and sounds like nonstop alcohol. Over five hundred people are packed into a large, crowded ballroom. Everyone is moving about as much as the limited space allows. Most of the people in the room appear to be intoxicated, and the noise level is overwhelming. We are all shoulder to shoulder, drinking, smoking, and eating hors d'oeuvres, yelling at each other because it is the only way to be heard. Most of these screaming furniture people are white males, overweight, and red in the face. No one pays any attention as the three of us push our way toward the bar. The cigarette smoke is so thick my eyes burn, and I begin to question whether free drinks are worth it. The marketers are wearing name tags that divulge their home states or corporate affiliations. The horrible din and recently swilled vodka make it difficult for me to concentrate. I try to focus on the two name tags closest to me. Moshe Cohen, Brahole Industries, is talking to Harley Sanders, Pennsylvania.

"We have some pretty exciting introductions at this market." Cohen shouts to be heard. "Don't you agree, Harley?"

There is no response from Sanders, even though his ear is less than a foot from Cohen's mouth. I cannot determine if Sanders does not hear or does not want to hear, but I decide to join the conversation and help Cohen out. Vodka on top of the amphetamine has made me gregarious, and irrationally optimistic to the point where I actually feel I might learn to like these guys. When I'm in this state of mind I always compliment people and tell them what they want to hear. These are the times when I even enjoy making shallow people smile, but I have learned that times like this never last for long.

"I think you people have come out with some really extraordinary stuff." I thrust my jaw forward and bob my head. "And I think it is going to sell like crazy." Cohen smiles at me. "Despite what all the detractors say." The salesman flinches at this last comment. I quickly return to the positive. "Who is the genius responsible for it all, Moshe?"

"It's a team effort, of course," Cohen says solemnly. "But I guess the man at the top deserves most of the credit."

"Who is that fantastic man?" I am surprised by the sincerity in my own voice.

"Old man Brahole, of course." Cohen says this with evident pride. "Where are you from?"

"California. This is my first market. Is Mr. Brahole here? I'd sure like to meet him and extend my congratulations."

We struggle through the throng and approach Brahole. He is talking and laughing with two other men. His much younger wife is off to his side. One of the few women present, like the others she is being ignored, but she is the best looking woman in the room. Cohen excuses himself and introduces me.

"He's a new dealer from California," Cohen explains to Brahole, and I decide to go for a joke.

"Moshe makes me sound like an FDR fanatic. Or a drug pusher." I can see that they do not appreciate my attempt at humor, or even understand it. "Ha ha, just kidding. I'm only one wide-eyed furniture guy who hopes that someday I can be half as successful as Mr. Brahole here."

The expressions on their blank faces do not change. Young Mrs. Brahole smiles and looks me over. She lays her head back and glances at my midsection, while slowly massaging her lower lip with the tip of her tongue. She is conveying the impression that brief encounters are greatly rewarded, and I nod in her direction despite the lack of an introduction. She opens her mouth and swirls her tongue around her lips. I suspect someone is going to have fun with her at this market, but it's not going to be me or Mr. Brahole. No one says anything until the old man finally speaks.

"How is business out west?" Brahole asks me.

"Oh fine, fine sir." I try to be as ingratiating as possible. "This is my first market sir, and I'm a little curious about something. May I ask you a question, Mr. Brahole?"

"Please do. That's what I'm here for. Ask me anything you want. Except how much money I make. Or the age difference between my wife and me."

Brahole guffaws and his employees follow his lead. Mrs. Brahole lights a cigarette and continues to examine me. I want to flirt with her but know all eyes are on me.

"Well sir." I face Brahole and look into his eyes. "Here we are in the middle of North Carolina, with wealthy business people from all over the country, including your home state.

And the only black people I see are the bartenders and the servants."

The only ones still smiling are the two Braholes. Their smiles are as different as their genders, and as always, I find the feminine much more convincing.

The old man's forced smile fades. "Well I hate to say it. And don't let me get caught being quoted on any of this, but let's face facts, white man to white man. Down here anyway, they aren't ready for ownership or management. And I think that's basically the situation around the world. Look at Africa. They're happier working in the fields and in the factories. I personally feel a tremendous responsibility to provide employment for them. Most of the workers in my plants are darkies. But I don't see them bettering themselves anytime soon. Besides, Jews are already locked into the higher-paying positions. And the greedy kikes aren't exactly anxious to cut their dark skinned brothers in on the action. Isn't that right, Moshe?"

Brahole pokes Cohen in the ribs and starts to chuckle. His friends laugh and nod agreement. Cohen looks glum. Kerry shakes her head before speaking pointedly to me and Cris.

"Despite the good food and drink, these racist paternalistic people make me sick to my stomach. Let's keep moving."

"Not my kind of crowd," Cris says as we work our way to the door. "But I think the booze has saved my molars, at least I'm not grinding my teeth anymore."

"I thought only doctors, lawyers, and car dealers had gatherings like this," Kerry says. "Now I know it's a universal phenomenon. Ugly people walk all paths of life. Even furniture." We get back in the Oldsmobile and cruise off down the road.

The next morning we pull into a truck stop and call the shipping agent back in New York. There has been another change in the itinerary. The ship is going to stop in Savannah instead of Mobile. The agent gives us a number to call. When

I do, a woman named Bonnie answers and confirms that the ship will dock in Savannah, but no one will be allowed to board for several days.

"They don't want anyone on board while the ship loads and unloads." Bonnie's voice sounds young and musical.

"Couldn't we quietly slip on board and keep a low profile?" I ask.

"The captain makes the rules. No exceptions."

"You've got me there," I say. "But I'm just an unemployed school teacher. My friends are doing cultural research. I guess you could consider me a scientific volunteer. Unfortunately I'm not rich enough to be a philanthropist. Where do you recommend three under-funded researchers stay until boarding?"

"There are plenty of cheap motels around town."

I can't resist. "When do we get to meet you?"

"After work I moonlight as a cocktail waitress on the riverfront. Come in for a drink when you get here. It's called The Warehouse."

"I'll be there."

Less than twenty-four hours later I am sauntering along the waterfront in old Savannah. Buildings have been restored to their original condition; the small city is charming and picturesque. At this hour only the bar scene along the river is awake and vibrating. When I enter The Warehouse, I feel fortunate to secure a stool. As I survey the crowded room I try to guess which one of the servers is Bonnie. After much conjecture I finally ask the bartender.

"She's a rather nice looking lady," I say brightly.

"They don't get much better." The bald overweight bartender sounds creepy.

When Bonnie comes over to the bar to place an order I introduce myself.

"I'm pleased to meet you." Her slight drawl adds impact.

"The pleasure's all mine." I grin while contemplating truth and guilt.

"I get a break in fifteen minutes. Would you like to go somewhere else and have a drink?"

"I'd love to."

Bonnie lights up a joint the minute we step out of the bar. We share it as we walk along the river. She is attractive and laughs easily. I ask her pointed questions and she responds with all the right answers. There is no doubt about it. The sweet southern belle is beginning to arouse me, and we make a lunch date for tomorrow afternoon. When we part ways at the bar she kisses me on the lips. Vanessa who? My guilt asserts itself, or at least tries to.

Why does all of this seem too good to be true? Does overindulgence really deserve its bad reputation? It appears to agree with me, because I have been doing everything my birthright allows, and I'm grateful that my punishment has been delayed. At this precise moment I feel terrific and envision this excitement lasting forever. Touching Bonnie's flawless body would go a long way in that direction. Nothing has happened yet, but I worry about my ability to control the future, because I have never been known for my self-restraint.

My sleep is tormented by dreadful dreams. The ski mask returns in all his monochromatic splendor. The details in the large room are the same as always. Once again I am tied to the chair. The dreams are getting worse.

"Will this ever end?" I ask.

"It will for you."

2

THE BOAT

ONNIE IS WAITING at an outside table in downtown Savannah when the three of us arrive for lunch. She is smiling and looks fresher and prettier than ever. More lustful thoughts cross my mind, and every time I look at her I have to fight myself to suppress them.

"I have some really good news for you guys!" Bonnie's face lights up with the announcement. "Your ship has come in. Literally. It docked this morning. Better still, my boss is friends with the captain. He agreed to make an exception and let you board early. It's not scheduled to leave for a few days, but you can get on whenever you want."

Cris is the first to voice a common sentiment. "Bonnie, you're too much. It's party time! Please be our guest on board."

"Guest of honor," I chime in. I have had a tough hangover morning. My dreams have stayed with me and they make the waking hours more important.

Bonnie agrees to help us celebrate after she gets off work. At five o'clock we all walk out of Bonnie's office toward the docks. We have champagne and are in high spirits as we charge up the gangplank. One of the sailors shows us to our cabins. We are all thrilled to be on board. For me, a first step toward escape and adventure. Dope and champagne pushes us all along. We explore the small freighter before settling into deck chairs for more drink. It is a very joyous time, and we toast our new friend Bonnie with compliments to her brains and beauty.

"If it wasn't for Bonnie, we'd still be in that shitty motel." Kerry says. "This is living life on a much grander scale. We're eternally grateful." Kerry raises her glass and offers another toast to Bonnie. "I know I'm a little tipsy, but I'm blaming the rolling of this stationary ship. In any case, I want to roll around in bed with Cris for awhile. We'll see you guys tomorrow. Sweet dreams."

Bonnie and I smoke another joint on deck and enjoy the view of the harbor. We are both drunk and feeling playful. I coax her down to my cabin on the tired premise that I have some etchings I would like to show her. One thing leads to another, and I find myself heading into a self-discipline disaster. My sexual energy seems to have a momentum of its own, and I've put myself into a very compromising position. I reason it would not be polite to the other person involved if I were to stop now, but I know I can practically justify anything at this moment in time. This type of situation never has been my best time to call it quits. She clumsily fumbles with her clothes and gets totally naked. I do the same. This is it. I feel it. This is what life is all about, and it is what eternity demands. My blissful trance is broken by the only two words I do not want to hear.

"Please don't." Bonnie breathes softly into my ear.

"Why not?" I stop salivating and try not to sob. It is the end of heaven. The total collapse of my kingdom.

"I have a boyfriend who is out of town working," she whispers. "We promised not to screw anyone else. I hope you can understand."

I hesitate because I wish I could not understand. I know that all of humanity castigates her for her brutal confession. My manliness has been rejected, but I won't allow myself to whimper. I also know that valor always wins, and that timing can't be dictated. Is she deliberately trying to be cruel and hurtful? I doubt it, but it really doesn't matter. I have no choice. I need to accept her decision and lose gracefully.

"I understand," I lie with great effort. "And I profoundly appreciate your candor at such an early interval. I was only kidding around anyway. This protruding appendage is for comic affect. When I'm telling jokes I use it for laughs. As a prop."

Inopportunely, my erection is pressing against her stomach. Right now I wish her boyfriend were dead, or worse. But I try to suppress such an evil thought. Bargaining with fate, I wonder if she will allow me to look at her beautiful nude body while I masturbate into the stainless steel sink. All situations present themselves as they are, provocative encounters included. My options have been limited, but I know, as Dr. Peterson told me, things can always get worse, and it isn't really all that bad at the moment anyway. Bonnie is fun to be around, but I wonder how this is going to progress.

"What should we do now?" I feel like whining but I am resigned to defeat and try to sound cheerful. "I hope you suggest the unspeakable. Please ask to tie me up and beat my naked ass with your slaps. Not really."

"Would it be okay if I did this instead?" She lowers her lips down below my waist.

"More than okay."

The radical change of boundaries makes it difficult for me not to chortle. Bonnie backs up her singular erotic question with immediate action. I am completely delighted by her efforts, but I ponder the fine line she has drawn vis-a-vis infidelity, and I hope Vanessa is not being faithful in quite this way.

When I wake up in the morning Bonnie is gone. My remorse is magnified by a horrible hangover. I walk into town and call Vanessa.

"I went to dinner with Peter Wilson last night," she tells me. "You're right about him liking me more than I thought. But I made it clear that any romance is impossible. And that I'm still your woman until you say otherwise."

"I feel the same way."

My hypocrisy makes me feel even worse. It's one thing to have no self-control, but to deceive in the aftermath is inexcusable. I figure if she doesn't know it won't hurt her. I can obviously rationalize anything, and I wonder if I should do the honorable thing and throw myself overboard. Or better still, walk the plank.

After two days aboard ship the three of us begin to

feel right at home. We do not see many officers but the crew is friendly, particularly with Kerry. We enjoy sunning ourselves, reading, and watching the bustling harbor activity from the top deck. The small bar is closed until the other passengers arrive, but the purser supplies us with inexpensive Yugoslavian beer and liquor. We look forward to meeting the other passengers, because we know we are going to be on the open seas with them for a while.

On our third morning aboard the others begin to arrive, a much different group than we had expected. Most of our early arriving fellow passengers have trouble walking up the gangplank. I think they must have a burning desire to be buried at sea, since they look like they could drop dead at any moment.

"It's renamed the S.S. Alzheimer's! We're talking geezer city here," Cris says. "Looks like we're in for an endless game of cards. I'll bet they know gin rummy."

"Maybe we can liven them up with a rousing game of Scrabble," I say. "My mother made me play. I'm quite good but she usually won. I don't like to play board games."

Kerry is visibly disappointed. "I expected swashbuckling Tony Curtis types would be traveling by freighter. Is senility contagious?"

"My arteries feel harder already," Cris answers. "Definitely not what I expected. But hey, we're sailing to Morocco with a stash. It's all good."

We are relieved to see younger people climb aboard later that afternoon. By nightfall all the passengers are accounted for and the loading is all but complete. The purser says we will sail tomorrow.

I spend my last night in Savannah at Bonnie's house. She has kept her vow of chastity, although I consider it to be on a very large technicality. Hey, everyone has their own definition of what sex is. I borrow her shallow excuse to make it easier to justify my own self-serving transgressions. She drops me off at the ship early the next morning. It is a cheery goodbye with promises to stay in touch.

All the passengers and most of the crew are on deck as we cast off and sail down the river toward the Atlantic. Kerry takes pictures while Cris and I drink champagne and congratulate ourselves. It is a warm, muggy day, and I feel terrific. When the ship hits the ocean the three of us gather at the rail. The strong ocean breeze is wonderful, and we all enjoy our last glimpse of American soil. Then, much to my consternation I discover I have been assigned a roommate.

Older passengers are making a round-trip journey. Most of the younger travelers, including my new roommate, will get off at the first stop, Tangier. My roommate is twenty-five and Jewish; he plans to travel across Europe before settling in Israel. He has never drank, smoked, or done illegal drugs. Most of all, he is very cautious about what he eats, and he is on the toilet constantly.

"Colitis." My roommate says this slowly and with a grimace. "It runs in the family."

I assume he is not attempting a double entendre and consider hazarding a personal anecdote about a time I had the runs, but I reason this guy wouldn't find the story funny.

"My father had to have his lower intestine removed." Apparently, my roommate does not want to let this flowing conversation die. "Now he defecates into a bag."

I do not know whether to laugh or scream.

"It's hell," my roommate continues unabated. "You can hear every time it happens."

This is not my idea of sparkling conversation, and I am afraid the roommate can only talk shit. The thought of discussing bowel troubles for the next two weeks on the open sea gives me a sour stomach and sends me up to the bar for another stiff one.

All the passengers eat together at appointed hours. The seating arrangement at the two long tables has been predetermined. I sit between Cris and Monica.

Monica is thirty; she is the only unattached woman under seventy on board. She is from Austria and teaches German literature at New York University, my old school. I like her immediately. Her aura sparkles and I see a beauty beneath her abundant flesh. She is carrying too much weight but that isn't my problem. I find her quick-witted and well informed. And she laughs at my sometimes inappropriate jokes. She acts wealthy and has booked a first class cabin for herself. I flirt with her during the meals, but always avoid watching her eat.

A middle-aged couple from Vermont sits across from us. They have been to every country on earth; they have even been on this freighter before. Their new, well-equipped Land Rover is making the crossing with them. After landing in Morocco they plan to rendezvous with friends and cross the Sahara. They talk about the amusement they get sending postcards from places like Timbuktu.

"One of the reasons we're making this trip is because we have to go to Upper Volta," Mr. World Traveler states emphatically.

"Why do you have to go there?" Monica asks between large mouthfuls.

"Because it's the only West African country we've never been to," he responds triumphantly.

This pair has taken traveling to the extreme. Is it all about bragging rights? There is more than a hint of elitism that pervades the entire conversation, but the compensation is that they have an infinite number of well-rehearsed travel stories. Whenever anyone else mentions some remote locale, they have an experience to go with it. I see them huddling together on deck and wonder what really goes on behind their pretentious facade. I marvel at the fact that they talk at the same time and can be understood simultaneously. It's like listening to a stereo, both sides say different things but they complement each other. There is something that intrigues me about them, but I'm not sure I want to know what it is.

The other passengers are more difficult to evaluate. There's a thirty-eight-year-old Iranian traveling by himself. He tells everyone he is from Persia. The older passengers think he is wonderful. He looks, talks, and acts like the actor Omar Sharif. He knows every card game ever played, and the women I talk to think he is the best-looking man they have ever seen.

"I swear to god," Kerry says as the Persian walks away from

his table, "that guy belongs in the movies. He's just too fucking much. Look at the ass on him. Omar Sharif never had it that good." The Persian begins to keep entirely to himself and becomes the mystery man aboard the ship. He sits at the other table during meals and says very little.

"He's probably some horrible deviant going back to his slave harem in Iran," Kerry says while admiring his backside again. "I'll bet they all lusted for him a lot."

Monica thinks the Persian is too pretty to be truly attractive. "Maybe he's a suicidal Palestinian terrorist. There's something about him that just doesn't add up."

There are also two widowed sisters who prove to be the life of the party. They look like they could be sixty-five-year-old twins, but they say they are only sisters. Both display an abundance of diamonds and gold jewelry. They wear a ton of makeup and are always overdressed. Since their husbands died they mostly cruise on luxury liners, but they felt they needed a change of pace and decided to try a freighter. After three days they tell me they are bored to death.

"To die of boredom is so inglorious," the older sister says as she pours herself another vodka lemonade. "There's nothing to do on this goddamn ship. I feel I should jump overboard just to give you people something to get excited about."

Her sister also pours herself another vodka. "I'd encourage you to do it for the common good. But where would that leave me? Guilt-ridden for not doing more for you, and doubly bored without you. I'd be compelled to follow suit." The sisters take pills, drink like fish, and are always extremely jolly, even when they are complaining.

By our third day out from Savannah, we are all hanging on and trying to avoid getting seasick. Most of us do not succeed. A powerful storm blows in from the north Atlantic, and violent rain with heavy seas soak everything not enclosed or tied down. Even the experienced crew looks green, and when the dinner bell rings only ten people answer the call.

Cris and Kerry have had difficulty since cast-off. They both have felt queasy and this storm has pushed them over the edge. They vomit for hours until have nothing left to give. I stop by their cabin on the way to dinner. They both say they want to die, and I assure them that they look like they already have.

"But you guys look much better than my roommate." I can sense that this astute observation annoys them. "The poor bastard has shit coming out both ends at the same time."

As expected, this bit of information does not seem to offer much consolation. They haggardly stare back at me as I bow out the door, and I'm secretly pleased that I didn't mention how good I feel.

I knew that Monica wouldn't miss a meal for anything. She looks downright hungry when she sits down at the table.

"I've always heard it's best to keep a full stomach when it's rough." She says this while eyeing the dessert tray.

The World Travelers are also seated. They say they have been on heavier seas than this many times. They don't consider it to be all that rough at all.

"I think our second time through the Straits of Magellan was the worst," Mr. World Traveler says.

"No," Mrs. World Traveler counters, "it had to be the icebreaker near Antarctica."

"How about that freak storm on Lake Titicaca?"

"Lake Superior!" she replies. "I thought we were on the *Edmund Fitzgerald.*"

I think I am going to get sick just from listening to them. I'm having a difficult time keeping food down, the ship feels as if it's breaking apart, and these two wandering souls keep talking about how much worse it can get. I think they're carrying it too far, but I admire their tenacity.

The two sisters are also at the table and say they are used to this kind of weather. The storm builds and it becomes so rocky that serving the food is difficult. Liquids spill and everything on the table rolls back and forth. This does not affect the sisters at all because they are not eating.

"We just came to socialize," one says. "Whenever it gets this rough we've found cognac to be the best remedy."

"What if it stays this rough for days?" I ask.

"We brought extra bottles of Remy in case the ship runs out."

"I admire your spunk," I say, "but I'm glad I'm not the one

who will have to biopsy your livers." They both take a big swig of cognac and laugh in unison. It makes me feel a little bit better.

I find it miraculous that these two look as good as they do. They tell me they want to have a party after the storm blows over. They are both anxious to meet the captain up close and personal, and they plan to throw the party in his honor.

The instant I awake the next morning I sense something is wrong. Either the ocean has become perfectly still or the ship is not moving. I bound to my feet and peer out the porthole. A lush green landscape awaits my view. The first thing I think is that we have discovered Atlantis, my true home, but when my mind clears I begin to doubt this theory. Atlantis wouldn't have a golf course, there wouldn't be any English cars on the roads, and there would not be expensive yachts cavorting around our ship. I run upstairs and find the bartender in the lounge.

"Borna, what the hell is going on?"

"What do you mean, sir?"

"I mean where are we? What do you think I mean?"

"We're in Bermuda, sir."

"What the fuck are we doing in Bermuda?"

"I'm not allowed to say. You'll have to wait until the announcement." Stories about the Bermuda Triangle flash through my mind as I charge out of the lounge.

"What's happening?" My question startles an older gentleman.

"What do you mean?"

"What do you mean what do I mean?" I wonder if this is how a nervous breakdown begins, right after a bout of heavy drinking. Maybe I should cut back a bit.

"I mean what are we doing in Bermuda?" I expect to see Rod Serling at any minute.

"Oh. Elmer had a heart attack and died last night. The captain decided to turn around and let his body off here."

The hospital boat shows up, Elmer is loaded aboard, and his wife leaves with him. I meet Cris and Kerry on the deck.

None of us knew Elmer personally, he was just another one of the old guys.

Kerry is upset by the untimely death. "Some of our earlier jokes aren't so funny now. It must be terrible for his wife. Elmer was such a good guy."

"Come off it, Kerry," Cris says. "We didn't even know him."

"I noticed him at mealtime. He looked like a kind old gentleman. He had a friendly face and a gentle smile."

"I don't want to sound too cynical," Cris persists, "but let's face it. No one knew who the old fart was until he died. He was probably an asshole and an idiot. A diehard Nixon guy. We're not all that sorry he's dead."

"Why don't you keep comments like that to yourself," Kerry shouts back with a devilish smile.

Because no one has anything better to do, the preparation for the sisters' big party becomes the major preoccupation on board. The sisters have browbeaten the purser into allowing the party to be held in Elmer's large and recently vacated first class cabin. I can sense that most of Elmer's contemporaries are glad to be rid of him, and the ghost of death has remained in Bermuda. No one gives a shit about Elmer anymore. They are happy it was him and not them. But sometimes I short-shrift good people, it's another one of many faults.

The sisters tell me the guest list for the party has to be selective because space is limited. Everyone under seventy is automatically invited. They say that age group will have the best chance of living through the night. All of the officers are invited too. The Persian has even agreed to come. The elusive captain says he will only be able to stay for a brief time—his responsibilities on the bridge will prevent him from making an evening of it. The sisters have made friends with some of the sailors and invited them as well. The party promises to be the highlight of the voyage. By now, the passengers are extremely tired of being at sea, day after day with nothing on the horizon but more water. Occasionally we see another passing ship, but so what? Even our smuggled dope and cheap liquor does not break the monotony for me. I torture myself every morning by watching the crew dump garbage overboard. It creates an appalling line of trash that snakes off for miles in our wake. I know things are really starting to get tough when Monica begins to complain about the food.

"I can't stand this greasy crap anymore," she wails during dinner.

Her criticism of the food catches me by surprise. Anyone watching her eat would think she was relishing every bite. Up until now, lapping up gallons of rich gravy has been her specialty. I have yet to see her return any of the generous portions, and I naturally presumed she was enjoying every large mouthful. But always, actions speak louder than words.

"I thought you loved this stuff." I know I should not go any further.

"These tasteless bastards have no imagination," Monica says. "All of this slop tastes the same. It's as if they're trying to make my crossing even more boring than it already is. The chef should be taken out and shot. Better still, make him walk the plank for impersonating a chef."

I reason that it is difficult to escape from cultural traditions. Her countrymen would not enjoy this tiresome food either. Fortunately, unlike certain of her German-speaking compatriots from the past, Monica does not have the authority, or the true inclination, to force the kitchen staff into their own ovens.

"You should go on a hunger strike." I know this is a mistake but I cannot resist. "It might convince the cook to kill himself out of shame."

"Fuck you!" Monica stands up and dumps her plate of spaghetti over my head. "I'm so sick of your not-so-subtle fat jokes. You think you're so clever. You're not! Any idiot can be insulting. You're just an egotistical asshole!" She has hit me on the mark.

She leaves the room in tears. I feel terrible. I don't care if I look goofy with spaghetti hanging down from my ears, because I deserve it.

"She's right, you know," Kerry says. "Humor crosses the line when it becomes hurtful."

"I know. It was inexcusable. The ugliest thing I've ever said."

"No it's not. You say shit like that all the time! You owe her a big apology. If I were her, I wouldn't accept it."

The sisters' much-anticipated party begins slowly. The hostesses have skipped dinner and greet their guests at the door. They are both wearing snug leotards and tights, and hoods that look like cat ears. Long tails are sewn onto their posteriors. Their painted hands and faces are made to look like felines too.

"We didn't know it was a costume party," Cris says.

"Oh, it's not really. We enjoy dressing and putting on makeup. And we love cats."

"You look great!" Kerry exclaims. "I love the costumes!"

"You should see some of our other outfits," the older cat smiles. "Do you guys happen to have any marijuana?"

"Well uh yeah, we might have a bit," Cris answers. "Not a lot."

"My sister and I would love to get high."

We finish the joints before the other guests arrive. The only effect it has is to make the two sisters a little more talkative. It is easy to see that the gals are old pros when it comes to smoke, and they have done a bang-up job decorating Elmer's room. Streamers and balloons hang from the ceiling; a folding table in the middle of the room supports dozens of bottles of liquor, beer and wine. Loud rock music is blaring from the four corners. It is a festive atmosphere and all concerned anticipate a memorable night.

Cris and I position ourselves to allow a good view of the door. We want to be able to see the other guests' expressions when they are greeted by the Cat Sisters. Everyone reacts differently. The Persian's face doesn't change. He acts as if this is the way he expected the ladies to look. The World Travelers look stunned but quickly recover. Most of the others appear to be embarrassed. The guest of honor, the captain, handles the situation with great aplomb. The Cat Sisters receive a deep bow and he kisses their hands. They act thrilled, turn around, and show him their tails.

"It is a certifiable pleasure to see you again, ladies," he

says with a slight English accent. The captain is fifty. He is a dignified man with streaks of gray in his shiny black hair. He has a slight paunch but looks handsome in his pressed uniform. He introduces himself, and then his officers, to all the other passengers present. The officers have a conspiratorial look in their eyes as they make the rounds. They look like they are ready to have some sailor fun, and they talk to each other in a language they think no one understands. But Monica speaks many languages and understands enough of this one to know what they are saying.

"They are making fun of most of us," Monica interprets. "Most of all, they talk about wanting to have sex with Kerry. She is the woman of their wet dreams. Their slang can't be translated."

Heavy drinking proves to be the order of the evening, and everyone is enjoying the party. Inhibitions begin to disappear as the night progresses. After the captain excuses himself to return to the bridge, the remaining crewmen become rowdy. They get progressively more stupid with every drink.

"What do you do with a drunken sailor?" Cris asks.

"Put him in the brig until he's sober?" I answer.

"Who's going to drive the fucking boat?" Kerry wonders.

"The captain looked all right when he left," Cris says. "But you never know."

Ten minutes later the drunken first mate asks Kerry to dance. She declines. He refuses to take no for an answer. She reluctantly relents. He propositions her as they swing around the dance floor. Kerry turns him down quickly in no uncertain terms. He tries to physically force her out into the hallway, which I know is going to be a big mistake.

"Get your hairy hands off me, asshole!" she screams. "Greaseballs like you aren't allowed to touch. That's a step too far." He laughs and she slaps him across his face. He grabs her wrists. Cris sees what is happening and quickly intervenes.

"You heard her!" Cris yells. "Take your hands off."

The first mate wheels around and glares at Cris. He pokes Cris on the chest repeatedly. Cris accepts a few touches before he grabs the officer's finger, and then the first mate tries to knee Cris in the groin but misses, and Cris sends him reeling against the wall with a straight right fist. The ship's doctor and second mate have witnessed the latter stages of this episode. They jump in front of Cris, and profusely apologize to Kerry. By now everyone in the room has stopped talking. The doctor begs forgiveness from all present. When the doctor finishes speaking he pours himself a tumbler of wine and drains it in one gulp, and then throws his glass against the wall. It shatters. The other crew members finish their drinks and do the same thing. The party continues as if nothing had happened. Is this is normal behavior on the high seas?

"It all caught me a little off guard," Cris says. "I didn't think that guy would go that far."

"Nice punch." I was impressed by the violence, and Cris's part in it.

"It's the first time I've hit anyone since I was a kid," Cris says.

"You did a fine job," I say.

"My hand's killing me." Cris does not look happy. I think he should be proud of himself, and maybe get his knuckles iced by the doctor.

"That fuckhead deserved worse," Kerry says. "No is the same in every language. It's the one word most men don't seem to understand."

"Put him in the brig until he's sober?" Cris asks.

"Throw the son of a bitch overboard," she replies with a shrug. "Get him out of the gene pool."

"I've got to say Kerry, it was a stylish slap. I'll bet you could've thrown him overboard all by yourself. I didn't realize I'm traveling with the dynamic duo."

Kerry decides to go out on the deck and get a little fresh air. The captain approaches while she is standing by the rail admiring the full moon. He is unaware of the recent events inside.

"Good evening, miss. It's a beautiful night isn't it?"

"Yes it is."

"It can be very romantic at sea," the captain continues. Kerry stiffens because she fears the captain's intentions are not honorable.

"Would you like to come up on the bridge with me? It's the best place on the ship."

"No thank you." Kerry steps away. "Not tonight. Maybe my boyfriend and I could come up tomorrow."

"No. I do not want your boyfriend to come. You must come by yourself. You are so beautiful. I think I love you. Please come with me now." The captain tries to put his arm around her.

"Don't touch me, asshole!" She forcefully throws his arm away.

"Please. I love you. Come with me." He tries to pull her to his chest.

Kerry screams for the second time that evening. She grabs both of his shoulders and raises her right knee very accurately between his spread legs. He doubles over, moans, and walks away. She wonders if this is ever going to stop, and if most Yugoslavian men behave this way.

"This is the worst group of sex maniacs I've ever run into in my life," Kerry says as she details her encounter with the captain.

"Now you know why sailors have the reputations they do," Cris says. "These guys deserve it because they've earned it. Top to bottom. Bad show. Men will be men."

"These guys are intolerable. Who takes care of the ship while they're all beating off?" Kerry asks.

Very few people have left the party, and even the doctor has returned and continued drinking. He looks intoxicated and unsteady, but still jovial and friendly.

"I hope no one needs medical attention tonight," Cris observes.

"I'll bet he writes himself a prescription in the morning," Kerry says. "But he's an okay guy."

The loud music stops while I'm chatting with the World Travelers, and they suggest that I go over and put on the next tape. While I am squatted down looking over the selection, I feel a hand slide between my legs and cup my testicles. I turn around and see Mrs. World Traveler smiling back at me. She makes an announcement that I would have found inappropriate earlier, but now, as she gives my balls a little squeeze, it is a statement I expect to hear, under the circumstances.

"My husband and I would like to have sex with you and Monica." I stand up, turn around, and look her right in the eye.

"You'll have to ask Monica yourself," I say with a crooked smile. "But count me out."

"Why?"

"It's just not my style."

"Maybe the two of us could make love while my husband watches."

"Thanks, but no."

I am more astounded than flattered, but now I know why they travel so much. They cannot afford to stay in one place too long, since they're always just one step ahead of the vice squad. I suspect they run an exclusive health care center in Vermont during their non traveling months, and that their kinky side is seldom bridled. They obviously like heavy women. I have made amends with Monica, and I hope she takes them up on their offer. She might learn something and have an orgasm in the process.

I am just about drunk and high enough to partly reconsider their outrageous proposal and see what happens, which means it's time to stop drinking. Is this the second stage of an alcoholic nervous breakdown? People try to kill me, people want to fuck me. But I do love being high and safe on the boat. I feel like a Steve McQueen character. This is *The Great Escape*, the remake, and unlike the original, I think it's going to work this time around. Despite the recurring nightmares, I feel completely safe onboard. I left my terminator back in New York.

The party room becomes so noisy and smoky that I decide to take a brief respite and get some air outside. The Persian follows me out the door, and then all the way up to the top deck. I pretend I do not know I am being followed. Six chairs are scattered about the deck, and I sit down in one by the rail. The Persian pulls a chair over next to mine.

"How are you tonight?" he asks sweetly. I knew before he sat down where this was going to go.

"Fine thanks. How are you?"

"Actually, I'm a little lonely. I would be much happier if I could get to know you better."

The Persian places a light hand below my crotch. I quickly remove his hand and stand up.

"I'm not into that. Please don't touch me again."

"Have you ever tried it?"

"No."

"You don't know how much you're missing."

"I'll risk it."

"Let me try to please you."

I get up and walk away, thinking the Cat Sisters must have spiked the liquor with an aphrodisiac. I cannot believe that I am running neck and neck with Kerry for the most wanted body on board. All my life I have dreamed about being used as a sex object, and now that it is a real possibility I back away. But being impaled by the Persian, or the meat in a Traveler sandwich, is not my notion of libertine satisfaction.

It is past two in the morning, and the Cat Sisters are performing an exotic dance. Everyone is whooping, hollering, and applauding. The crew is yelling for them to take it all off. It looks like the Cat Sisters are about to heed their call. I return to my cabin. The ski mask continues to dominate my dreams, and I get little more than a touch of sleep.

At breakfast Monica tells me I missed quite a show.

"The two old gals got completely naked. You could never see everything because of the fans and feathers, but it was the closest thing this ship will ever see to professional entertainment. Unbelievable."

"What happened when they finished?"

"I don't know. Most everyone left, including me. Rumor has it they had sex with some of the crew. From the way they were acting, it certainly wouldn't surprise me."

"I'm sure it was mutually beneficial," I speculate.

"I hope so. Some of those Serbian guys look pretty good." Monica gets more alluring every day; because she has an allure that goes way beyond the shallow side of the physical. It's ethereal.

The Cat Sisters make it to the dining room for lunch and act as if nothing has happened. They thank everyone for attending, and for making the party such a success. After the meal I am headed to the upper deck when they intercept me in the hallway.

"Do you think we could beg another joint off of you?"

"Sure. I don't have any on me right now. How soon do you want it?"

"There's no hurry. Anytime before eight would be okay. We're entertaining some of the crew after dinner. We think it will be a kick to turn them on. If you know what we mean. It might improve their imagination."

"Be careful," I laugh.

"Not at our age, sweetie." They both pinch my cheeks, synchronized, no doubt from long practice.

The remainder of the voyage is uneventful. Gossip circulates around the Cat Sisters but nothing is substantiated. They appear for meals but spend most of their time in their cabin reading and entertaining.

"I think the elderly nymphomaniacs are having a lot better time than any of us," Kerry says.

"You had your chance," Cris points out. "I'll bet the Cat Sisters are in charge."

In our conversations, Monica has convinced me that I do not want to make the tough Sahara desert crossing with Cris and Kerry. She says I should go north to Europe.

"You've never been to lots of places in Europe. See the First World before the Third," Monica advises. "Take my word for it, that desert crossing is going to be hell."

I also know I need to be a single wheel and not a third. Besides, Cris and Kerry require their privacy. They are beginning to climb the walls with cabin fever. The constant confinement has made them irritable. Kerry paces the gang ways while Cris broods over his maps. He has carefully charted a course across the western Sahara to Senegal with precise connections.

The Persian and the World Travelers have been seeing each other constantly since the night of the party. They behave as if they share a deep, dark secret. They are all fit and trim, and I imagine some stunning positions, with the woman always on top.

The three of them have decided to travel together in Tangier.

Three days before our scheduled arrival, the ship's daily bulletin announces that we will not be docking at Tangier after all. Minor repairs have to be made on the ship, and we are told that the maintenance can only be performed at the port in Casablanca. All unloading of passengers will be done there.

That evening another strong storm roars in and begins to rock the ship. As usual, Cris and I started imbibing in the lounge early. The storm catches us both off guard. Kerry has sensibly gone to bed early.

"Let's smoke the rest of the dope," Cris says. "Maybe I can mellow out and sleep through the storm. My sea legs have failed me in the past. I can't wait to get off this fucking boat."

"I want to go up to the very front of the ship for this one," I say to Cris. "I'm going to get high and watch the waves break against the bow. It should be quite a ride up there."

"Watch yourself. You've had a few."

"I'm fine."

The front of the ship is always off limits; if the cargo shifts, it can crush anyone in between. The deck is crowded with cargo containers and heavy equipment, and the World Travelers' Land Rover is strapped near the port side.

I climb under the boundary rope. There are no crewmen about and I dash toward the bow. It is very rough and I have to push off the sides of the containers to keep my balance. It takes longer than usual to get to my favorite place, between the two large holes that accommodate the huge anchor chains. It makes a great perch because it allows unobstructed views to the sides and straight ahead. It is raised from the main deck and not exposed from above. This is where I want to be. No one knows I'm here, and I am happy to be where I am.

I have a firm grip and am admiring nature's fury when a white flash consumes my entire being. Later I would know it signaled a major turning point in my life. It would be a long time before I would understand what happened. But one thing was settled right there and then. The great fear I hoped would never materialize was proven to be true. For the third time in my life, someone tried to kill me. I had known all along, but had hoped I was just being paranoid, like everyone said.

The next thing I remember is waking up and lying on my back in the ship's small infirmary. The doctor, the captain, and two crewmen are looking down at me. I have a ferocious headache.

"What happened?" I ask the doctor.

"You tell us," the doctor replies.

"How did I get here?"

"These two seamen found you up by the anchor chains. They were making sure everything was secure and just about stumbled over your body. They saw blood on the back of your head and presumed you fell over backwards."

"I didn't."

"Well then, what did happen?" The captain does not look friendly.

"I don't know. But I do know I didn't fall."

"It's very rough and you smell like you've had a lot to drink."

"Right on both counts," I say. "But I didn't fall. Someone hit me from behind."

"Who would that be?"

"I don't know."

"You were drunk," the captain says, "and somewhere you should not have been. That area is off limits for a reason. It's slippery and dangerous."

The captain's assessment is shared by everyone else, including Cris and Kerry.

"You were pretty shit-faced," Kerry says. "But I have to admit, you were fairly steady under the circumstances."

"Most importantly," Cris says, "who would want to knock you off for Christ sakes? There's no motive here. You're talking nonsense."

"Someone was trying to kill me. I'll admit I don't recall much after the blow, but I vaguely remember being pushed toward the front. Toward the holes in the bow."

"I'm sure it was just the sailors trying to get you to the doctor," Cris says. "And I repeat, old buddy, why would anyone want to kill you? Get real. Your jokes aren't *that* bad. It must be embarrassing, but face reality, you're lucky you didn't kill *yourself.* You've been drinking a lot."

"Goddammit, man! Someone on this boat tried to kill me, and shove me overboard," I say. "I told you what happened in New York. It's the same fucking thing. I thought I was safe out here in the middle of the fucking ocean. But I can't get away! They've followed me onboard!"

"Get a grip, Andreas. There are no murderers on this boat. Perverts, but no murderers. Do the Cat Sisters want you dead? I doubt it. Where would they get their smoke? Who on this ship could possibly want to kill you? Maybe the horny captain wants to kill you now. He's obviously had enough of your shenanigans. The Persian wants your body too much. I hate to use this term, but you're at a dead end here concerning suspects. Think it over. Stop drinking so much," Cris says emphatically. "I'll bet the accidents stop happening."

Excitement grows on board as the ship passes Madeira and approaches the African coast. It has become even more confusing and difficult for me. The nightmares are worse than ever. They end in the big room with the ski mask conducting affairs.

"You should be overboard," the ski mask says, as calm as always. "You're lucky those sailors blundered onto me. You won't be so lucky the next time."

3

MOROCCO

SATURDAY MORNING our ship docks in Casablanca, and it immediately begins to vibrate with activity. Within minutes of docking there are dozens of unusual vendors aboard. Most of the passengers have never seen the likes of this crowd before. They are dressed in shabby clothes, and the older passengers find the contact intimidating.

These newcomers handle themselves differently. Their physical presence is anomalous. They prowl around the ship looking for customers, and they are very persistent salesmen. Some are wearing caftans and djellabas. They speak to the passengers in French, which mostly the travelers do not understand. Between each other they exchange low guttural grunts and wicked laughter. Personal hygiene and cleanliness does not appear to be a large part of their daily routine. Conspiratorial smiles reveal badly stained and irregular teeth. The products they are trying to sell range from scarves and beads to pornographic pictures and knives. I can't imagine anyone wanting to buy any of it, but I enjoy having them aboard.

"This group sure looks great!" Cris exclaims. "What a variety! I had forgotten what a big change it is when you leave the sacred shores of America."

"I like these guys," I say. "No slacks or suits here. I can see that the Yasser Arafat look is still in."

"I want to know where Humphrey Bogart is," Kerry says. "These guys look like bad news. I'm sure Ingrid Bergman wouldn't tolerate this rabble."

Cris has spent time in the Middle East, but he has never been to Morocco.

"You haven't seen anything yet," he says. "I'll bet you'll learn to dislike most Arab men before this is all over. They're basically misogynists. They might even make you homesick for southerners."

Cris leads Kerry, Monica, and me down the gangplank and onto the pier. Unlike on American docks, labor in this harbor is mostly done by hand. There are hundreds of men doing it. The two women receive attention as we make our way down the wharf toward town. Monica is the only one who speaks any Arabic, but it is easy for all of us to see that these scruffy longshoremen are not being subtle. Catcalls and profanities follow us like a wave hitting the pier.

I am immediately struck by all the different aromas; they are spicy and exotic, but urine and garbage smells complicate the mix. This is my first experience outside the First World, and I am loving every minute of it.

The scene in town is an amalgam of styles, unlike anything I have ever seen. Attractive women in western dress and mini skirts walk side by side with women completely covered in veils. Men in business suits converse with men in expensive tunics and turbans. I stop to look across a wide boulevard. High-rises stand next to ancient structures. Jewelry stores are filled with well-dressed patrons. Mangy dogs sift through uncollected piles of trash. It is all too much to absorb at once, and I'm looking forward to seeing more.

We are all exhausted by midafternoon. Kerry has not enjoyed her first day in mysterious Morocco. She finds it "dirty and unpleasant." The leering local men annoy her; she has nothing but bad things to say about Casablanca. I wonder what she expected. Cris will have his hands full, but thankfully that's not my problem.

Despite mildly unpleasant realities with persistent peddlers, Cris and I, however, have a great time in town. We meet a pleasant hustler at the bus station and purchase some hashish. Kerry is sure we are all going to be arrested, thrown into a dingy jail, and never be seen again.

We check into an old French hotel near downtown. It has a pleasant inner courtyard that shields us from the chaos on the streets. We sit down at a table and order mint tea, the national drink. Two young Frenchmen sit at the table next to us and strike up a conversation. They are headed south across the Sahara to Dakar, Senegal. It is the same route Cris and Kerry plan to follow.

"You two should come with us," they say. "We have good connections through Mauritania."

"I have to see Tangier first," Cris replies. "It's too famous to resist."

"Forget Tangier," they say. "It's been ruined by tourists. But don't miss Fez. It has the largest medina left in the Arab world. There's no place on earth quite like it."

We spend two nights in Casablanca before taking the bus to Fez. The ride affords us our first look at the Moroccan countryside. It becomes even more beautiful as we leave the coast and enter the foothills. Pastoral fields and acres of tangerine trees drift by as we bounce along. Pedestrian traffic is heavy, and the congestion is compounded by oxcarts, sheep, goats, and chickens.

I have a difficult time comprehending my situation. A month ago I was pounding the streets of Manhattan, confused and frightened. Now I am on a magic bus ride traveling through time. The Cat Sisters gave me some Valium when they said goodbye, and I wash one down with wine as the bus bounces along. It helps take the pain of the worry away; or is this chemical relief only in my imagination? I do know that the bloody attack on the boat was all too real, and that no one would ever have found my body, if the crewmen had not found me. But what really happened?

Darkness has fallen when we arrive at the bus station in Fez. A welcoming party of touts awaits us, and once we are spotted there is no escape. We graciously allow two young boys to lead us to a nearby hotel in the French part of the city.

Kerry has been complaining all day. She does not like being the main attraction in what she considers "an Arab freak show." Women who look like her inevitably draw attention, but we all think these Moroccan men are even less subtle than the Yugoslavian sailors.

"There are only a few things I don't like about Morocco," she says. "The people. The food. The transportation. The accommodations. Other than that, it's perfect. The scenery is great. Just get rid of the men." I bring up that she should be traveling with her feminist heroes, Betty Friedan and Germaine Greer, and she tells me to shut up.

Cris and I are pleased with our new hotel, which is clean and inexpensive. At one time the compound belonged to a wealthy French family, who retreated from their mansion years ago, and it is now a two-story structure with all the rooms surrounding a central courtyard. The building looks as if it has not received any paint or maintenance for decades. Kerry thinks there are too many seedy people lurking about. She does not know if they are fellow guests, part of the establishment, or random wanderers, but she does know she doesn't like any of them. One particularly grim looking old man crouches against an inner courtyard wall, sharpening his large knife. We all hope he is a security guard since the doors to our rooms do not lock properly. Kerry is convinced the knife sharpener is a psychotic slasher intent on making a blonde woman his next victim. She piles all of our gear against the door, and reasons that it will at least slow the madman down long enough for Cris to jump into action.

"Don't misunderstand me," Kerry says. "I want Cris to win of course. But if he doesn't, he's the one who brought me here, and I hope to have the satisfaction of seeing him go first."

"A very noble thought, my dear," Cris says.

"How long does it take to sharpen a knife for Christ sakes?" Kerry asks. "What's the purpose?"

"I told you what Arab men are like before we left. Few of them support women's liberation. Didn't you ever take any comparative religion?"

It is getting late by the time we go look for something to eat.

We find a small outdoor café. One of the four tables is empty and we sit down. It is the most exotic eating establishment I have ever seen. Kerry thinks it looks like "a minus five on the one to ten cleanliness scale." All of the other patrons are slurping a thick soup, and we order three bowls of the same. The delicious concoction is accompanied by heavy dark bread that even Kerry cannot resist. She has been eating tangerines all day, and I have not seen her this happy in a long time.

"This is wonderful!" she exclaims. "I'm lucky I have two great guys by my side. Good men are hard to find, particularly around here."

Tuesday morning brings a crisp, clear day to the valley around Fez, the kind of weather that makes everyone feel better. We are served coffee and croissants in the courtyard. After breakfast, Cris and I smoke hashish on our exterior balcony overlooking old Fez. We can see that the city occupies a position of outstanding beauty. It is surrounded on all sides by verdant hills. The French section of the city, where we have spent the night, is landscaped and quite pleasant. We wander around town and pick up maps at the nearby tourist office. The old section, the famous medieval medina, is a ways off, so we hail a taxi and speed down a wide boulevard toward the old city.

Cris has the driver drop us off at the far end of the Bou Jeloud Gardens, a large square just outside one of the ancient gates to the medina. It is the highest point near the old city and it has always commanded its defenses. The guard is still up when we arrive, and touts swarm all over us when we exit the cab. As usual, Kerry draws the most attention, and she is dealing with it better all the time, but I can also see it is not easy for her.

"It looks like we're back at the circus," Cris says as he politely declines all offers.

The public area inside the blue-tiled gate of Fez is larger than I had expected. It is a major hub of commercial activity. Cheap hotels, open air restaurants, small businesses and inexpensive food stalls line the perimeter. We book two rooms at the nearest hotel and sit down at a small café for mint tea. I appreciate a place away from the omnipresent salesmen, and I love the sweet tea. There is a subdued frenzy all around us, and it is so much more than I had imagined, because it is further away than I can comprehend. The Marinid Sultanate controlled this medieval city for two hundred years, and much of it looks the same as it did in the fifteenth century.

Kerry decides to escape the frenzy and returns to the room to read and relax. She feels safe in there. Cris and I head out to explore the inner reaches of the vast medina. The usual bevy of unofficial guides harass us as we slog our way inward. The Rue du Grand Talaa, the main street in the medina, descends from near our hotel. It is a winding path covered in places with trellis or matting to provide shade. The narrow street is lined with little shops. It is also crowded with people, donkeys, oxen, and carts. Fountains with beautiful tile basins seemingly at every corner. Most buildings have white walls; some are cracked and crumbling, but the ancient and the contemporary blend well in this setting, and the labyrinth of stone and dirt byways are incomprehensible.

We walk for over an hour. The streets and byways become narrower and narrower. One by one the self-appointed guides have left us. However, a poorly dressed old man stays with us, his malformed leg requiring the use of a crude crutch. Whenever he is rebuffed he retreats while still following our course. It seems to me that everything the world has to offer is at our fingertips. Many of the goods have been sold on these same lanes for centuries. Modern electronics are readily available as well. I suspect I could find liquor if I asked.

We stop at a small shop opposite the entrance to a major mosque. An old man is selling a dazzling array of pipes. We buy two expensive models and are talked into several extra clay bowls.

Cris jokingly accuses the vendor of trying to pad the sale.

"We pay your asking price," Cris points out. "And now you say we must spend more for extra bowls. Maybe we should talk more about the price of the pipes."

The old man looks up and smiles. "You Europeans are all

the same. Rich and cheap. Pay me for the pipes, and the extra bowls are free. You are clumsy and will break them easily." He pauses and smiles at both of us. "And in the future you will thank me for my generosity."

"We thank you now," I say. "And we know Allah will smile on both your wisdom and your generosity." As I've said before, I like telling people what they like to hear.

"What do people use these pipes for?" Cris asks the vendor.

"They're for smoking kif," the old man replies. "Some use them for tobacco and hashish."

"Would you happen to have anything we can put in these pipes?"

"You'll have to find that on your own," he says with a laugh. "It won't be difficult. The old man with the crutch is a reliable source."

We do not walk more than fifty feet when our crutch-bearer hobbles out from a cloth stall. We are both surprised to see him in front of us. He straightens his bent back, takes his cane in both hands, and looks us in the eye. We stop and meet his stare.

"Are you looking for something to put in those pipes?" The old man's English is strong and clear.

"What do you suggest?" Cris asks.

"What do you want?"

"Show us the options."

We are led down a small alley that widens to about six feet after several hundred yards. The stone walkway is slippery and it makes the going slow. However, our new friend limps with a steady pace. We now know we are in a section of the massive maze that the tour groups do not visit. After fifteen minutes we enter a tiny wooden doorway that leads upwards. Before approaching the steps we look at each other.

"Well, what do you think?" Cris asks.

"I say we risk it. Go boldly where no white man has ever gone before."

We lower our heads and walk up a dark damp stairway. Our infirm guide steadily leads the way. The first flight of stairs is wet, slimy with moss. We have to feel our way with both hands on opposite walls, as there is no visibility. The footing is treacherous, but the narrow passage makes the climb easier; bouncing off the walls keeps us on our feet. At this stage the only undesirable direction is down. We both stiffen when a burly local approaches at the first landing, but are relieved when he humbly apologizes in French on his way past. To overtake anyone in this tunnel means bowed heads and backs against the wall. The confines make physical contact almost mandatory, and in places there is barely enough room to turn around.

We pass through another doorway and enter a small smoky room. Large open windows on either side reveal our position, which is on a wide bridge that looks down on the narrow cart way below. A dozen small tables line each side of this archway. The large windows provide a good view of the street. Our guide sits us at the only unoccupied table and tells us he will be back soon.

A middle-aged man serves us mint tea while we wait. All of the other patrons are Moroccan. They are all talking softly, drinking mint tea, and smoking dope. To my amazement, no one pays any attention to us, and to my great surprise, several women are present. The ladies briefly glance at us, and I notice all of the smokers have their own pipes, which are similar to the ones we have just purchased. Leisurely, they draw in the smoke, and expel the dying embers onto the floor. Some of them are laughing, some are eating. It appears to be a very relaxed atmosphere, and I like it because there is not a person on earth who could find me here. I felt this same way on the boat until my head was nearly crushed from behind.

We have nearly finished our tea when our guide returns. He has brought several varieties of hashish. Two inhalations from my new pipe puts me where I want to be. It is elation on a sublime scale, and the euphoria provokes a feeling of soulful kinship with those around me. Our guide chuckles and asks us what we think.

"I think you know more than you say," Cris says.

"I would hope so."

We have another glass of tea while the transaction is

completed. Cris buys enough to last for the remainder of his stay in Morocco.

"The vendor is friendly and the deal is easy. It will be something less to think about as I travel south." Cris redirects his attention back to their supplier. "By the way, what's your name?"

"Muhammad."

"Everyone in this country is named Muhammad. How do you tell each other apart?"

"That is not your concern."

I rise early the next morning and walk the ring road around the old city. Fez commands splendid views of the vast medina. To the south the hills climb to over five thousand feet. The new town's tall buildings gleam on the distant plateau. The flat, watered valley shines with the gloss of fertile land, and beyond the river there is a long ridge. It is the highest part of the Middle Atlas Mountains of Morocco and its snowfields are sparkling bright. I take in the physical heart and soul of a great Moorish metropolis, finding a pleasant place to sit on an uninhabited hillside overlooking it all, take out my recently purchased products and have a few heavenly hits.

On my way back to the hotel I stop at a small café and write to Vanessa. It is a difficult undertaking because I do not know where to begin. I tell her how much I miss her, and how I wish she was here. It sounds banal when I read it back. I avoid specifics I can't articulate on paper, and I purposely omit any mention of the attack on the ship, because I am the only one who knows it's true.

When I return to the hotel, my two companions are sitting outside having coffee and croissants. I greet them cheerfully and sit down.

"It's certainly a beautiful day," I say. "How's it going?"

"Not perfectly well," Kerry says. "Put it this way. It could be better, but I can't do anything about it."

"I take exception," Cris says. "I agree with you, Andreas. It's a splendid day. And I'm doing everything I ever wanted to do. Well, not everything. I've always wanted to wake up and have happy people around at breakfast."

"Fuck you and your happy breakfasts," Kerry says sarcastically. "There are things I've always wanted too. Like sheets that haven't already been slept in. Or men who look beyond my tits, ass, and crotch. I'm not as happy as you because I'm not a male in this wretched place. I lack that precious little appendage. You assholes can go wherever you want. I can barely leave the table without being accosted by a throng of lecherous jerks. You chuckleheads are starting to piss me off. These men are pigs. I wish they'd break with their stupid religion and eat each other. Pigs should eat pigs."

"She woke up on the wrong side of the bed," Cris says to me. "I don't think she's going to get that job at the UN."

Muhammad becomes our spiritual advisor and traveling mentor in Fez. He takes us to places even the locals do not usually frequent. Smiles and handshakes greet him wherever he goes. I can see that he is a popular fellow. His disability is more of a trademark than a handicap. The high pressure furor of the medina seems to dissipate with his presence; laughter accompanies us wherever we go. Even Kerry enjoys the treks into the mystifying medina, and begrudgingly agrees with our assessment of Muhammad.

Muhammad leads us through a warren of pathways to the large tannery in the middle of the ancient city. Several acres of the medina are devoted to this enterprise, and we are stunned by the enormity of the operation. Hundreds of hides are drying in the sun. There are great vats of dye. Half naked red bodies wade about with the skins. Muhammad says the best view is from above. He hobbles up ladders and leads us along catwalks. Eventually we reach the top. The stench is very strong, but it is one of the most incredible sights I have ever seen.

"From here you can see it all," Muhammad says, "the mountains, the medina, and the misery."

It is a breathtaking view. We marvel at the tremendous amount of work being done directly below us. There is not a modern machine to be seen. We are transfixed by the vista, and no one says anything. Time briefly stands still as we forget ourselves and think of the thousands who have come before.

Kerry breaks the silence. "It's too much. But it's all too much, including the smell. Let's keep moving."

On our way back to the hotel, Muhammad stops at some of the historical sights. He loves his city and takes great pride in its history, art, and architecture. Fez contains the oldest continually operated university in the world, and the largest mosque in Morocco. We catch several glimpses of the interior of the great mosque. There are fanciful marble pavilions with hundreds of colonnades. We see splendidly engraved bronze plaques, deeply carved cedar wood windows, and sumptuous vestibules. The huge courtyard looks like the most peaceful place in the entire city. It is early evening by the time we make it back to our hotel. To please Kerry, we have dinner at a malt shop down the street and prepare to move on.

The next morning we catch an early morning bus to Chefchaouen. Initially the winding road takes us higher into the mountains through forests of cedar and pine, along a scenic route on a bumpy road. Cris is tempted to get off when the bus makes a brief stop in Ketama.

"This is the cannabis capital of Morocco," he says. "It's famous with all hashish smokers. For a doper it's like going to Mecca for the Hajj. But I think we should save it for another day."

Four hours after leaving Fez the bus stops in a park-like square near the center of the small town of Chefchaouen. To our surprise and delight there are no high-pressure salesmen waiting for us here. Cris and Kerry stay in the square and watch the gear while I climb up the hill into town to find a hotel. The second hotel I look at is ideal. I know it the moment I enter the small lobby: there is a well-stocked bar adjacent to the front desk, an unusual feature in this price range, especially in Muslim Morocco. The owner serves as the desk clerk, and proudly shows me around the premises. Everything is scrupulously clean and the view is spectacular. I book two adjoining rooms that share a large rooftop balcony. It is more than I wanted to pay but I know Cris and Kerry will love it, particularly Kerry. The cleanliness is up to her standards, and the relaxing location will be a relief from the frenzy of Fez. I hustle back to the square to deliver the news.

"I've found paradise!" I exclaim. "Completely on my own. I'm quite proud of myself, actually. This place is like no other. You guys are going to love it."

"No doubt it's the cheapest place in town," Kerry says.

"You're going to regret that comment." I rub my chin and point my finger at her. "It's right down your alley. And it's not the cheapest, but it's worth every dirham, because it's the best."

We spend the rest of the afternoon on our rooftop balcony admiring the view, smoking hashish, and drinking red wine. The setting against the mountains is magnificent. We are quickly flushed with good spirits. The French did a terrific job with their Moroccan vineyards, and I consider the fruit of their efforts to be the country's best-kept secret. Religious intolerance works for some, but it doesn't prevent everyone from falling victim to the liquid appeal. My theory is confirmed later that evening when we find ourselves the only non-Moroccans at the crowded downstairs bar. There are women present, and heavy drinks are consumed all around. For the first time since getting off the freighter, Kerry makes friends with the locals and loosens up. The Moroccan women laugh at all of her assessments; she is brilliant at going with the flow when she wants to impress.

The people of Chefchaouen are easygoing and friendly. A congenial small-time atmosphere prevails around the area. Visitors can move about without being constantly accosted by vendors. We hike on the well-tended paths above the town. The mountain air is clean and clear, and the streams are cold and pure. We see another side of this country and its people, and the more we see the more we like.

"It's postcard perfect," Kerry says after another long hike. "Get rid of the men and it's paradise. The women are great, but their odds aren't that good. Unless they're rich."

We savor our active days in Chefchaouen. I am happy to have some quiet time to write to Vanessa. I go on extended hikes by myself and try my best to give Cris and Kerry their privacy. We pursue separate paths and usually only meet up around the bar at night. All of us would like to stay longer, but our reality is the desire to keep moving and see new places, improve upon perfection. I feel that Cris and Kerry have much more reason to be upbeat and optimistic than I do. Their lives are not under a dark cloud. I do not talk about my own fears anymore. No one has listened and no one believes. The fear is mine alone and seems to be gathering steam. The nightmares persist. But the road show has just begun and we hope for a long run. Tangier and the rest of the world beckon. The lure of unseen geography pulls us onward. We feel healthy, well rested, and ready to move on. A convivial late night in the bar ends a flawless, relaxed stay.

We pack up the next morning, walk back to the main square, and catch a bus to Tangier. The bus makes a brief stop in Tetouan on its way to the coast. Thirty minutes after leaving Tetouan, the bus is stopped on the open highway by Moroccan soldiers who inform us that they are searching for illegal drugs. Everyone is ordered off the bus while the interior is examined. Most of the luggage is opened. I am panic-stricken because both Cris and I are carrying hashish. My new pipe protrudes from my pocket. The authorities select unlucky passengers and perform perfunctory body searches. Miraculously, the foreigners are spared. Everyone is declared clean, and after a half-hour delay the bus continues its journey toward Tangier. I have slipped through the legal net once again, but my nerves are shattered, and I look at Cris.

"Strike two."

"Valium is my drug of choice from here on out."

Nothing prepares the uninitiated for the turmoil of Tangier. Its location contributes to its uniqueness, and on a clear day Europe can be seen across the straits from Africa. But it is the people that set the city completely apart. The cultural collision of the two continents has always commenced in Tangier. Muslim, Christian, Jew, Hindu, Buddhist, Berber, European, Asian, Turk, Russian. All are present in Tangier, which has been a major crossroads since the dawn of travel and civilization. All languages are spoken here, and everyone has a different story to tell. The varied inhabitants are consistent with the international nature of the city, and I've learned that they are like no other people on earth. The constant influx of visitors has helped hone their talents. I have read everything Paul Bowles ever wrote, and here I am, like someone stepping into a book, or off its pages.

When we exit the bus, we are swarmed by a beehive of activity in search of someone to sting. It's make a sale, get a job, or pay the price by going hungry. We shed locals quickly as we trek across the new town to the Grand Socco. This large and unparalleled open marketplace looks like a carnival sideshow in a blockbuster movie. It boasts a variety of types. But the players in this scene are not acting. This is great drama and it is all real in one way or another.

An elderly street vendor approaches us carrying his product on his back. The holy drinking water is dispensed into a communal copper cup. I buy a cup and drink it down.

"It's delicious," I say after licking my lips. "I just hope my shots are still good."

"No shots are that effective, "Kerry says. "I don't expect to see you live through the night." My impending death jokes aren't funny anymore, even to me. It's all too real. I'm the only one who knows.

Tangier sprawls out around the small medina, on a steep hillside that slopes down to the spellbinding harbor. From the Grand Socco, outside the medina's main landward gate, we head downhill to the appropriately named Petit Socco, where we find an inexpensive hotel overlooking the small square below. It is a relief to dump the packs and be off the crowded walkways. The high windows in my room provide an unobstructed view of the square. Groups of tourists are guided through the maze, while locals sip mint tea at outside tables. It is a functioning open-air museum coexisting with a charming tourist trap.

I am admiring my view when Cris and Kerry suddenly appear on the far side of the square. They settle in for mint tea at a café on the edge of the Socco. I can see that they are talking very seriously, and I decide to allow them some alone time. After a few minutes, Kerry leans back in her chair and spies me up in my window. She waves for me to come down and join them.

"Kerry and I have been talking," Cris says when I sit

down. "We've decided to split up here in Tangier. I'm going to continue with my original plan. South across the desert to West Africa. She's not too keen on the idea."

"At this stage I think I would lose my mind," Kerry says. "I'm not the hardy traveler I expected to be. The trip sounds too difficult for me. I'm just not into any more Arab bullshit. I've had just about enough of this." She spreads her arms and looks around the square. "I've seen enough. Marrakesh is not on my wish list."

"What are your plans?" I ask her.

"That's what I want to talk to you about," she says. "I was hoping I could tag along with you in Europe for awhile. I want to fly back to L.A. from Paris or London. Be honest. If you don't like the idea, say so."

I do not know what to say. The dramatic change of plans catches me completely off guard. I stall for a moment and try to formulate my thoughts.

"I really don't know what I'm going to do," I say. "What vague plans I do have could change at any time. I'm feeling paranoid and playing it day to day. Right now I think I'll check out Europe for a while. Why not? I've always wanted to go. After that who knows? Maybe I'll be dead. Just kidding. I just want to keep moving. I might try to rendezvous somewhere down south with you, Cris. Where do you think you'll be in January?"

"Hard to say. If everything goes well I hope to be in East Africa. I'll try to stay in touch as best I can."

"Well, what do you think?" Kerry asks me. "Do you mind if I travel north with you for awhile? Be honest."

"Of course you're welcome to come along. If you think you can stand me. That's a big if. I'm flattered. And honored to be asked by such a lovely lady." I am tempted to lay it on even thicker but decide not to. "Let's agree to let each other know if we start grating on the nerves. And try to remain friends at all costs."

"For sure," she says with conviction. "I appreciate it. We've already traveled together for a while. Thanks. I promise not to give you any trouble."

Her assurance does not relieve my suspicions, in that my observations have convinced me she is seldom compliant. Kerry yields when she wants to yield, or when it is the lesser of two evils. She is moody at times and complains too much. She can be highly aggressive when she feels things are not going her way. I also knows she is sharp, clever, amusing, intelligent, and open-minded. But I do not think I really know her, because I have always only known her in conjunction with Cris. They have been the couple. I have been the odd man out along for the enjoyable ride.

"What do you think of this, Cris?" I ask.

"I think it's for the best," she says. "I'm in a hurry to get south and I don't think Kerry would enjoy the trip. I'm on the train to Marrakesh day after tomorrow. After that I expect it to start getting tougher. I hate to say goodbye but that's what's happening. It's easier going north and I'm sure you'll both enjoy it. I've been there done that. I want to see things I haven't already seen. Places I've never been. People and cultures I've never met. A trip of a lifetime. I've been planning this one for quite awhile."

We finish our tea, walk to the top of the Casbah, and sit on a ledge overlooking the straits. Some of my memories have now become uncertainties, and my anxiety is mixed with anticipation. The rapidly changing relationships make it difficult to evaluate anything. I wish I could simplify my thoughts because I seem to be moving fast in all directions at once, but I gaze toward Spain and know I am headed north.

I write a letter to Vanessa but carefully omit mention of Kerry's new travel plans. I rationalize that there is no need to arouse suspicions, because I am sure that she would not look favorably on this new arrangement. I know the relationship with Kerry is platonic, but reason that distant explanations may not be convincing.

Later that evening I hear music from below my room and go downstairs to investigate. There is nothing happening in the square, just the usual crowd sipping mint tea. The sounds are coming from around the corner, away from the Socco, down one of the small alleyways. I head in the direction of the music, and soon discover its source. A group is playing in a corner café and I sit at a small table by myself. The only other listeners are a diverse group of locals who occupy three tables opposite me. They are laughing, tapping their feet to the music, drinking mint tea, and smoking hashish. I soon become absorbed in the powerful sound. I feel more relaxed and calm than I have in quite some time, and as always, I enjoy being by myself in situations like this.

By midnight the café has become a major gathering spot. All the tables are full. The room is crowded, dark, and smoky. And although several of the musicians are over sixty, this is primarily a younger audience, and the splendid music dominates. I am happy that I do not have to deal with anyone. I am enjoying my solitude, but my feelings about traveling with Kerry are mixed at best.

Without warning, a Moroccan guy suddenly pulls a chair over next to me. The newcomer is dressed like he is doing a Zorro impression. He is wearing tight black pants and a snug black shirt. The full black cape tops it all off. His leather boots and hat match the cape. His mustache looks fake. I think Zorro must be gay. Either that or it's Halloween in Morocco. I do not really care about Zorro right now. The gay blade could be a long-lost childhood friend and I would not be pleased to see him. I am doing fine listening to the music by myself, and I studiously ignore my new tablemate.

"Where are you from?" Zorro asks in perfect non-accented English. I pretend to be absorbed in the music.

"I said, where are you from?" Zorro's shout can't be ignored.

"Australia."

"That's funny. You don't sound like you're from Australia." I don't say anything. I know I am being pushed.

"I said you don't sound like you're from Australia."

"You don't sound like you're from Morocco." I turn and look at Zorro. "But right now I don't give a shit why. I'm enjoying the music. Please allow me to do it by myself."

"I want to know where you're from."

"In a few words or less, what's it to you?"

"Sounds like you're an American."

"Suit yourself, cowboy."

"I guess you're a pretty smart guy."

"It depends on who's making the call," I say.

"Do you ever smoke hashish?" Zorro asks in French.

"I don't speak French."

"That's a lie. You speak it as well as I do."

I can't understand why this guy is engaging me like this. What's in it for him?

"I have the best stuff in Africa. It's pure." Zorro leans over. "Do you want to try some?"

"No thanks."

"Why not? Are you too good for me? Rich white boy does not want to be friends with dark-skinned African. Is that your story?"

"I'm into the music, my friend. It has nothing to do with you. Maybe we can talk later. I've had difficult times lately and would prefer to be by myself."

Zorro prepares a large chunk of dark hashish and mixes it with stringy tobacco. The music heats up and I regret not taking Zorro up on his offer. To my delight, he pushes the pile over and hands me the pipe. I take two deep hits and put the pipe down.

Two minutes later the room and the music seem to be exploding. This Zorro smoke is very strong. I grip the seat of my chair and pretend nothing is happening.

"Well, what do you think?"

"I said, what do you think?" He raises his voice.

"About what?" I ask.

"Anything."

"Nothing."

"What about the hashish?" Zorro asks. "I'll bet you can't think straight."

"That's a pretty good bet," I say.

"I know everything about you," Zorro says.

"Why do you care?" I ask.

"I don't really. But I think you might want to hear it. It's intriguing."

"Like what do you know?"

"Like you're from New York. You've been traveling with a couple from California. You're headed to Europe and the woman is going along with you. You're not sure it's the right move. She's very attractive."

"Not bad. What else do you know?" I ask nervously. Zorro has captured my attention big time.

"Right now you're wondering how I found out about you and the people you're with. You think I must have followed you into the hotel, or something. You're thinking maybe I can read your mind and it's making you incredibly anxious. You hope it's the hashish but you know it's not. Now you're thinking you'd better get away from me. Back to your hotel. I'm starting to really scare you."

Zorro has hit the mark. This guy is reading my thoughts, and I am shocked. Nothing like this has ever happened to me before.

"Test me, man," Zorro chides me. "Concentrate on something remote."

I am frightened by this taunt. Zorro looks wicked and acts confident. The challenge is difficult to accept. The tension within me is scrambling everything. I direct my energy to the small round table in front of me, but I gaze out at the crowd and look around the room in an attempt to throw Zorro off.

"Get your mind off that table and start thinking about me," Zorro says softly. "Now you're petrified. You wish I didn't exist."

Zorro is right. We both know it. Zorro holds all the cards. This African stranger has got me good. I worry about what comes next. Does Zorro know why, when, and where I will die? Is Zorro part of what happened on the ship? Does Zorro know who was driving that car in New York? Who pushed me in front of the train? Was Zorro on the boat? Does Zorro want me dead? Is Zorro going to kill me right here and now?

"Relax, my friend." Zorro touches my forearm. "I most certainly do not want you dead. On the contrary, I want you on my side. Alive and well."

This statement takes a little of the edge off, but I am disappointed with myself. I crossed an ocean to stay alive. Zorro is not the image I want. I need an ancient, smiling, benevolent sage. This guy is young, flamboyant, and threatening. Zorro makes me realize that there is another league, where they play the game with an understanding beyond mine. I grope for an explanation and wonder if Zorro ever changes his disguises. Does he own a ski mask?

"I don't ski," Zorro says with a friendly smile.

"What should I think about you?" I ask.

"You tell me. They say first impressions last. I'm a guy you just met. Up till now I've had both the questions and the answers. You've had neither. It's up to you."

"What do you want from me? Why bother?"

"I just want your friendship. See the world from my eyes. There are millions of people like me. Every voice is important. Educate the ignorant. Do more. Actually, you are a better guy than you give yourself credit for."

I am having trouble with everything Zorro says, but I like that last statement. "Why me?"

"You're all I've got right now." Zorro laughs, reaches over and shakes my hand.

"There is something I just recently learned. It's important. You're in a very dangerous situation. You are not safe here in Tangier. Your life is in jeopardy. That is all I know. But I know it for sure. I like you. I can't imagine why anyone would want to kill you. But it's true. Someone wants you dead." Zorro stands up, turns around, and walks away.

Cris, Kerry, and I have our last breakfast together in the Petit Socco. We take a taxi to the station and Cris catches the train south. Kerry and I are left alone on the platform. We do not say anything to each other as we make the long walk back to the hotel. Since her room only has one bed, and mine has two, Kerry decides to move into my room. I like having my own space but do not object. The desk clerk thinks this is a funny development and laughs with his assistant in Arabic. I wish I could share their bemusement. Kerry deposits her pack in the corner of my room and flops down onto her new bed.

"It feels like there's been a death in the family," she says.

"It's not quite that bad." The death analogy startles me. "After all, Cris is still alive."

"I wonder if I'll ever see him again," she says. "I'm not sure I even want to."

"Why's that?" I wish I was not in this deep already. It was a major worry when the pairing was first proposed, but I find her spirit sublime, and know by now that she generally says and does what she wants to. I find her beguiling.

"Cris is a great guy, but I don't think we could ever have a lasting relationship." She is starting to cry. "He always wants to keep moving. It's like he's addicted to the road. I think I want to settle down and raise a family. I'd lose my mind trying to stay with his itinerary. He'd lose his trying to play house with me. It was great while it lasted, but I doubt if we will ever be together again."

"People change. Circumstances change. You never know." I hate my clichés but do not know what else to say.

"Some things never change." Kerry looks away to hide her tears.

Right now I would like to go over to her bed, wrap her in my arms, and slowly make love to her, probably the most inappropriate thing to do under the present circumstances.

Instead we spend the remainder of the day sightseeing in Tangier. Kerry enjoys visiting the chic shops in the new city. She is more considerate to the locals than I have seen in the past, and I like being one-on-one with her.

"Let's splurge and go to an expensive place for dinner," Kerry says, "and after dinner, let's go to the casino. Maybe you'll be my lucky charm."

"Sounds good to me." I know that it is in my best interests to keep her as happy as I can. So far it has been the easiest job I've ever had, but I know that my first day isn't even over yet.

The desk clerk recommends a restaurant frequented by locals and tourists alike. The spacious, ornate room is crowded when we arrive. There are low tables and dozens of sofas draped with tapestry. Musicians are seated on the floor, and dancers entertain while diners eat. Kerry is in the best mood since she got off the boat. I stuff myself with roast lamb and wash it down with way too much red wine. The excessive drinking and the hashish bring visions of well-stocked harems. The nubile young bodies frolicking in front of me excite my prurient interest. It is a male condition that cannot be denied within this environment, and I feel like I'm part of a giant movie set again.

"I know it's a terrible thing to say," I announce, "but I'm beginning to empathize with King Farouk's worldview. The more women the better. This is a blatantly chauvinistic society, but from a man's perspective, things could definitely be a lot worse."

"That's true. But it's hard for me to look at things from a man's perspective. The one thing, and I mean the only thing, that could make men here worse would be for the government to encourage drinking. The dope mellows them out a bit. 'Drunken Arabs Run Amok'— the world's worst screenplay. Women can't trust them. With good reason."

After dinner we take a taxi to the modest casino. It is still early and there are more croupiers than customers. Kerry gravitates to the roulette wheel and begins to place bets. After fifteen minutes she has won over a thousand dollars. The only other player at the wheel is an overweight Frenchman who chuckles through his large nose whenever she hits a number.

"I told you I felt lucky," Kerry says with a smile. "I think we're just going to keep it going. We're a good pair."

"I think you ought to take the money and run," I reply. "I've always thought gambling was synonymous with losing."

"When I get to twenty-five hundred I'll quit."

I stand behind Kerry and survey the action. It is apparent that the croupier enjoys having her at his table, and I would not be surprised if the spinner could determine the final drop, because she continues to win, despite the odds.

After an hour she has passed her goal, and a small crowd has gathered around the table. A stunning blonde attracts attention, and gamblers like to be around winners, particularly sexy winners. Every time Kerry hits a number she shouts and gives me a hug. My fourth cognac makes it difficult for me to conceal my jubilation, but I think I can get even higher with no problems.

"I'll get us another drink," I say. "Keep winning while I'm gone."

"Don't be gone long." Kerry puts her arm around my waist and pulls me closer. "You're bringing me luck."

I wander over to the bar. When I sit down, two middle-aged Moroccans in business suits position themselves on either side of me. They do not look friendly and I ignore them. The older of the two whispers in French that he would like to talk to me in private. I remember Zorro's admonition to be careful. How can that be accomplished? I try not to show fear, and grin at the older man.

"This is as private as I get," I reply in French. "What do you have to say?"

"We've been sent to tell you that you have to leave."

"Why?" I ask. This is high anxiety.

"I do not know why. All I know is you have to leave."

"What about my girlfriend?"

"She can do what she pleases." They follow me back to the roulette wheel and I tap Kerry on the shoulder.

"I've just been told I have to leave." Now I wish I could have grabbed one more cognac.

"What did you say?" Kerry asks as she reaches out to place more bets.

"These two guys here just told me I have to leave."

"Why?"

"They won't tell me."

Kerry turns around and looks at the two Moroccans and then back at me. I shrug and raise my palms. She looks at the Moroccans again, extends her raised upper fist, and slowly lifts her middle finger.

"We prefer to stay," she says. "Fuck off."

"You can stay, miss. He has to leave." The Moroccan is all business.

"Why?"

"I cannot say."

"Then fuck off!" She says with a snarl. "He's with me and

were both staying. Go back to your perverted little brothel and leave us alone."

She turns around and directs her attention back toward the wheel. The ball drops on one of her numbers and she rakes in more chips. The croupier looks at his two countrymen, excuses himself to Kerry, and walks away from the table. Kerry watches him go, then swings around on her stool.

"What the fuck is going on here?" Kerry screams at the two Moroccans. "The house doesn't tolerate winning. Is that it? You can only gamble if you promise to lose? This is a classic move coming from you spineless bastards. Why don't you tie me up like you have to do with your own women. Better still, just go butt fuck each other. It's obviously part of your DNA."

Her tirade justifiably draws a crowd, and everyone is looking at this shrieking beauty. We are all captivated by her outrageous harangue and wonder what will happen next. I am aghast but silently supportive. Kerry calms down a bit when she sees how much attention she has received. She looks at the two Moroccans, then over at me, and flashes her confident grin. I give her a nod and two thumbs up.

"I'll cash out and then we'll get the fuck out of here. This is unbelievable."

"You can stay if you want," I say. "They're only telling me to leave."

"I wouldn't be caught dead with these fucking assholes. They'd sell me into slavery if they could."

I wish she had not used the dead word. I fear I might be the one caught dead. Why are they kicking me out? I'd hoped my experience with Zorro would spark a crystallization, but instead I am more confused than ever. The older Moroccan accompanies us to the door.

"I'm very sorry about this, sir," the bouncer says. "Management didn't want any trouble."

I am incredulous. I don't think I have ever caused trouble. I pride myself on being a happy drunk. Kerry and I get on the elevator and return to street level. Neither of us can understand why my presence was unwelcome. I tell Kerry about meeting Zorro and the warning he gave. She thinks I am becoming "unbelievably more paranoid than ever. These people are fucking with your mind."

"Getting kicked out of the casino? Isn't that a tad too coincidental? A little too much?"

"Zorro's warning was bullshit. Arabs love to scare people. They never really deliver the goods. That's why they are what they are. The only thing they've got is oil, and it's not working well on their brains. If their women could take over, it would be a much better place, but so would the rest of the world."

"The guy was reading my mind. Everything I was thinking." I can see that Kerry does not believe a word of it.

"These people have made you crazy." She grins. "Plus you drink too much, and the hashish isn't helping. But you're amusing. And you need a change. I know I could certainly use one. Let's catch the ferry to Spain tomorrow morning."

I agree that it's high time to get out of town, beginning to feel like I've really started to run, from and toward what I don't know. As for Spain, why not?

4

THE SPANISH AFFAIR

IT IS LATE AFTERNOON when we leave the ferry and enter Algeciras, Spain. The contrast with Morocco is like night and day. A short physical distance, it's a long economic and societal divide from where we have just been. The staggering frenzy that whirled around us in Morocco has disappeared and been replaced with unusual calm.

I can see that Kerry likes Spain immediately. She enjoys the absence high-pressure salesmen, and she can see that there are many scantily clad attractive women out and about by themselves. None of them are wearing veils. There are also no "guides" and we have to find a hotel on our own. Kerry enjoys the search because she can speak the language, and her fluent Spanish impresses me. After looking at two hotels she books a room. It is spotlessly clean and she sighs as she removes her backpack.

"I knew things were going to improve," she says with a contented smile. "That country was just too fucking much. I can't imagine being a woman there. Hell hath no fury."

"I feel like we've entered another world. It's almost too mellow. Let's explore and find something to eat and drink. Not necessarily in that order."

Kerry likes the Spanish and feels comfortable in their country. We spend our first week here exploring the Costa del Sol.

We discover that the Mediterranean coast north of Gibraltar is a hodgepodge of conflicting economic interests. Beautiful beaches have been sold to wealthier northern neighbors, and ugly tall buildings dot the horizon. We pack up and take a short bus ride north nearly every day. The paella and sherry remain consistent, but the world around us changes constantly, and we both appreciate the variety.

We always have black coffee and brandy before we get on the bus. It gives us the energy to keep moving and invariably improves our outlook. And it's great to be back in a country where everyone is so openly alcoholic. Unlike Muslim Morocco, there is no under-the-counter nonsense here. The Spanish are proud of their ability to drink and maintain. They show off their skills around the clock, and much of the drinking is done standing up, to prove, I think, that it takes more than a few stiff ones to put these people down.

Unfortunately my own tolerance for alcohol increases every day. A week of constant inebriation reaches its climax in Nerja, a little town north of Malaga. We spend the day walking the quaint streets and admiring the fantastic views from the Balcon de Europa. But later that night unbridled excess catches up with me. Too many sardines, too much sherry, and too many hits of my smuggled hashish combine horribly. I awaken and bolt upright in bed. Vomit gushes from my mouth. It sprays the low ceiling and all over the opposite wall. It is like the room is aflame and I am using my mouth as a fire hose filled with partially digested particles. I have never gone this far before, and I know I'm in big trouble with my traveling companion.

Kerry leaps from her bed and turns on the lights. Regurgitated red wine, miniature fish chunks, and soggy bread dribble down from the ceiling and wall. Kerry is deeply appalled by my lack of control but does not say a word. I try to clean it up but quickly realize the task is beyond me. The filth is everywhere. I have no equipment, and only two small towels. My efforts are futile. I can tell a major cleaning crew will be required for this job. It is the worst awakening I have ever had, and I've had bad ones before.

"I think we'd better check out of here," I say lamely. "I'm

horribly embarrassed and feel like shit. I do know one thing, I will never drink again."

"You said that yesterday morning," she says disgustedly.

"This time I mean it."

"You also said that."

"Please don't rub it in, I feel bad enough already. I promise this horrendous display won't happen again. I mean that deep down."

We pack up and check out at dawn. Kerry explains our early departure by telling the desk clerk that I have become ill and must return to Malaga for treatment. The clerk is sympathetic, but I know she will not be when she sees the room. I look down at my feet, say nothing, and skulk out the door.

"Death should be the only excuse for leaving a room the way you did," Kerry says.

"I wish you'd get off your death talk. I'm beginning to think you're the one who hit me on the boat. I was dreaming about being murdered when I woke up this morning. So give me a break. Now I feel like I am dying."

"You should." She displays no sympathy. "You drank like a fool."

"I'll always remember your compassion in my hour of need." I am not amusing her and we both know it.

"Where to now?" She points her finger at me. "And if you say the nearest bar I'll slap you. I shouldn't say this…but you were pretty hilarious last night."

"Let's catch the bus to Seville," I say. "Everyone says it's a beautiful city, and they're having bullfights over there right now. I can't be in Spain and not see a bullfight. It's fate. The bull and I share the same destiny."

"Stop with the fucking self-pity. You're a paranoid drunk is all. When you start talking about snakes I'm leaving. Funny only goes so far. And if you do throw up again, I'm going to dump you."

By the time the local bus rattles into Seville I am about ready to pass out from anguish and exhaustion. I nearly soiled myself along the way, but thankfully passed gas instead. Kerry selects a moderately expensive hotel near the center of the city.

The adjoining bathroom is a supreme luxury.

"My insides are eternally grateful," I say from behind the door, while trying unsuccessfully to muffle the noise.

"I'm just glad to be off that smelly bus," Kerry replies. "It was like you were battling the locals with your foul farts. They fought back bravely with their stinking black tobacco. Unfortunately you all won. I needed a gas mask."

"If I didn't feel so vulnerable right now I would respond to that," I say from behind the door.

"Respond! How? By cutting another fart? Maybe you should see how flammable they are. Do your small part for the energy crises. Sell your gas back to the grid."

"Toilet humor is beneath you." How long will she be able to stand me, I wonder.

By morning I have recovered sufficiently to take a walking tour of the city. Seville turns out to deserve its reputation; it is quaint and engaging, a genuinely beauteous Spanish city. It charms us with its wide boulevards and small back streets. This is the city of Don Juan and Carmen, the spiritual capital of Andalusia. We wend our way through the fascinating quarter of Santa Cruz with its twisting byways, dignified old houses, and flagstone patios, splashed with the water of drowsy fountains the color of potted plants. Kerry insists on stopping for lunch at a sidewalk café near the Cathedral. It is the largest gothic building in the world, and we marvel at its magnificence.

"I like this place a lot," Kerry says softly. At this moment she is more breathtaking than I have ever seen her, but I'm still following my mother's admonition that "if a woman wants to be touched, she'll touch you first."

One feature of the city I soon learn to adore is the tapas, and we are told they are the best in Spain. We eat mostly in drinking establishments, from small plates, one little delicacy at a time. The offerings are unlimited and we do our best to sample it all.

"This is the only way to eat," I say enthusiastically.

"Only if you're an alcoholic, because it allows you to keep drinking. But I admit it's exciting. And all of this stuff hits the spot. It's the best bar food I've ever had."

We also both love the pinball machines. Every good tapa bar has an old machine that works well and costs next to nothing. Most of them make it easy to win games. They make me feel like Pete Townshend and I sing "Pinball Wizard" while I move the flippers.

On our third day I talk Kerry into going to a bullfight. She is not pleased with the prospect but reasons it should be seen at least once. As we approach the bullring I am struck by a strong feeling of déjà vu. We circle the exterior of the building while I try to interpret the feeling.

"I could swear I've been to this place before." I purse my lips and look around.

"Maybe you were a matador in a previous life," Kerry says.

"I doubt it. Their pants are too tight."

"I think you might be cute in tights. Even cuter if they made you sound like a soprano."

"That's it! It's Lincoln Center," I say. "The final act of *Carmen* at the Met. The sets were fabulous. It looked just like this place. It's uncanny."

"Are you trying to impress me? If you are, don't bother."

"I'm just actualizing my cultural heritage. My parents had season tickets for the opera."

"You're a lousy elitist. Save it for your rich friends back in New York. I don't give a shit. I've never been to the fucking opera."

Kerry wisely insists on paying more for seats in the shade. She thinks the spectacle is going to require heavy consumption and she does not want to do it in the sun.

"Big time drinking and direct sunlight don't mix," she says. "And alcohol makes bloodletting easier to watch. You're a natural for sure. I just hope I can put up with this. At least you're drinking a little less."

Once the action begins our attention is captured. The showmanship and carnage are impossible to ignore. Kerry has to turn her head away at times, and is nearly sickened by the brutal display, but she drinks steadily and sticks it out.

"It would be more enjoyable if they'd substitute Moroccan men for the bulls. I guess balls are balls." She keeps talking while she covers her eyes. "They have a lot in common. Subtle approaches. Intelligence levels. And mating habits."

There are more killings than either of us had anticipated. Bulls are continually released into the arena and the inevitable occurs. The beasts are slowly tortured to death in ritualistic fashion, and the triumphant matadors act like dandies. Kerry and I feel tortured along the way, her more than me. Several horses are wounded and two matadors are seriously injured, but the gory show goes on. We are both transfixed but sickened. After a while we find ourselves rooting for the bulls, despite the impossible odds. Our alcohol consumption, and the pomposity of the killers begin to make us rancorous. We cheer wildly whenever the bulls make contact, but we know it is to no avail. The lack of suspense is the fatal entertainment flaw here. Every one of these bloody dramas ends exactly the same. Kerry looks away during the endless death throes, and when the final bull is dragged from the ring, we are both drained by the entire affair.

"I'll admit those matadors looked pretty cute in their tight little pants," Kerry says as we leave. "What I can't understand is why anyone outside of the sadomasochistic community would bother to attend. Tight pants are one thing. Ritual torture and killing is another thing altogether."

"Are you saying that only sick, macho guys or gals would like this stuff? The derrieres don't do it for you?"

"You have such a delicate way with words. I was only theorizing that it has limited appeal. Once you've seen it, why come back?"

"Hemingway wouldn't agree."

"But he was a misogynistic, anti-Semitic, white supremacist. I can see its appeal to that crowd. Let's find a peaceful place for dinner and call it a day. Anything but steak tonight. I say let's share a vegi paella and keep drinking."

It is past midnight before we leave the restaurant. We are both drunk and decide we had better go straight back to the hotel. For the first time she takes hold of my hand and I can feel my inhibitions plummeting. I have grown extremely fond of her since we have been alone together, and I often awake with dreamlike morning erections that involve her. I reason that neither of us is particularly prone toward sexual abstinence, and at this intoxicated moment I have no hesitation in initiating my thoughts when we reach the room.

"Do you remember our last night in Tangier?" I ask.

"I sure do." She giggles. "I'm still living off my winnings."

"Something's changed in a big way since then," I say.

"What?"

"Me. My self-imposed celibacy is cracking under the strain. It's hard for me to keep my hands off of you. I think you're just great. Everything about you. To say nothing about being sexy beyond belief. You are just about too much to resist. In fact, I think you're irresistible."

"So what do you think you should do about that?"

"I suggest we take off all of our clothes and see what happens."

"Me first," she says with a tipsy grin. "But only if you promise to do the same thing when I'm finished. And only when I'm finished."

"Ladies first has always been my motto."

She cautions me with her finger to stay where I am. I remain in my chair and watch with tanked excitement. She sways sensuously about the room, and then slowly raises her blouse above her shoulders. It is an outrageously sexy display, and her presentation is enhanced when she removes her bra and exposes her breasts. I always knew they were beautiful, but they look better than ever right now, and I hope to be able to put her taut nipples into my mouth soon. It is all I can do to not run across the room and tackle this beauty. She senses my desire and wags her index finger, silently cautioning me to be still. She smirks at me as she moves around the room and strokes her breasts.

If I had known earlier what I was in for I would have initiated it much sooner. Now I understand some of the things she has said about reincarnation and predispositions. Kerry must have been a stripper in a previous life. No one could be this seductive without training and practice. A pole would be a superfluous distraction, because my own will be the only one of any importance tonight.

Erik Erickson

91

"That's a very tantalizing dance you're doing." I get right to the point. "I want to lick you all over."

"I'm just getting started," she whispers. "You'll get your chance."

"Will I live to see it end?"

"If you're lucky." She flashes a smile the likes of which I've never seen before.

She lowers her jeans and panties below her knees and slowly steps out of them, one cautiously smooth shapely leg at a time. Then she does a quick totally naked pirouette. I'm happy to see that her high ass is even more perfect than I thought it would be, and I cannot ever recall being in such a state of heightened anticipatory arousal. I know I'm close to exploding but also know it is far to early. When she finishes her second twirl she spreads her legs and masturbates briefly before telling me to take off my clothes.

"It's your turn now. But I want you to stay in the chair. Just show me what you've got. Don't stand up."

"You're starting to pique my interest." I understate my case to the extreme.

"Take it all off and be as still as you can. I want to tease you some more."

"I'll have to warn you." My eyes are riveted on her. "There's not much theatrical talent in my family. We're mostly professional people. However, maybe I just need a better opportunity. This could be it. We could be porn stars."

She swings over closer to my chair and begins to run her fingers up and down my back. It is the first time she has ever touched me this way, and I'm glad she didn't wait any longer. She moves around in front of me and gets down on her knees. And then she slowly lowers her head and touches me with her mouth. I cannot stifle my loud groan. When my hips begin to writhe, she gets back on her feet, spreads her legs, and starts to masturbate again.

"I don't want this to sound like a complaint," I say, "but don't you think you're being a little hard on me? As you can see I'm pretty hard already. If you want me to be so still it seems like the least you could do is tie me up."

"Next time," she laughs as she lowers herself back to her knees. And then she straddles me and inserts my penis between her spread legs.

Her up and down routine is repeated until I can no longer contain myself, and we both blissfully reach for eternity. It was a long time coming but worth the wait.

"That was just about too much," I say while still trembling.

"The pleasure was all mine. Well...we did share. We'll have to remember to pick up some sex toys and rope. I think you might like it."

I am awakened the next morning by the sounds of the shower. My head feels thick and cloudy, but when I think about what happened last night my spirits soar. Kerry emerges from the bathroom and is surprised to see me awake. She is naked and looks fresh and lovely. I remain expressionless and say nothing.

"How do you feel?" she asks.

"I'm a bit hung over. And I know I should feel guilty. But when I look at you the guilt goes away. In case you're wondering, no, this is not a tent pole underneath the sheet. It's my homage to last night."

"You are so reserved. That's why I like you so much. You're not just another pretty face."

"Go lie down on your bed and be as still as you can," I tell her.

"Is turnabout fair play?"

"You deserve a dose of your own medicine. Like you, I'm going to begin by administering it orally."

"What's good for the gander is good for the goose?"

"You got it. Now please go lie down and be as still as you can. You'll find it difficult. But rules are rules. You'll break sooner than I did."

"I was hoping you'd say that. But talk is cheap. Feeling's believing."

I try to repay her for last night. It is a major debt, but I hope I will be able to work on paying it off for a while. The first installment is marked with tenderness and consideration. I know she deserves my best and I try to provide nothing less. We have become gentle lovers and our relationship has become much more complicated. We hold our embrace and do not talk or move for what feels like forever but is less than an hour.

"Where do we go from here?" Kerry sighs and strokes my cheek.

"Straight to hell I suspect. No one should have it this good without paying the price. Where do you want to go next?"

"I've always dreamed of visiting England," she says. "And the cheapest flights back home are out of London. I'd like to get there as soon as possible. And I'd love to have you as my escort. I like having good-looking men on my arm, particularly when I'm fucking them. It makes traveling much easier."

"Let's catch the train north tomorrow," I say.

"I'm easy."

"I only wish I'd known it sooner."

"It was soon enough," she leans over and kisses my cheek.

The train glides out of Seville's station. Our movement is developing its own momentum and we both enjoy being swept along. After awhile, Kerry decides to go to the bar car and bring back a couple of beers. I have been looking out the window evaluating the weather, and wondering if the rain in Spain stays mainly in the plain. It is midafternoon before Kerry returns, wearing a wide smile and a slight alcohol flush. She's getting prettier every day.

"You have to come and meet this guy I met in the bar car," she says. "He's amazing! You two will really hit it off."

"Who is he?"

"His name is Rowalyn Cummings, but he calls himself Mousa."

"What's his story?"

"That's a tough one. His mother is Kenyan and his father is English. He's been in Morocco for the past month, just like us, and he's got great stories, but now he's headed back to England to see his father. He's really a nice guy. Absolutely gorgeous. I tell you, you'll like him. He's special."

"How old is he?"

"Around thirty."

"How'd you meet him?"

"When I entered the bar car he started singing to me. 'The Most Beautiful Girl in the World.' He was so funny I couldn't resist. He wouldn't let me buy anything. I ate like a queen and drank like a whore."

"Don't tell me I'm losing you already?"

"Not yet." She laughs. "But come and meet the competition. He's pretty strong stuff. You two will get along great. You've got things in common."

She leads me through the train to the bar car. When I see Mousa I fear I might be fighting a losing battle. Kerry has not exaggerated this time. Mousa is very handsome.

He bounds up from his chair and shakes my hand. His smooth brown complexion is lighter than I had expected, but I can understand Kerry's enthusiasm for his attractive attributes. Mousa has green eyes, a long muscular neck, a chiseled chin and high cheekbones. His lean body is crowned with dark, wavy hair. But his most striking feature is his smile, and he displays it often. He looks like he uses whitening toothpaste three times a day. They are even more dazzling against his milk chocolate background. Five minutes with Mousa convinces me that if it comes to competing for hearts, and losing, it is preferable to be beaten by such a formidable foe. Is this guy too good to be true? His aura is special, and I like him immediately.

Mousa orders a bottle of Spanish champagne. He continually asks us questions. Where were you born? When did you meet? What are your plans? We talk for hours as the train speeds toward Madrid. The champagne contributes to our universal infatuation with each other, growing stronger with each glass. Mousa is charming and full of information about where we have been and where we are going, and we are flattered by his undivided attention. Mousa reminds me of Zorro, but I keep that to myself.

Two members of the Civil Guard enter at the far end of the car. Their goofy hats are humorous, but the machine guns at their sides are no laughing matter. Mousa pours more champagne and raises his glass when they approach.

"Viva Espana," he says to them. They walk past and ignore him. "Unfortunately, cops are almost all the same. All over the world. They are either humorless dimwits, or fascists. It must be the nature of the job. Some are born and some are made. But I do think there would be much less crime if women were the only ones allowed on the force."

"Hear, hear," Kerry says.

"To be honest," Mousa says, "I hoped Kerry was lying when she said she was traveling with her husband. It's rough when the most beautiful woman in Spain is already taken." Mousa looks at Kerry and flashes his irresistible smile. "I offer a toast to a very attractive couple, and I hope it's a lasting friendship for us all. Viva Espana!"

"Here's to your continued good health, my friend." I raise my glass.

"Kerry says you're headed my way," Mousa says. " If you can find the time you'll have to come out and stay with me for awhile. My father will be in America. I'll be house sitting for him."

"Where's your father's house?" I ask. I find myself wanting this guy to like me.

"Somerset. Near Glastonbury. It's a lovely area. I'm sure you two would enjoy seeing it."

"Kerry told me your mother is from Kenya. Where does she live now? If you don't mind me asking." I have always thought that I pry well; and most people like to talk about themselves.

"She's a Kenyan citizen, but she's actually an ethnic Somali. Most of the time she lives on a farm near Mombasa. I spend three or four months there every year. I'll go down and visit her when my father returns to England."

"No job worries?" Kerry asks. "More money than you know what to do with?" I like her style, and I've learned her inappropriate questions are usually answered.

"I love you Americans," Mousa laughs. "Let me say that I'm in between jobs right now. I help my father here and there in his business dealings. I help my mother on the farm when I'm there. She needs my assistance for a project she's presently undertaking. And if you ask any more questions about my economic situation I'll consider it rude." He laughs again. "I'm only joking. Ask me anything."

By the time we reach Madrid, the champagne and fellowship have us roaring. Mousa knows the city and has a favorite hotel. We follow his lead and share a taxi from the station. I quickly see why I like Mousa so much. I have never seen anyone who so purposefully invites attention, and whose robust friendliness reaps only positive returns. He cuts a wide swath with his elevated spirits, and I can tell that everyone who comes in contact with him is swept along in his wake.

"Let's start with the old streets of the Malasana district," Mousa says. "It's a fabulous area. There are still plenty of plump fascists chomping on fat cigars and bemoaning the loss of the good old days, but the section is alive with fresh thoughts and new activities. The music doesn't stop till dawn."

We follow Mousa from one club to the next, and he is often the main attraction. I feel like I'm cruising the East Village again. The language is different but the sounds are similar. Kerry takes to the bohemian nightlife, and as always when she dances she takes pleasure in the attention she attracts. We are both elated to be with Mousa. He is the ultimate man about town. The pulsating tour does not end until three in the morning. We stagger back to the hotel drunk and in high spirits. Kerry crawls up the final flight of stairs to our room on her knees, but only for comic effect. For the first time since I have known her she falls asleep without brushing her teeth.

We are awakened the next morning by a loud pounding on our door. It is still early and we try to ignore the sound. Mousa will not be denied.

"Hey, you two," he shouts. "Wake up! Rise and shine! I have to be on the train in two hours. Let's get something to eat and I'll give you my address and phone number in Glastonbury."

It is a crisp fall day without a cloud in the sky. We sit at a table on the sidewalk and Kerry complains about the cold weather. Mousa is his usual jubilant self and maintains that the brisk weather makes him feel terrific.

"I apologize for being contrary," Kerry says. "But I have a nuclear hangover, and the reflection off your gleaming white teeth hurts my eyes. How can you look this good? It's inconceivable."

"Thank you." Mousa's incomparable smile shines even brighter. "You might not feel it, but you're strikingly beautiful at this moment. Looking at you makes me feel even better. Since I was a child, women have always been the loves of my life. Andreas is a lucky man."

We accompany Mousa to the train station. It is tearful goodbye for Kerry, but Mousa assures her they will see each other again in England. Kerry and I spend the rest of the morning meandering around Madrid. A visit to the Prado Museum leaves us exhausted. We go to bed early and resume the tour the next day. Madrid is a sophisticated city, very much a cosmopolitan world capital, and I am tempted to stay longer but Kerry is anxious to keep moving.

"I'm ready for England," she says. "Let's take a bus to Bilbao and catch the ferry to Portsmouth."

"I can't believe this pace." I pour more brandy into my coffee. "You're not even allowing enough time for surface study. I feel like I'm being pushed around by a budget tour guide.'

"You're right. I'm a bargain. I like the fast lane." She is animated. "We'll slow down when we get to England."

"Your wish has always been my command. That's why I beg so much."

"Tell me about it."

The crossing to Portsmouth feels hellishly long. The sea is rough and I get extremely drunk. Halfway across I get violently ill.

"What do you think?" I ask Kerry. "I just might throw myself overboard."

"Promises, promises," she responds. "Remember? You were going to cut down on your drinking."

5

THE BRITISH ISLES

B
Y THE TIME we dock in Portsmouth I have made a miraculous recovery, grateful to have both survived and arrived. It is heartening to be on solid ground again. Kerry finds the British customs agents to be delightful and is reassured to hear everyone speaking English again. All the different accents combine to bolster our spirits even more. We smile at everyone and pass through the port of entry with ease. Kerry hugs me and I feel like a heel for betraying both Vanessa and Cris, but that unpleasant thought passes quickly; I want the moment to dominate, but it's difficult to get the attacker off my mind, and my nightmares are always the same.

Unlike in Spain, the trains run on schedule here, even if British Rail makes everyone pay dearly for the convenience. The price of public transportation in Morocco and Spain has spoiled us. However, unlike Morocco and Spain, the rail cars are remarkably clean and tidy as we ride toward London. A pleasant, polite gentleman pushes a refreshment cart through the cars. His immaculate uniform and courteous demeanor are movie-perfect. We talk, and acting like teenagers, buy more junk food than we can eat.

"It's right out of the travel brochures," Kerry gushes. "Too quaint to believe."

I gaze out the window and have to agree. The countryside is greener than any we have seen since leaving Georgia. Large trees and thick hedges separate open fields. There are dairy cows grazing on the fertile rolling hills, and the farmhouses look enchanting.

"I feel right at home here," Kerry exclaims, "I love the English already."

Our first impressions change when we pull into Paddington Station. There are many different shades of people, and most of them are not nattily dressed. Blacks and Asians predominate. It makes me feel right at home. The colors, clothes, and mannerisms remind me of Penn Station, except cleaner. We charge up the stairs to street level. I begin to notice that all of England does not look like a folk tale, unless this locale is merely the set for a Masterpiece Theater Dickens movie.

"It's a little gritty around the old station," I say as I survey the scene.

"But genuinely old." Kerry is still enchanted. "This is the real thing."

We fan out from the station looking for a place to stay. Every establishment we investigate has a person in charge with a decidedly non-English appearance. After an hour we begin to question whether there are any native English left in London. Greeks and Asians have absorbed the bed and breakfast industry. We ask likely looking contemporaries for accommodation advice. No one offers any real specifics but people tell us to take the underground to Earl's Court, where there are a lot of cheap rooms, and maybe some deals.

Kerry stays in the station and watches our belongings while I comb the Earl's Court area. I purposely saunter by the arena where Led Zeppelin recently played. There are low-cost rooms nearby and a surprising number of lowlife individuals to go with them. I move from one place to another looking for the ever-elusive best deal in town. The prices don't vary much in our category and all the rooms begin to look the same. My choice is eventually determined by its quiet location and the pretty young desk clerk with a Mohawk haircut. Kerry is grateful to find that the shower is en suite, but she is not impressed with the hygienic standards of the cleaning staff.

"This place must be owned by Moroccans," she says as she inspects the room. "They're probably holding that girl at the desk as their sex slave."

"Your racism is my favorite thing about you."

"Fuck you. My cleanliness standards are higher than yours."

"You find a better place and I'll share the rent. I'm just happy to have a place to lie down, and it doesn't look all that bad to me."

"Give me a day and we're out of here. Right now I need food and sleep."

The famous English breakfast is served in the dank basement, four floors beneath our room. There are no white tablecloths, and no rosy-cheeked maidens serving marmalade. There are also no eggs, no bacon, no fruit, and no butter. I look around for the kindly grandmother serving juice. She has been replaced by a fat surly punk rocker with green hair and a ring through her nose. Stale white rolls and margarine are dropped on our plates with a glare. I look at the offering and wish I had slept late.

"I guess this is what they call a continental breakfast," I say with a mirthful frown.

Kerry shakes her head. "Continental rats couldn't survive on this shit. These buns are even harder than yours. I couldn't eat this crap if I was starving to death. But it strengthens my resolve to find a better place to stay."

Kerry insists on seeing the changing of the guard at Buckingham Palace. She thinks it is overrated but she enjoys walking the streets of Chelsea. We walk for hours, take the tube occasionally, and explore the city together.

"I was slightly disappointed with the Statue of Liberty." Kerry's wide eyes dart around Trafalgar Square. "But Lord Nelson looks a hell of a lot better than I expected."

"It's impressive, all right," I say. "But I wonder why they decided to turn it into a pigeon breeding ground. They are one of the few animals I detest."

I am astounded by the number of birds, and silently

curse their presence. If experience is any indicator, it will be impossible for me to walk through this flock without being dumped on from above. The bowels of birds have always had it in for me. I figure I must have been a cat in a previous life, and I hope I get nine.

We see a group of demonstrators off to the side and walk over to investigate. South Africa House is being picketed by a large but orderly crowd. The building is cordoned off and the entrance is guarded by police. People are marching quietly and distributing literature.

"We should see what's going on," Kerry says. "I'm sure we would agree with what they're saying about apartheid. But I have to get my mail first!"

We are both exhilarated by the walk around Trafalgar Square. Kerry resolves to send postcards and points out that pictures do not do the place justice. We turn right on Haymarket and stride down the street to the American Express office, where a security guard directs us downstairs to the mailroom. I am delighted to receive four letters. Kerry gets twice as many as I do.

"Let's walk to Hyde Park," I say. "We can sit down on a bench and read them there."

We stop at Piccadilly Circus to look at the crowded scene. Kerry finds Regent Street more enjoyable. The wide storefronts have an irresistible appeal to her, inveterate shopper that she is. We keep a brisk pace as we pass through Oxford Circus and head down Oxford Street. I find it all to my liking, and curse modern architecture.

"The walking visuals here are great," I exclaim. "I love this accessibility. All we ever build in the States are huge pylons, giant marble slabs, and large reflective windows. It's boring shit. I like to be amused when I walk down a street. This does it."

"Windows full of clothes and jewelry amuse me."

"You're a complicated person."

"Don't I know."

We enter Hyde Park at Speaker's Corner. There is only one person in the immediate area, a lone orator on a soapbox. A middle-aged woman, she is railing against the evils of abortion to a nonexistent audience. Kerry and I pause briefly to analyze her argument.

"You know," Kerry says as we move on, "abortion foes are their own worst enemy. The longer I listen to them the more I wish they had been aborted."

"I love how you never take a position."

"You're worse."

I sit down on a bench and read two letters from Vanessa. She is enthusiastic about her career and says she has been busier than ever because she has been selected to play the lead in a new off-Broadway musical. It doesn't pay much but she thinks it represents the opportunity of a lifetime. "Some of the best people in New York are involved." She tells me she will have a month free before rehearsals begin. She wants to fly to London and meet me here. The news throws me completely off balance. I've always been told it is best to be careful about what you wish for, and now, all of a sudden, I might have too many women on my hands. Perfection shouldn't be this complicated. I am riddled with guilt.

Cris has written me from Ghana. The Sahara crossing was even more difficult than he had expected, and he hopes to be in East Africa within two months. "Get your shit together and join me there."

The last letter is from my mother. It is filled with family news, gossip, and local events. She wonders when I will regain my senses and come home. "Haven't you got that traveling bug out of your system by now? Your father and I can understand you not wanting to teach anymore, but does that justify dropping out and leaving everything? We think you should come back, go to law school, and work with your father's firm. You should at least give it a try. We will pay for your schooling, but not for traipsing around Europe and not accomplishing anything. We know you have savings, but not much, and the only money you'll get from us will be for a plane ticket back to New York. Remember, we will always love you and only want what's best for you. Maybe you don't always believe that, but it's true."

I believe it and know it's true, but I also know one person's dream is another's nightmare. The thought of working with my father sends shivers up my spine. Father and son in the same workplace would not be the ideal match my mother imagines. However, I will miss their money. They were quite generous when I lived in Chelsea. I've got more of a stash than they know about, but I worry how long this death threat is going to last.

When I finish my letters I look over at Kerry. She is serious and pensive. When she is finished reading she stares off toward the open field in front of us. An errant soccer ball rolls up nearby and I kick it back to the players.

"Well, how were they?" I ask. "Good news or bad? What are you thinking?"

"I think you have a stupid, shit-eating look on your face," Kerry says inquisitively. "Good news for you I presume."

"Pretty good, Vanessa is going to fly over here in a few weeks."

"Lucky you. Her timing couldn't be better. I'll be out of here by then. You'll be moving from one grade-A piece of ass to another."

"That hadn't crossed my mind."

"You're lying! I know you."

"I'm going to miss you. I really mean that. You're a wonderful person. And you're very funny on top of it. You've put up with a lot of shit from me, and I appreciate that. I've had some phenomenal times with you. Unforgettable."

"Hey, we've had an understanding from the beginning. It still holds. I've had a hell of a lot of fun with you too, but we both knew it wasn't meant to last. Stick with me for a little longer. Help me see all I can. Do me one more big favor."

"It's my pleasure! What do you want to do first?"

"Find a better place to stay," she says. "I struck out. The filthy shower, the inedible breakfast, and that bitch with the safety pin in her nose are too much. After that I'd like to do some more sightseeing. Then I'd love to call Mousa and see some English countryside. What say we stay partners for the next fortnight? You have to do everything I say."

"You're on. But we haven't got any rope yet."

"I'll get it when I buy the vibrating dildo." She smiles.

"Don't forget the butt plug."

She pinches my ass. "I won't."

We start to formulate a basic itinerary as we stroll through Hyde Park. At the British Museum we meet a young American named Sandy. I go out to smoke a joint and walk around while the two women talk, and then rejoin them for lunch.

"Sandy here has given me a fabulous recommendation, Kerry says. "She's been staying in a great bed and breakfast, but she has to fly home tomorrow, and we can have the room when she leaves. The family that owns the house is evangelical Christian, but I don't think that matters. I'm sure we can keep to ourselves. She says it's plush."

"The landlady is a bit too much," Sandy says. "But the room is terrific. The price is right, and you can't beat the location!"

"Jesus freaks never allow you to keep to yourself," I reply. "I might be better off staying with the heathens; at least they don't think god is on their side."

"Humor me for once in your life for fuck's sake," Kerry says. "Let's make the move up to Holland Park. The crowd where we're staying make the Manson gang look adorable."

I have always had a penchant for taxis and London cabs the real deal. Every time I get into one I feel powerful and confident. Unlike New York, there are never any threatening undertones here. Better still, all the drivers speak English and know where they are going. It is tantamount to having a chauffeur at my disposal, and the cabs invariably reinforce my sense of well-being. It's a great pleasure when I hail a cab at the Earl's Court Station and tell the driver our new lodging address. Kerry and I both settle back in civilized comfort, look over at each other, and burst out laughing.

As we approach our destination I begin to notice that our new accommodations are in a considerably more expensive part of town. There are no signs advertising bed and breakfasts in this neighborhood, and no poor people on the streets. At this early hour the morning traffic consists mostly of well-dressed nannies pushing luxurious prams.

"I can't believe anyone around here is renting rooms," I say to Kerry.

"Just for us," she replies. "I'm more important than you realize. Everyone is on my side when I think they should be. Who can blame them?"

There are sumptuous houses on one side of the street, and a manicured park on the other. It is obviously a very wealthy neighborhood, and thankfully I do not see any pigeons in the park.

"I expect to see a famous princess jogging next to one of those miniature carriages," I say. "God knows she wouldn't want the likes of us invading her private little scene. What a location! This is the high end. American riffraff is supposed to stay somewhere else."

"I knew you'd love it!" Kerry exclaims. "And speak for yourself when it comes to riffraff. You're the only one who always looks like a vagrant."

The driver passes the address and makes a quick U-turn. The large vehicle nearly swings around in its tracks. We stop in front of a three-story townhouse, the most stately building on a baronial block.

"I can't believe this is a commercial operation," I say. "I hate to say it but it looks too legit for us. We're basically young peasants."

"Easy for you to say, rich boy. Besides, who cares what it is? Count your blessings and don't be so fucking skeptical. You owe me. This is a shit load better than that dump you found."

Why start to argue with her now? I have the driver wait until I check the door. A teenage girl answers after my second knock. She has blue hair and blue eyes. I have experience with this age group from my teaching days, and I am confident when I'm around them.

"May I help you with something, sir?"

"I might be mistaken, but I was led to believe that my wife and I have room reservations here."

"We've been expecting you."

"Thank you. Those are welcome words. We feel fortunate to be here. Please excuse me while I gather our gear and pay the driver."

The teenager leads us up three flights of stairs. She opens the door to a room overlooking the park. Kerry smirks and gives me a knowing nod. It is the best room we have had on the entire journey. The spacious interior has two queen beds. A pair of chairs face each other at either end of an overstuffed sofa, and the strikingly large bay windows make the room. They provide an impressive view of Holland Park from three different angles. A massive desk occupies most of this outward extension, which is the focal point of the room. Kerry is also impressed by the opulent bathroom and its antique fixtures.

"Mother will be up soon to complete the registration formalities," the teenager says. "Please make yourselves comfortable. In the meantime I'll bring you up a cup of tea."

"That would be lovely," Kerry replies. She leaves the room and we look at each other.

"I told you so," Kerry says. "It's the perfect base for seeing the city. We've got a palatial suite with three views overlooking the park. It's even better than I expected."

I settle down in one of the chairs and admire the view. Kerry investigates our surroundings and finds everything exemplary, particularly the immaculate bidet. She triumphantly parades around the room and compliments herself. I justifiably agree with everything she says.

Suddenly there is a loud knock. Before we can respond, it flies open and a hefty woman with grayish hair barges in. She introduces herself as the owner and places a tray on the console table near the door. Then she sits down in the other chair and begins to talk.

"Please have some tea and cake."

It sounds like a command and we instantly obey. She looks like Miss Marple but acts like Winston Churchill. There is no doubt in my mind about who is the queen of this castle.

"You've already met my daughter. I also have a son. We are happy to have you here with us. During your stay we want you to make yourselves at home. We provide accommodations because we enjoy the company of people who share our beliefs. I hope we will get to talk often."

I clear my throat, look back at Kerry, roll my eyes, and

107

wonder if the landlady will ever shut up and go away. She takes a deep breath and keeps talking.

"We particularly enjoy Americans. You are so different than most Europeans. You have been fighting the racial battles. We must prevent our vital genes from being diluted. Evil ethnic theories have to be resisted. White people have to band together and stay united. Protect the purity of the race at all costs."

Kerry gets up and turns her back on the landlady. I can see that she is seething. I hope Kerry kills her before we leave, but only after our stay is over.

"You've seen it all first-hand," the landlady continues. "We have to keep the darker races subjugated. That's the way the Lord wanted it to be. God's natural order is being threatened. Satan's black hand reaches farther everyday. If we are not vigilant the white race will cease to exist."

She pauses and peers over the top of her glasses. We are paralyzed. She is so blatantly insane we do not know what we could possibly say. It is the first time ever that Kerry and I have been simultaneously speechless. I wish the landlady would have a massive stroke and die right now, although I am afraid it might adversely affect our luxurious accommodations. It looks like a no-win situation, and I figure I'm just along for the ride anyway. Kerry glares at the landlady, while possibly contemplating having to relocate.

"I'll bring up some literature for you to read," the landlady says, then suddenly gets up and strides out the door. We hear her march down the stairs.

"I don't know if I can deal with that monster again," Kerry says. "I thought that maniacal bullshit was only an American thing."

"Racism is everywhere, my dear. Don't forget. God is on her side. Let's just not let her in again."

"There's no lock on the door."

"I'm going to take a walk in the park," I say. "I'm glad you don't have a gun. But if anyone deserves a bullet, it might be her."

The landlady is still on my mind as I head back to rejoin

Kerry, but I decide to stop for a few drinks. This section of London is on an economic par with my upbringing in New York. I know my way around these type of people, and with my smiling face, I am welcomed everywhere I stop. Privileged people put me at ease, because, like me, they are usually so self-satisfied they rarely pose a threat.

"I've come up with a plan concerning our new landlady." Kerry says when I enter the room. "It's devilishly brilliant."

"If you've killed her and think I'm going to help dispose of the body, forget it."

"I should kill her but I didn't. The fucking bitch barged in here twice since you left. She never bothers to knock. She just marches right in."

"Does she act like she owns the joint?"

"Worse. She acts like she owns the truth."

"Don't forget the move here was your idea," I say. "I was fine mingling with the serial killers over at Earl's Court. In any case, what's the plan?"

"It's a great idea but a little fiendish." She rubs her hands together. "In fact, it's downright nasty, but I think it will allow us to enjoy the room and maintain our privacy at the same time. This evil deed does require major participation on your part. You're the co-star. And you're going to love it. It's right down your alley."

"Count me in if it's legal. Or make me an offer if it's not."

"We'll throw sex in her face. And I mean right in her face."

"I repeat, what's the plan?"

"We can tell when she's headed our way. The stairs creak. We'll teach her a lesson about privacy that she should never forget. She'll learn that it's impolite to enter a room without being invited. When we hear her coming, we take off all our clothes. She's slow coming up, so we'll have enough time. I'll bend over the desk at a provocative angle. And you feign that you're fucking me from behind. We'll need lots of sound and action. Groan blissfully like you always do. She'll charge in and we'll be center stage, baby. Two white people in the act of keeping the white race alive. Doing what she knows those dark people are doing all too much of. We pretend everything is okay and continue. In between moans we ask if she would like to stay and watch. What do you think? I think it's hysterical."

"I've got to admit it's not a bad plan. But there might be one fatal flaw. What if she accepts our offer to watch?"

"Religious right wing racists are afraid of sex. She'll freak. But if she doesn't, make sure you back off from time to time. I want to shove my ass in her face. She's a nightmare. What do you say?"

"Well, she deserves it."

"Take a look at her literature. It's unspeakable."

"Any other news?" I ask.

"I called Mousa out in Somerset. He sounds as friendly and inviting as he was in Spain. I told him we'd do some more exploring here and then head out in his direction."

I start to ask another question but Kerry cuts me off. She cocks her head toward the door. A slow creaking sound is coming from the stairs below.

"Here she comes," Kerry says excitedly. "Let's do it!"

I have never seen anyone disrobe so quickly. She is naked before I have undone my belt, and I hurriedly tear off my shirt and slide my pants down around my ankles. I have always felt silly in this condition, literally caught with my pants down, but the time frame allows nothing else. Kerry is already bent over the desk and has her posterior pointed toward the door. Timing is essential here, but I pause briefly to admire the perfect bottom I feel lucky to have been in touch with as often as I have.

I shuffle and hear the door flung open behind me. We both start to moan and move. I feel like laughing, but the naked nature of things helps keep me in character. I cup Kerry's breasts and look over my shoulder toward the door. The landlady takes several strides into the room before she realizes what is happening. She is momentarily blinded by bewilderment, and I can appreciate her confusion. I find the scene outlandish myself. Kerry grabs my buttocks, arches her back, and exhales loudly. It is a sexual sound of hers, but greatly exaggerated for effect.

"Can we help you with anything, madam?" Kerry asks while panting.

"Oh my god!" The landlady is frozen in her tracks.

"We thought this was our room," Kerry says calmly, and continues to rotate her hips and lick her lips. "Didn't we pay in advance?"

"It is your room," the landlady sputters. "I am so terribly sorry."

"We would prefer to be alone." Kerry looks straight at the landlady and throws her head back. "But you can stay and watch if you're willing to pay for the show."

The landlady is stunned by this offer. She is obviously transfixed by our coupling, but horrified by the possibilities presented.

"No," she whispers at first. "No! Never! Excuse me! I am so sorry! Excuse me!"

She turns on her heels and leaves. Her hurried footsteps go down faster this time, and we hear her fall at the bottom of the stairs.

"Did you see that look on her face?" Kerry is beside herself. "It should have been filmed. She delivered more expression than I thought she would."

"She liked what she saw," I say. "I loved your pay-per-view proposition. A nice touch. It caught her a little off guard."

"She looked so aghast I couldn't resist. I was afraid she might accept. Hey, I forgot to tell you. I went to the toy store today. The woman had recommendations."

"I'll bet she did. Let's try them out," I say lustfully.

"They're in the armoire." Kerry walks over to the bed, lies down on her back, and starts to masturbate.

"Let's do it for real right now," she purrs. "Get those toys. I want to do the unimaginable."

"Good god! What if we get caught?"

"She'll have to pay."

Our contrived sex show for the landlady delivers the intended results. She never enters our room again, and we see her only fleetingly throughout the remainder of our stay. When we do run into each other, she bows her head and looks down. We continue to act as if nothing happened that could not happen again at any moment.

Kerry becomes an insatiable tourist. American life looms ever nearer on her horizon, and she sees it is going to come only too soon. London is her "all time favorite city." She wants to visit all the famous places but discovers there is always another sight right around the corner. Five days of nonstop movement takes a toll, and Kerry suggests we take our rest and recuperation in the countryside.

"Let's rent a car and drive out to Somerset. I think it's time to visit Mousa," she suggests.

We head south on the motorway. It is a rare sunny day and the scenery is beyond compare. Fantasies are fulfilled for both of us as we drive across rural England and peer out the windows. Kerry compliments me "for adapting to the wrong side of the road so quickly." Shifting with my left hand is no problem, and I find that only the ludicrous roundabouts give me any trouble.

"I wish we'd rented a convertible," Kerry says. "We deserve it. Look at us!"

Stonehenge is like the Stature of Liberty for Kerry, a minor disappointment. From a distance it has great potential, but that notion is gradually dispelled as we get closer. The parking is difficult, and the throngs of people in tour buses make us think we have seen enough.

Our drive turns into a leisurely trek across Somerset. I take the smallest roads I can find and stop at village pubs along the way. The rolling green hills are lush, the old country England of popular imagination. Manor houses, thatched roofs, cider apple orchards, and winding country lanes lead from one little hamlet and valley to the next. It looks right out of the tourist brochures.

"You're the kind of woman who makes all men wish they had more to give." I am trying to be funny.

"You're right." She laughs. "But full of shit. However, I do make your wishes come true."

"Prove yourself." I look over at her. "I'm wishing for oral sex right now."

"For me or for you? Either way, I don't want to miss this scenery. Plus you won't fit on the floor, and I don't feel like driving."

"In other words, my wish is not your command?"

"Never has been. Never will be. Unless we agree. Which we do, thankfully, most of the time."

It is early evening but still light when we eventually get to Glastonbury. I take a brief drive around the famous Tor and find it very impressive, more than I expected. The small market city is bustling with activity, but there is no place to park on the crowded downtown streets. We drive a short distance from the city center and park opposite a pub.

The public house is crowded when we enter. It takes me a while to work my way to the bar and ask for two pints of beer. The big woman behind the bar, Jane by name, sets me on my heels. She yells, she laughs, and throws her large breasts around. I decide it is the way buxom barmaids in Britain were meant to behave. I always enjoy it when a positive stereotype comes true. The hefty Jane has a smaller companion behind the bar with her, a little fellow who watches the action and acts irritated by her theatricality and inefficiency.

Even by English standards it is an unusual crowd. Some of them look like they are auditioning for a part in a new *Star Wars* movie. It is a diverse gathering spot with all ages represented. Contemporary fashions mingle with the more traditional. There are some expensively dressed drinkers scattered about, but despite the obvious economic disparity, everyone is getting along famously. Many of the patrons appear to be intoxicated but there is no alcohol aggression here. They are drinking to have a good time, and for the moment anyway the booze brings out their best. I like the community spirit; it's refreshing to see barristers and layabouts rub elbows so congenially. Kerry and I have two beers and talk about calling Mousa. We are comfortable where we are, so we decide to get a room in town for the night and get in touch with him tomorrow.

"Nothing is worse than unexpected guests at dinnertime," Kerry says.

"At least we don't have kids or dogs. Let's have another round and find a place to stay."

I wade my way back to the bar and get two more beers. When I sit back down at our table the noise level in the pub suddenly increases. The uproar is coming from near the entrance.

"This isn't the peaceful place it appeared to be," Kerry observes. "Looks like the early merrymaking was just a temporary façade. I told you so. These people probably drink like most drunks. Some asshole has no doubt summoned the courage to beat the shit out of his neighbor. Everyone is cheering them on. I thought some of those guys at the bar looked pretty obstreperous."

"No way," I say.

I stand up and peer around the small partition, toward the door. My attention is instantly riveted on a familiar face, the only face I recognize here. Mousa has entered the pub and received a tumultuous welcome from the patrons; it would be considered a standing ovation if everyone had not already been on their feet.

"It didn't sound like a fight to me. Take a look."

"We should have known," Kerry says when she stands up and looks around the corner.

Mousa does not see us across the room. People demand his attention and he works the crowd like an experienced politician. Like everyone else, he has to struggle through the crowd to get a drink at the bar. Mousa turns around to scan the crowd after he is served, wades into the room, and spots us against the far wall. He moves smoothly through the crowd of well-wishers and joins us at our table.

"Welcome to Somerset." Mousa hugs both of us at the same time. "I'm so pleased you came. But tell me, how did you know I'd be here tonight?"

"Women's intuition," Kerry says. "I'm drawn to great men. Look at Andreas here."

"Beautiful women have the best instincts," Mousa says. "You know you couldn't find two better men."

Mousa is different with different people. His words are invariably welcoming and complimentary. Kerry obviously thinks he is super. I am always relieved when someone of his caliber at least pretends to give me a warm reception. I very much want to be Mousa's friend, having never met anyone with such captivating charisma. It's not just me, everyone thinks he's great to be around. And this is his home turf.

"I want you to meet two of my mates," Mousa says. "I came here specifically to see them. Seeing you two is a major bonus. This is a good omen."

Mousa hails Nigel and Dave from the end of the bar. They come over and join us at our crowded table. The newcomers are particularly taken with Kerry, and they behave accordingly.

"Good-looking women are always popular around men like us," Nigel says raising his glass and offering her a toast. Kerry eats up the attention and responds appropriately. She knows how to play their game as well as anyone.

"The English are the most civilized people on earth," she gushes. "I love your country."

"You'll change your mind when you get to know us better," Nigel says. "We look okay on the outside, but beneath this thin veneer lurks an underlying depravity that foreigners seldom see. There are two key facts about the English. Our teeth are really bad because of our insatiable craving for alcohol, and we don't rinse our dishes after washing them. We're too drunk. That's just the way we are."

"I wasn't saying I want to live here!" Kerry laughs. "But it's a great place to visit. I want to see what you people do for fun. No stiff upper lips need apply."

"Touché," Mousa says. "We English do play games very well. In fact, these two old friends are my teammates. We have a dart match scheduled for tonight. It's in a small pub nearby. Please join us and be part of our cheering section. It's no big deal, but we like it."

"We'd love to," Kerry says. I very much appreciate her being my new spokesperson. I have always liked her style and am learning to support her decisions. After all, I would not have met Mousa if she had not introduced us. And since she is on short time now, it's all her show from here on out.

"I'll go with my guests and meet you guys at the pub," Mousa says to Nigel and Dave. "Don't be late. This is a big match."

"We'll be there." Nigel replies. "Dave wants to stop by and

pick up his girlfriend. She's always late, but we'll be there."

Mousa talks as we drive the dark, winding roads to the next pub. "You'll enjoy your stay in Somerset. This is the real England. And these are the best of the English. I'm not the same color, but we all live together here with a minimum of stress or tension. Until it comes to darts!"

Mousa has not exaggerated. The rural pub is packed with drinkers and dartsmen. Both sides have boisterous supporters. The proprietor calls Mousa aside and tells him that one of his teammates has been arrested and is still in jail. He won't get out in time for the match.

"What's the charge?" Mousa asks.

"Possession of stolen property."

"That's what he does for a living," Mousa says. "My American friend here will take Tony's place. Put his name on the board. Andreas."

"This American thinks you must be out of your mind. I've never thrown a dart in my life. Plus I always buckle under any kind of pressure."

"There's no pressure here," Mousa says. "I expect you to lose. Against anyone. Therefore I'm matching you against someone none of us can beat. He seldom loses. They'll save him, their best, for last. I'll save you, our worst, for last. They'll think you're a ringer I brought in from America. The outcome of the match will already have been determined before you throw one dart. I'm a brilliant tactician when it comes to darts. Trust me."

Dave shows up with his girlfriend, Heidi, just in time for the opening match. Heidi is precious beyond words, but I also think someone should ask her if she is truly old enough to be here. Young women this gorgeous always draw everyone's attention. Men gawk and women steal surreptitious glances.

Kerry looks her up and down. "I have to say, she's got it and she flaunts it." Kerry pinches me in the ribs. "You have a woman on your arm. Try not to stare."

"I didn't suspect Dave of being a child molester." I reexamine Heidi. "Maybe the age of consent is lower over here."

"Come off it, turd face." Kerry rolls her eyes. "She doesn't talk beyond a giggle and she can't keep her hands off Dave, but she's obviously older than she looks."

I have noticed that Heidi constantly touches Dave in ways that are more appropriately done in private. Her sleek leotard is tucked into skintight jeans, and they are so close they form a crease through her crotch. Her high, small breasts protrude through the worn elastic top. It is a fetching display and most of the men in the pub eat it up. I have reservations but ultimately side with the lechers. I enjoy being around women who invite attention; generally, they never slap anyone for just looking.

"My father would have shot me if I'd gone out looking like that," Kerry says.

"Maybe her father is proud of her on this level."

"Don't get creepy on me."

The hoopla builds when the match begins. Mousa is the first player at the line for his team. He wins decisively and his side hollers, stomps, and cheers. The succeeding contests are much closer. Team spirits temporarily sink when Dave loses. Heidi offers Dave way more sympathy than is called for, but she is able to pull it off in her nubile way.

Mousa's strategy works as planned. Our team has won before I even step to the line, and the last game is merely a formality. I lose quickly and don't score a point. Mousa's team is chivalrous in victory.

"We owe this triumph to the two gorgeous women who stood by their men. Even though they both lost." Mousa is being a card and everyone loves it. He raises his glass and buys a round for the house. "It was a difficult struggle and we couldn't have done it without you." He looks at Kerry and Heidi. "This toast is for you. I propose I throw a party in your honor."

"We don't deserve it," Kerry says modestly. "We only watched. Have a party for yourselves. You're the ones who won the match."

"I think we do deserve it." Young Heidi surprises me with this loud statement. "Get real. We're the sexiest women in Somerset. We deserve everything we want. When's the party, Mousa? We want a party in our honor."

I never expected to hear this kind of talk from such a sublime source. It removes all my doubts. She enjoys the attention for sure, and the bold expression mildly shocks everyone but Mousa.

"Of course you deserve it." Mousa's eyes twinkle and he smiles at the two women. "And it's a pleasure to hear honesty so accurately stated. It will be the best party of the year. And you two beauties will be to blame. Plus, my accumulated social debts will finally have an excuse to be paid off. It's the least I can do. Let's all party at my place next weekend! I look forward to seeing everyone there. Tell all of our friends. It's open house at the Cummings Estate."

Over the coming days, party preparations begin to take on mythical proportions. It promises to be an epic event, and Mousa's invitations extend beyond my comprehension. News spreads quickly in the local pubs. Mousa spares no efforts and spends long hours organizing the affair. He hires caterers and books two bands. Cases of liquor are stacked in the ten-car garage. Kegs of cider and beer stay cool in the basement. Kerry works tirelessly on Mousa's behalf. Everyone we meet looks forward to the gathering. Most of them have attended Mousa-thrown parties before, and no expense is ever spared.

Plus, the two-hundred acre Cummings estate is the ideal location. Days of preparation have transformed the house and grounds. The three-story main house has ample room for entertaining. It has held sizable gatherings for over a century, but it was designed for more formal occasions. Mousa has made temporary modifications that he maintains will facilitate his "contemporary entertainment concepts." Rugs have been removed. The furniture in the capacious ground floor rooms has been placed against the walls. The dining chairs have been scattered about because Mousa plans to use the fifty-foot table for a continuous buffet. By Friday afternoon the stage has been set and everything is ready for action. I have been to extravagant upstate New York affairs but nothing like this.

"This is the biggest party I've ever been part of," Kerry says to Mousa. "How does it feel to be producer, director, and star?"

"If the weather holds," Mousa says, "it's going to be quite

a production. I owe these people a lot for their kindness throughout the years. I wasn't the easiest kid to get along with. Wealthy, with a black chip on my shoulder for those who weren't either. These people have always been kind to me. It's up to Mother Nature now."

Kerry and I have often discussed our shared curiosity concerning Mousa's sex life. "He's the hottest guy on the planet," Kerry exclaims. "If you weren't in the way, I'm sure I would be his first choice, and I wouldn't even pretend it wasn't mutual."

"I'm lucky you haven't left me already."

Our reciprocal speculation about Mousa's private life is resolved the morning before the big night. Ingrid, Mousa's girlfriend, shows up in a limo while I am wandering around the extensive grounds. She sashays to the front door and lets herself in. My standards are high, and when I see a woman like this, even under these circumstances, Vanessa still tops my list, Kerry is a close second, but this Nordic beauty belongs on the podium. I've always preferred being around women, particularly those who know their way around, and this one has an outstanding presence.

"Mousa has changed since Ingrid arrived," Kerry says. "I didn't think it was possible, but he's gotten even more charming. He confessed to doing everything Ingrid tells him to do. She's a Norwegian biologist slash environmentalist. The guy is totally in love with her, and despite her supermodel looks, she's about the most informed, reasonable, and sweetest person I've ever met. They are a completely committed couple and get together as often as their time allows. I love being part of shit like this."

The first guests begin to arrive early Saturday afternoon. I am surprised by the nature of these early arrivals. Most are local women with children in tow. Some are dressed like royalty and others look like farmhands. Mousa greets everyone with enthusiasm and introduces "the Americans." The children play outside while their parents admire the gardens and peruse the grounds. It is a cordial and sedate beginning, but in the next few hours I meet more people than I can remember, and the energy picks up as more guests arrive. Kerry and I receive considerable polite attention, everyone shakes our hands and wishes us well. By nightfall there are over five hundred people roaming about. The intensity level continues to increase as more guests stream through the door. Relaxation and camaraderie are the bywords of the early evening, and although many of the guests appear to be quite high, everyone is friendly and under control.

"I haven't seen a crowd partying like this since that horrible furniture convention," Kerry says.

"But that's where the similarity ends," I say. "These people are not white. The color is comparable but that's it. That group in North Carolina only had one interest, and they all worshipped only one god. The same god, money. And they will put no god before it. *These* people might not always agree on their idol, but they sure as hell worship a more benevolent spirit."

"Well, excuse me," Kerry says sarcastically. "I stand corrected. On the other hand, I think you've had too much to drink and are starting to pontificate."

"Kick me when I become intolerable."

"To me or to everyone around you?"

"Is it possible they'll coincide?"

"Hey, I'm fed up with you already." She laughs and kisses me on the cheek before walking away to rejoin the crowd.

I go outside to take another blow and am admiring the English moon when an elderly couple approaches and introduces themselves. The gray-haired gentleman is the headmaster of an exclusive prep school near Glastonbury. He remembers Mousa's early years and tells me witty stories.

"Rowalyn, or Mousa as he calls himself now, has always been a most remarkable young man," the headmaster continues. "Relationships were not always easy for the brown boy with the absent African mother. It was not easy to fit in with the rest of the boys. But he possesses magical qualities. He can see through people, and he has a unique ability to make friends when he wants to."

"I'm living proof of that," I say. "I love the guy!"

"You're lucky to have met him," the old man says. "He's special. Much better than his father."

"Who is his father?" I ask. "And where is he?"

"Oh, he's still around. He goes all over the world making money. Mousa helps him out from time to time, but they're not close."

As expected, the revelry ratchets up as the evening progresses. The hard-core party people enjoy the heightened excitement. I have a few more snorts with Nigel and they make me feel even better. As always, Kerry dances with reckless abandon and draws considerable attention. At midnight the musicians take a break, and Kerry and I take a stroll. We haven't gone far when Dave calls to us from the gardens. Young Heidi is clinging to his arm.

"Do you remember Heidi?" Dave chuckles.

"Doesn't everybody?" I say.

Kerry smiles thinly at Heidi. "How could anyone forget? The party is for us. We're both just about too alluring."

"A few of the couples are getting together upstairs," Dave says. "We'll do some drugs and get naked. Nothing really kinky, you understand. Just good visuals while having sex with our partners. You two are invited to join us. Heidi and I would love to see you there. Most of us have done this before, and it's a lot of sexy fun, believe me. Trading partners is against the rules."

Kerry is astounded but seldom speechless. "We've never thought of trading partners, and group sex is not our thing."

"Speak for yourself, my dear." Sobriety has deserted me, and once again I am exaggerating the quality of my own humor.

"Jesus!" Kerry says. "You're drunk." She looks over at Heidi and Dave. "He gets this way all too often. It makes him frisky."

"I didn't mean to offend anyone," Dave says. "I was hoping to encourage participation by explaining the ground rules. We plan on watching the show and enjoying ourselves. It's all quite harmless really. Think it over. I hope we'll see you there."

"Thanks for the invite," Kerry says.

"Turn to your right at the top of the stairs," Dave says. "It's the first door on your left." Turning to me, he emphasizes, "don't show up alone. Couples only."

We watch Dave and Heidi climb the magnificent spiral staircase. My eyes stay fixed on Heidi until they disappear. I try to suppress my pervy inclinations, but the alcohol, smoke, and speed dominate me at the moment, and I cannot gain control of my sexual fantasies.

"I'll give you credit for one thing," Kerry says.

"What's that?" I ask earnestly. "At this juncture I'm glad you're giving me credit for anything."

"At least you didn't run over and look up her dress while she was climbing the stairs."

"Only out of respect for you."

Kerry plucks another gin from the passing drink tray. "This is just about too much."

"What do you really think?" I ask.

"About what?"

"About making love with a bunch of English people looking on?"

"I think you're high enough to want to do anything. Mostly to watch Heidi fuck."

She's got me there. I'm afraid I am about to sound bad, but I do not really care, and reason that anything is worth a try. Opportunities to join an orgy of attractive people are not offered every day, and right now I would like to be part of one. It sounds like a blast, just like Dave said.

"Maybe you're not looking at it from the proper perspective," I venture. "This really will be just one on one. We'll only touch each other. In fact, we could just take off our clothes and fake it. Practice our performing techniques. Pretend we're actors perfecting our craft. Remember the landlady. We could make a lot of money being porn stars. We'll never see any of these people ever again, either. You'll be home to reason and sanity soon enough. Wouldn't you hate to go through life and say you never saw a real orgy? This might be our only chance to be in a safe one. I remember your dancing that night in Seville. Any audience would love it. This will allow us an option to check out the competition." I know I am out of arguments, and I'm also aware that I've been blabbering, but hope it works.

"We don't have any competition." It is the first time I have ever heard her sound this naughty. "Let's grab a bottle and enter from the center."

I cannot believe my self-serving argument worked so well.

I begin to wonder if I don't sound as stupid as people say I do when I'm drunk. It doesn't matter now. It's enough that Kerry seems more than ready, so I locate a bottle of champagne and I am titillated by the prospects upstairs. We take our time on the spiral staircase and have a couple of swigs at the top.

The invitation-only party is in full swing when we arrive, with at least three dozen couples scattered about the room. They are all behaving in an extremely uninhibited fashion. The lights are low but the images are quite clear. Everyone is nude or in various stages of undress. I can see that there is a substantial amount of physical contact going on. Several couples are smoking hashish while fornicating. Others pour champagne, fondle each other, and watch the action. I look around for precious Heidi, and spot her standing lewdly in front of Dave. Her legs are spread and her clothes are gone. Dave's face is burrowed in her buttocks. His tongue and chin are invisible between her thighs. She brings out a vibrating dildo and uses it on herself. I wonder what her mother would think of this stance, and ponder what it might be like to have a mother and daughter at the same time, but I bury that thought quickly. I scan the room carefully to see if Mousa and Ingrid are participating in the festivities. They are nowhere to be seen. It would have been the big cherry on top for me, but I'll survive, thanks to Heidi and her bag of tricks.

All of this looks like my dream come true, but at the same time I feel self-conscious. The situation is more intimidating than I had expected, and I smile at my fellow carousers while looking for a comfortable nook away from the limelight. It looks like my type of gathering, but I do not want to stand out, and I am hoping to be the fly on the wall with my eyes wide open.

Kerry, on the other hand, has very different ideas, and starts to oscillate and move about the center of the room. The driving music provides her with the perfect backdrop, and she begins her performance by keeping time to the heavy rhythm. It is much like what I have seen before, only this time I am not the only member of the audience and she is not telling me to be still. The show is better than ever, and I love the sideway visuals as she moves sexually about the room.

It does not take her long to captivate the appreciative crowd. This is what everyone is here for, and I cannot fault them for their rapt attention because even I take my eyes off Heidi to watch her. I know what it is like to see this for the first time, although it never gets old. Kerry is dancing to her type of music now. She has more room to maneuver. I very much appreciate her subtleties.

By all indications the audience is having a whale of a good time also, and I think that sharing has reached astronomical proportions. Everyone is aroused by Kerry's active participation. Her universal sensuality lowers the gender boundaries. The women are as engrossed as the men, and for the first time I notice several gay couples on the scene. The fondling of partners continues, but all eyes are on Kerry, while she keeps time to the music, and removes her clothes.

I now agree with Kerry's earlier statement completely. She has no competition. Her performance is in a league of its own, but I have foreseen the conclusion, and I am upset at the prospect of my own importance. It is a star performance and I'm part of it, but she knows she deserves top billing, and is playing it for all it's worth. When she makes contact with me, I succumb. She draws it out much like she has in the past. There is the slow advance, a quick retreat to more dancing, and then more contact. She is up and down on my erection, with her lips and her vagina, one after another. I am in heaven when Kerry is the boss, dictating the terms. I love every minute right until I pass out from release and exhaustion. I am proud that most of the other attendees exploded before I did.

It is a night to remember; the rapture never seemed to end, but it must have, since I wake up in the early morning on a sofa wearing Kerry's underwear, and it takes me an entire day to fully recover. The big party affected everyone who attended. Kerry says the mental is much worse than the physical. She deeply regrets her public performance and acts sheepish around everyone who was there. I won't have it, and I tell her that she has become a cult hero, a woman that other women envy, but it does not lift her sagging spirits, and she keeps a low profile.

Her emotions sink even lower two days later. It is cold and rainy. We drive onto the motorway and head toward Heathrow. Both of us are lost in our own thoughts and we say nothing to each other. When we approach the airport I break the silence.

"It's not going to be easy to say goodbye."

"Then let's not." She puts her arm around my shoulder. "I'm not much for goodbyes anyway."

"Then I'll change the subject. What are your plans when you get to L.A.?"

"I'm not going to do anything for a while. Hang out with mom as much as I can. She's the best. I may need to investigate the possibility of a liver transplant. The boozing has taken its toll. I can hardly even remember what it's like to wake up without a hangover. You're mostly to blame, but it was all nothing but high fun."

"I always bring out the best in people. Seriously, thanks for being such a great friend."

When we enter the Heathrow complex Kerry tells me to drop her at British Airways. I stop in front of the terminal and look over at her. She gives me a quick kiss and grabs her pack from the back seat.

"Write me now and then," she says with tears in her eyes.

I blink away my tears. "I will."

Kerry closes the door and walks into the terminal. I get back on the motorway and drive back toward Glastonbury. I feel as if I have parted company with a sister, albeit an incestuous one, and hope to see her again, because I liked her more every day. I do know that I will be making this same drive again soon, and contemplate the fact that next time I will be picking up a woman, not parting company with one.

For the first time in months, I am on my own, but I find it difficult to be completely alone when staying with Mousa. There is a constant throng coming and going at all hours. I marvel at his ability to handle the multitudes. Everyone who visits is welcome. People come in from all over the world. Most are not there for long, but some stay for days. I find it hard to believe that one person can know so many people and be on such positive terms with all of them. The constant host is almost oblivious to the partying by some of his guests, but no one ever doubts who is in charge, and when Ingrid is there, he is seldom seen.

A week later I make the return drive to Heathrow. Unlike the first trip, my spirits soar during this drive. After I park the car, I can barely contain myself. Vanessa's flight is two hours late, and my positivity degenerates into a nervous frenzy. I am convinced that my immoderate ways have prompted a cruel twist of fate, and that my grand expectations will not be fulfilled. I rush to the gate when they finally announce the arrival of her flight. Hundreds of people stream out but there is no sign of Vanessa.

"My fucking god," I say aloud. "Where is she? Did she come to her senses and stay in New York?"

At that moment she emerges from the gate. I am stunned by the reality of her presence. She is even more lovely than I remember. Vanessa does not see me immediately. I look at her for several seconds before walking toward her. She smiles when she sees me approaching. We hug each other before saying anything. A warm, fuzzy glow flushes through my body. It is a feeling that I have only had with her.

"Long time no see." I hug her tighter.

"Too long," she says.

"I can hardly believe it," I cup her face in my hands.

"What about me? I've never crossed an ocean before. I'm afraid I'm going to wake up and find myself back in New York."

"You cut your hair."

"The director wanted it short. What do you think?"

"You've never looked better."

"You always say that."

"It's always true. God it's great to see you!"

"It's mutual. I've missed you so much. What now?" she asks. "I really don't have any idea what I'm doing here. I just had to see you."

"We'll drive out to my new friend Mousa's and spend the night there. He made me promise to take you to Somerset for your first night on English soil. After so much talk he's anxious to meet the real thing."

"I hope he's not disappointed."

"That's an impossibility. You're beyond perfection."

We talk constantly on the drive to Glastonbury. Vanessa is excited about everything, particularly her part in the upcoming play. She has the script with her and wants me to help her prepare. It is a major role and she has a considerable amount of work to do before rehearsals begin. I have always enjoyed listening to her talk, but now more than ever.

She also wants to hear everything I have done in the last few months. The days since I last saw her have passed like the blink of my eye. The people and places have moved too quickly to be accurately absorbed, assembled, or related. All I have are dreamy recollections of my heady early days in Morocco; the details are too transitory to be explained out of context. Kerry's name will not be mentioned in any regard. I have decided not to tell her about the events that dominate my thoughts. The blow to my head on the boat, Zorro, and the scene at the casino will not be brought up. I have not been able to make any sense of it all, and I see no reason to needlessly worry Vanessa. I debated telling her about it long and hard since my preoccupation with it is so intense. In the end I decided it would only be selfish, that sharing my deepest fears would serve no useful purpose.

She becomes even more enthusiastic as our ride continues. She looks younger with her short hair, and I am delighted to see her so high-spirited. Simple sights have her wide-eyed with wonder, and she is thrilled by a stop at a country pub. She is experiencing the exhilaration of movement into new territory, I know it well, and I enjoy sharing her euphoria.

"For once the American braggart has not exaggerated," Mousa says when he meets her. "Your loveliness makes overstatement impossible." He smiles and kisses her extended hand.

"Watch yourself, Mousa," I say. "We're in the process of rekindling a committed relationship."

"Committed to what?" Vanessa asks me. "Exchanging letters while you tramp around the globe, pretending you're on the run. My continuing commitments are questionable."

"I hope I sense an opening." Mousa is always lighthearted, but I do not share his levity, because I'm afraid he might inadvertently mention Kerry's name.

"You'll be the last to know," I say. "We're off to Wales tomorrow. I thought we'd take the evening ferry from Swansea and be in Cork the following morning. There is something about Ireland that draws me there."

"I hate to see Vanessa go so soon, but I was wondering if you would ever leave. You know I'm just kidding. I wish you were both staying longer. But it's a lovely plan. You'll have a splendid time. The Irish are enchanting. It's a perfect place for lovers."

It is midmorning when we clear customs and make our way into Cork, Ireland. The city is completely deserted. There is not a living being in sight, and we both find it eerie to be driving through an empty town.

"What's going on here?" Vanessa asks me. "Where is everybody?"

"Maybe the English inadvertently nuked the place during the night."

"What did they do with the bodies?"

"This could be the result of some type of evil research. Test the system in Ireland, against the real enemy. An English style final solution. Vaporize the populace and do away with any more troubles from these pesky Irish."

Vanessa gazes around. "I was prepared for culture shock, but I feel like I'm in the Twilight Zone."

The city streets are wide but there is no traffic. Near a major downtown intersection, I pull the car over to the curb. All of the businesses are closed but we spot human movement for the first time since leaving the dock area. Two older men glance in our direction and then turn the corner. We get out of the car and walk down the empty street.

"Maybe this is the first feature of a furtive folk festival," I say to make conversation.

"Your obtuse observations are obnoxious." When she's right she's right.

"As usual, our alliterations are always admirably adversarial," I fire back, holding my own.

We walk several blocks, turn a corner, and are startled to see a throng approaching from the opposite direction, several blocks away. Most of the male pedestrians are dressed in black suits, but none of the clothing seems to fit well. The jackets are too tight, or the pants too short. This incomprehensible horde disperses as quickly as it appeared.

"I was afraid our future was to be forever frequented by that frightful phalanx," I say.

"You're incorrigible." I love her laugh. "You've got to stop."

"Thank you. Now let's check out the pub over there and see what the hell is going on here."

It is a small public establishment, with a fireplace and a low-beamed ceiling. Six older men are at the bar. Vanessa is the only woman present. All eyes are on her as we make our way to the bar. I order two pints of Guinness, and the bartender winks while the dark stout slowly settles into our glasses.

"Excuse me," I say to the bartender. "May I ask you a question? What's going on here?"

The bartender looks at his compatriots, several of whom are inching closer. "Could you please be a little more specific?" I've always been fond of the strong southern Irish brogue, and this guy has got it. And I also know that whenever I've been around the true Irish, they are always looking for a laugh.

"Well, actually I have three questions." I smile broadly and look at everyone. "First of all, it looked like a ghost town here this morning. Where was everybody? Secondly, why do all these men look like overdressed alcoholics? And lastly, where are all those good-looking Irish women I've heard about?"

This set of questions comes close to bringing the house down. The patrons raise their glasses and drink heartily. The bartender's eyes are on me, and they twinkle when he responds.

"First of all, welcome to Ireland. I can answer your first two questions by pointing out one simple truth. It's Sunday. We're a Catholic country and religion is taken seriously here. If you're not in church, you'd better keep out of sight. Everyone wears their Sunday best even if they don't go to church. These lads look like they're homeless the rest of the week." He points to his customers who are smiling. "Most importantly, I'll answer your last question by offering you a piece of advice. If I was lucky enough to be with the lady you're with, I would count my blessings and not look around. She's even prettier than a Galway gal, and that's really saying something."

Vanessa steps off her stool and bows deeply. "He may not be with this woman for as long as he thinks. But right now I love him, despite the fact that he's not that smart. I like him because he's rich and handsome." I'm amazed by how effortlessly she has immersed herself into the swing of things.

More boisterous chuckles are exchanged, and more patrons enter the pub, including some women. They are an unusual looking group, but decidedly friendly. The tall bartender jokes with his customers. He is obviously considered to be a wit, and most of the drinkers look like they are merely biding their time until the next eruption of laughter. I find their joviality contagious. We say goodbye after two pints but the bartender buys us a third to detain us, only because he has more jokes to tell.

"Let's drive out of town a bit and find a farmhouse that offers bed and breakfast," I suggest. "Maybe we can take a hike around the countryside tomorrow."

"I feel like I'm starring in my own play right now," Vanessa says. "Which in real life opens in two months, I might add."

"I want you to screw New York. Join me on the road. We'll never have to wake up."

Vanessa responds sharply. "I've made commitments and I have obligations. People are counting on me. Besides, who pays the bills in this dream world of yours? Can you live off your parents forever?"

"I wish I could, but they've ruled that out, and right now I can't see that far ahead. I'm still on the run."

"Your limited vision makes me feel insecure. I'm beginning to think our directions are different. That our paths were only meant to cross in passing."

"I want to be with you forever. I mean that," I say. "I need to solve a mystery first."

"I guess I just don't understand then." Her voice gets sharper. "How can we share a dream when you're here and I'm there? We should solve things together."

"I want you to wait until I come back."

"How dare you ask that? Until you come back? When, pray tell, is that? And back to where and back to what?"

We spend the night near Blarney Castle and head south the next day. My carefully planned itinerary changes drastically as we traverse the rural roads of southern Ireland. I had allotted five days for this section of our travels, but I did not anticipate the unmatchable attraction the color green would generate within me.

As we travel along, both of us feel like we are drifting through a magical fable. It is cool and misty, but the foliage glistens with a brightness that transcends the temperature. We spend hours strolling hand in hand, winding along hedges and through fields, always keeping our eyes open for leprechauns.

The terrain varies but the green dominates everything, and the variety within the color surprises me. It can be thick and lush, or rocky and sparse. We are completely immersed within it. I had allocated one day for the drive around the Ring of Kerry, but we spend three days romping around instead. During which the pixies start to play tricks on us. And friendliness takes on elfish forms. Refusing invitations becomes our most difficult task, and some offers are impossible to decline. One day, while we are hiking near Limerick, Vanessa befriends a young mother and her two children. We enjoy two nights with the family on their small farm north of town. Vanessa thinks she might see the family again back in New York, as our hosts have extended family there. She is on cloud nine when we drive down a country lane toward the Dublin road.

"What a great family. This country is unbelievable!"

"The first synonym for hospitality is Irish."

We arrive at Dublin in late afternoon and feel lucky to find an inexpensive bed and breakfast near Trinity College. I like everything about the city. It seems as if there's a pub on every corner. Vanessa thinks Kehoe's Pub has the best pork ribs on the planet and we use it as our home base when we explore their captivating city. We make fast friends with a bartender who is from Belfast. On our last night I'm drinking pints of

Guinness when I go to the restroom to take a pee. The Belfast barman follows me into the small men's room and tells me what I don't want to hear.

"I shouldn't be saying this to you but I'm going to risk it anyway."

"Saying what?"

"I'm a member of the Irish Republican Army. I can't tell you everything but I will tell you this: your life is in danger. Someone, I don't know who, has offered my superiors a considerable amount of money if we kill you. It has to look like an accident. We want to fight to unite Ireland, not kill Americans. That's all I know. Take it from there." I return to our table but I don't say a word to Vanessa.

After five days in Dublin we make the ferry crossing back to England. Vanessa's vacation is coming to an end, so we concentrate on the time at hand and postpone any talk of our future.

It is late afternoon when we enter the old imperial port at Liverpool. I can see that the once great harbor city is a shell of its former self. The birthplace of the Beatles looks like it died long ago. We had planned to stay the night but find it so depressing we keep moving. Vanessa consults my travel maps and recommends we spend our last days together in the Lake District. She pinpoints Windermere because there is a town with the same name near her home in Alberta.

The small guesthouse we find is the perfect choice. It is an idyllic setting, and I am thankful for the privacy. The entire area, with its lush hills and calm lakes, is preserved as a park, and has been consecrated in the words of poets. There are footpaths around the lakes, and not many people about. We wear our rain gear, ignore the mud, and wander among hills, vales, and somnolent villages. At this time of year, and with the poor weather, we have the countryside completely to ourselves. At times we feel like we're the only people on earth. There is enough tranquility here to recollect a lifetime. We fall further in love every day.

The daylight is short-lived, so we spend long evenings around cozy inglenooks, talking and warming ourselves by the fire. The days slip by quickly and I feel myself growing closer to her all the time. The inevitability of our looming separation overwhelms us both, and I try to assure her that she will see me again sooner than she thinks.

"Exactly when is that?" Vanessa asks sarcastically. I can tell that she has grown closer to me as well, but she cannot believe that I will not relent, and return with her to New York. "Lovers should be together," she says. "We should be together for as long as life allows. Why be separated if it's not forced on us? Come back with me. Or at least set a date. Not a marriage date. I don't care about that. I need a together date. When will you be back?"

"I don't know for sure. Please let me follow some things through on my own for a while. I know it sounds crazy to you, but it's not, I swear." The bartender's warning is still with me.

"Okay," she says, but does not sound like she means it.

Her position makes me wonder how much time I do have left, but I reason that it's anybody's guess. Everyone says a moving target is harder to hit than a stationary one, and I know I can move faster by myself. My fear is still real and the nightmares never goes away.

"Try to understand it from my perspective." She starts to cry. "I work hard every day and go home alone. I worry about you all the time, and I want you with me. I'm lonely."

She does not cry often but when she does it breaks my heart. I have to swallow and fight back tears before continuing.

"There are some important things I have to find out. I'm in the middle of a sinister mystery. I have to solve it before I can do anything else. I want you to stay with me, but I have to work this out alone."

She clutches my hands. "I don't know if I can make any long-term guarantees. You'll be the first to know if anything changes. I shouldn't tell you this, because all you'll say is "I told you so" but Peter wants me to marry him. He tries to be suave, but he's coming on pretty strong."

"That fucking asshole." I lower my voice. "I told you so. Are you having sex with him?"

"You have no right to ask me that! I might ask you the same.

I don't want to hear your answer, and you don't deserve to hear mine. But I'll tell you anyway. No. I like Peter but I could never make love with him. You should thank him really. He takes up so much of my free time that I don't get a chance to see other men. I've told him that as long as you want me, I can't think of any other man. But like I said before, I can't guarantee how long I'll wait. There are other men in this world, don't forget."

This is the moment I know I should use my best card and I do. I have thought it over and hope it plays.

"I've been thinking about this for awhile," I say. "I want to make you a proposition. My guarantee for yours. Let's make a deal."

"What's the deal?" She sounds skeptical.

"I'm offering two pledges for the price of one. I promise to stay abstinent until we meet again. I'm asking you to promise the same. If either of us breaks the vow, we have to notify each other. I swear you can trust me on this one, and that I will never deceive you. Furthermore, and this is the free bonus from your end, when you absolutely can't go on alone any longer, I promise I'll come and join you. When you truly get to the end of your rope, I'll be there. I swear to god. I promise to keep my side of the bargain."

"You've got a deal." She sighs, puts her arms around my neck, and lays her head on my shoulder. "I hope you come back on your own volition before I have to ask."

Our agreement mollifies us both and makes our last days together easier. We stay in Windermere until the day before her flight, then drive south and get a hotel near Heathrow. Vanessa laughs about being the only tourist in history to ever visit the British Isles and never see London.

Our final night outside the airport is agonizing. We both cry when we make love, and neither of us can sleep. We remain in a naked embrace and talk about our future. She is reconciled to our parting, and gives me a free pass, for now, on my "someone is trying to kill me" fixation. She hopes it will pass and has faith we are meant to be together. For my part, I feel noble. If worse comes to worst, I want her to be far away from my violent end. Her life is more important than mine.

Neither of us knows what to do or say when flight time arrives, but we accept our circumstances with dry eyes and embrace one last time before walking in opposite directions.

6

RETURN TO THE
CONTINENT

D RIVING BACK into the center of London is more difficult than I had expected, particularly when I have to read the confusing map and drive simultaneously. Burly lorry drivers help keep me alert by blasting their horns and making ugly faces. I respond with my finger, but only when I am sure that my getaway is clear. I learned early that it is much better to be a big shot when I have a safe escape, but now the ultimate escape, the one that means survival, eludes me. I finally find a place to park near Trafalgar Square. I run down Haymarket to American Express, pick up my mail, and rush back to the car. I have an easier time driving out of town, partly because I adopt a more aggressive attitude. My horn is an important tool as I slash my way back onto the motorway. Most of the victims of my reckless driving are annoyed but respond civilly, unlike most Americans. I eventually get into the slow lane and begin to relax. After an hour I exit at a rest stop and read my mail.

Cris has sent several brief letters from the Central African Republic. He raves about a beach in Ghana, says he has heard nothing but fabulous things about East Africa, and plans to be in Nairobi soon.

Erik Erickson

"Meet me there. Let's go on safari and party on the fabled white sands of Mombasa."

Monica has written from Vienna. She is working for a travel agency and will be visiting Paris soon. She says she would love to meet me there and asks that I give her a call as soon as possible.

I ponder my predicament while continuing to drive back toward Somerset. Vanessa's departure has yet to sink in, but my primary consideration is my immediate future, which I want to extend as long as possible. And crucially, since I'm certain someone is out to kill me, why can't I determine a suspect and a motive?

The return to the Cummings estate changes my mood and elevates my spirits. It is good to see Mousa again, and Glastonbury provides me with a sense of security amidst the confusion.

"How was Ireland?" Mousa asks when we shake hands.

"Fabulous!" I answer. "They are the best people I've ever met."

"I'm glad to hear it hasn't changed. Where is your lovely lady?"

"I put her on the plane this morning. Your place looks like it's in more disarray than usual. Where's Ingrid? What's going on?"

"She left a couple of days ago. She's got a UN gig in Kenya. I'm flying down to Nairobi on Friday. My mother needs help on the farm. I can't wait to introduce her to Ingrid. I expect I'll be there awhile. Why don't you come down and see me?"

"You're the second person today to suggest Kenya. My friend Cris expects to be there within a month. This is auspicious."

"You'll love Kenya. It's full of awesome people and breathtaking places. I'll give you my mother's address on the coast. I'm not sure where I'll be at any given time, but she'll know where I am. Phones don't always work down there. When you get to Nairobi, ask about me at the Iqbal Hotel. Someone there will know where to find me."

I call Monica and arrange to meet her in Paris. She says she can't wait to show me around. I appreciate her enthusiasm, and also hope she may be able to provide some insights into the ship's passengers. Together, maybe we can figure out a suspect. Monica says she has a favorite hotel near Luxemburg Gardens and that I can stay with her for free.

"I get special rates," she tells me. "I'll book us as Mr. and Mrs."

"I must warn you that I'm celibate and I'm saving myself for another woman. That's actually true," I say.

"Does that mean I won't have to put up with any more of your forced sexual attempts?"

"I've never forced sex on anyone except myself. All too often lately. "

"You'll regret your decision in Paris."

"How's that?"

"You'll see."

I drive Mousa to Heathrow early in the morning. He talks incessantly about his return to Kenya and encourages me to make a reservation early.

"Look around now," Mousa advises. "If you pay in advance you'll be able to get a cheap seat. I can tell you're ready to go back to Africa."

"I'll see you there," I say.

I have already decided to go to Kenya after Paris. It is the perfect destination because no one on earth will suspect it, and unusual movement is hard to follow. Before joining Monica in Paris, I decide to go to a discount travel agency in London and book a ticket to Nairobi from Heathrow.

"Have you ever flown on this charter before?" the travel agent asks.

"No, I sure haven't," I respond.

"I didn't think so."

"Why's that?"

"You'll be surprised."

"Pleasantly?" I ask.

"Probably not."

"Do they crash a lot?" I ask.

"I'm not sure about that, but I don't think so. Are you afraid of flying?"

"Not flying. Just crashing."

"That's the least of your worries."

I decide not to pursue this topic any further with her. I cannot fathom how crashing could possibly be the least of anyone's worries. Right now death is at the top of my list, and crashing is simply another way of doing me in. If I do die en route I reason that it's my own fault. I should have hired a private detective a long time ago. In any case, I am booked into Nairobi on Sudan Airways. I have a plan, set in stone.

The ferry across the Channel is uneventful, but the train to Paris impresses me. Everything runs on schedule and the rail cars are clean and comfortable. When we approach the city I am thrilled by the sight of the Eiffel Tower. It is a more dominating presence than I had expected, and reaffirms my belief that seeing is believing, and that I have to be there to really know. The wonder of the Paris skyline heartens my determination to stay alive and see as much of the world as can before I die, hopefully of old age. It would be tragic to have lived and not seen this in real life. Next, I want to see the tower up close and personal, and I wash down an upper with a glass of red wine.

I take a taxi from the station to Monica's hotel and discover that she has not yet arrived. I leave my pack at the desk and head back out onto the street. Open spaces within large cities always attract me, because of some innocent, youthful forays into Central Park with my mother. I take a stroll through Luxemburg Gardens and check out the surrounding neighborhood. My fellow pedestrians are very well-dressed, making me feel like an eyesore in my ragged jeans and bulky sweater. There are prosperous mothers with children in tow, and joggers in stylish outfits. I conclude that First World wealth looks about the same everywhere, and regardless of nationalities, the upper classes successfully conspire to maintain their favorable conditions, although Parisians might be a serious cut above. The park is peaceful and pleasant, but I decide to keep moving.

I quickly down two glasses of wine at a corner café, and

then, after a quick tour of the Sorbonne, make the short trek to Notre Dame, which is not as grand as I thought it would be. Maybe only the French can understand why some consider it the center of the universe. The longer I walk around, the more I begin to understand their perspective.

I return to Monica's hotel and find the staff at the front desk friendlier this time around. When I deposited my backpack three hours ago, they were reserved and formal, but now they are downright ebullient. The change in their demeanor catches me off guard, but I am always gracious when I get the royal treatment. And once again, I thank my mother for making me learn French.

"Your wife anticipates your arrival," the desk clerk says happily. "She instructed us to send you up immediately."

The clerk gives me a wink. This change in attitude bewilders me. I know it has everything to do with Monica, and I understand that Frenchmen are excited by "the womanly presence," but I cannot grasp the attraction of the overweight Austrian. I know she is special, but not at first sight. Though certain segments of this population are irresistibly drawn to Renoir women with very high standards and aggressive personalities. When I knock on the door, I am greeted by the loud voice I remember so well.

"Come in," Monica screams.

I open the door and see no one.

"I'll be out in a second," she yells from the bathroom.

"How have you been Monica?"

"Fine thanks. How about you?"

"I've been okay. I'm still alive anyway."

"Didn't you expect to be?"

"It's a long story. We'll talk about it later. What's going on in there, anyway?"

"The minute you knocked I was sitting down to take a pee. Now I'm opening the champagne."

I hear the cork pop. She makes her entrance with the bottle and two glasses in her hands. I gasp when I see her. I would not have recognized her on the street. Only the familiar voice is unchanged. My mouth drops open but I say nothing.

"Well, what do you think?" She throws back her arms, does a tight spin, walks over and hugs me.

"I'm speechless."

"I thought you would be. That's why you're the best. You're never speechless."

"What happened?"

"I decided to become anorexic." Monica moves away and does another spin. "How do you like the new me?"

"I can't believe it! You're gorgeous! You're ravishing."

"Thank you, my sweet. It's so nice to be rewarded. I've always loved talking with you. You're honest. Now it's better than ever. Let's drink and talk."

"What happened?" I am still having a hard time taking it all in.

"I finally got sick of being the fat chick with the winning personality. Well, some people might even question the personality part. In any case, I just decided I'd had enough. Food that is. Sometimes enough is enough. You might be responsible. I'd never met anyone with such a vast arsenal of fat jokes. And now, for the first time in my life, everyone looks at me like you are looking at me. They don't avoid me visually. Sometimes they stare to get a better view. Not only men, and that's what really blows me away. Women look me over from top to bottom. I love it. Nobody ever glanced below my neck before. Now everyone wants to see what I look like naked."

"Pretty good I bet."

"Real good."

"How'd you do it?"

"I willed myself thin. All my life I was overweight. I went from baby fat to chubby to plump to obese. But when I got off that freighter I didn't eat anything for a week and I started to exercise, then ate nothing but fresh fruit, vegetables, and tofu. The longer it went the better I felt. Now I'm just like all those other trendy, self-righteous, health food freaks out there. I'm addicted to good food and workouts. And I'm more intolerable than ever. Just like you."

She pours the champagne and I toast the new and improved Monica. We spend the next hour sitting in the room, drinking champagne, and bringing each other up to date. We have a second bottle and laugh at each other's stories, and except for the striking change of appearance, she is the same, only better. She is still open, sensitive, and outspoken, but there is a confidence in her manner that was lacking before, and a look on her face that exudes sensuality.

"So what's on the itinerary for this evening?" I ask.

"It's changed since you brought up your celibacy. I bought a few sex toys and thought we could use them together."

"I think that might technically be against the rules."

"We won't be touching."

"I wouldn't be able to stop myself."

"You're the first person who turned down the new me. I'm shattered."

"It hurts me more than it does you."

"Suit yourself, cowboy. I respect your vows. But you don't know what you're missing."

"I think I do. You make it hard to refuse."

"Hey!" she says, "it's going to be a special night even without the sex. I'm sure our friends will like seeing you."

"Our friends? What friends?"

"You'll see."

"What do you mean I'll see?"

"You'll see, that's all. I refuse to discuss the subject any further. We'll get some strong smoke and go to dinner."

"Am I going to stay alive and have a good time?"

"You're going to have an amazing time, but I don't know about the staying alive part. Judging from your past behavior patterns, I suppose you could drink yourself to death."

She leads me on a brisk walk up the Left Bank of the Seine. We cross a bridge onto the Isle de St. Louis and through some of the most exclusive streets in Paris. Near the center of the island we enter an inconspicuous restaurant. The interior rooms are much larger than they look from the street. Rough wooden tables on old stone floors; it makes me think that not much has changed since the Three Musketeers dined here.

"I adore this place," Monica says. "It's a hedonist's heaven. This is the first time I've been here since I've been thin. No guilt tonight. Wait until you see what they offer. A feast with all the trimmings. Everything but a sex show. That comes later. First we have to get in the mood."

She gulps down a glass of wine, pours us both another, and sashays over to the nearby oak casks to fill up another pitcher.

"This is the part you'll like the best," she says when she returns. "All the wine you can drink. No extra charge. I've always loved it. It's right down your alcoholic alley." I survey the room, look at the kegs, raise my glass, and we toast each other.

Hours later we are still eating and drinking. Pitcher after pitcher of heavy red wine has numbed my cognitive powers. It reminds me of the meals we shared on the freighter. Monica ate like a horse then, and she is doing the same now, only this food is gourmet. I wonder how she was able to take off those pounds, and begin to think the stories of willpower are invented, that a fiendish Austrian fat farm doctor is behind it all. Perhaps she was sliced open and had all the corpulence sucked out by some unpatented German machine. She is certainly not displaying any self-restraint this evening, unless unabashed gluttony requires effort. Maybe she is willing herself, against all odds, to eat and drink everything in sight. I hope she is not bulimic. The thought of seeing it all come up again scares me. Still, it is easier to watch a thin person gorge themselves than a fat one, and for the first time since we met, I can tolerate watching her eat. We both get theatrical throughout the meal and have a grand time. When we leave we are so satiated we have trouble moving through the crowded room, but we excuse ourselves and laugh all the way along.

"I think it's time to catch the show," she says on our way out.

"What show?"

"You'll see."

"Not this shit again."

"Follow me."

We weave our way through the dark streets and walk for thirty minutes along the Left Bank. Eventually Monica leads me into a cabaret on the water's edge. We pay a cover and enter a long tunnel-like hallway.

"In the old days this place used to be a jail," Monica tells me. "When they needed to dispose of a dead body they just tossed it out the window, right into the river. Rather clever, really."

"Only from a German perspective," I reply. "Disposing of bodies is one of your specialties."

"Fuck you and shut up. Some of these old jails have been converted into nightclubs. This is one of the most exclusive. There are different rooms connected by these corridors. We're headed to the main cabaret area. The more popular acts appear in the main room."

We continue down the hallway and descend into a room with dozens of tables surrounding a stage. Monica pushes her way through the crowded entrance and finds two chairs up front. A comedian is making jokes about recent political events in France. Monica and I can both understand him perfectly, but we don't find him amusing. The audience thinks he is funny, and so maybe we're missing something.

"I've never been able to understand the French sense of humor," Monica says. "And believe me, I've tried."

"They think and do things differently. That's why the French fight with their feet and fuck with their face."

The next act is a young female singer. She is followed by another male comedian. When the comedian is finished, the master of ceremonies takes the microphone and begins to introduce the main act. He spends an inordinate amount of time on the buildup, pointing out that they have become the rage of Paris and that everyone is talking about them. He finishes by urging the audience to give them a warm round of applause.

When the two performers come onto the stage I am so shocked that at first I am not sure what I'm watching. After rubbing my eyes I realize that it is true, and that I have seen parts of this act before, months ago, in the middle of the Atlantic. I can hardly believe my eyes.

"My god! It's the Cat Sisters! Jesus Christ! What's going on?"

"Enjoy the show," Monica says.

It is quite a performance. The Sisters have refined their act since their freighter days. Their makeup and costumes are impeccable. They have added sexual innuendos, and it is a highly charged routine with heavy lesbian overtones. They do not make a sound as they slowly undress. Their timing is perfect and their lithe, flexible bodies handle the energetic material with ease. Despite their removing everything except the masks and tails, the audience never sees it all. It is masterfully teasing. The crowd gives them a standing ovation when they finish. There are no encores.

"Those two deserve the Nobel Peace Prize!" I say when the applause dies down. "I almost don't believe what I just saw. How on earth did they end up here?"

"It's a wild story," Monica says. "They got "bored on board" and jumped ship in Marseilles. I'm not sure how much is true but seeing is believing. That's why I had to keep it a surprise. I knew you'd love it. Let's go backstage and say hello. I told them you were going to be here tonight."

"How did you find out about them?"

"Completely by accident. A French couple brought me here. It was a random decision. I nearly died when they came out onto the stage. Cardiac arrest time. My friends didn't know what was happening. You must admit, it's pretty sexy for sixty."

"Incredible!"

The sisters are the same as always. If anything, even more over the top. They saunter fluidly around their dressing room with ear to ear grins.

"No more card games on the decks of slow-moving freighters for us. We're booked for three weeks in Munich starting next month. We've got an agent and everything."

"How did this meteoric rise to stardom come about?" I am still having trouble absorbing it all.

"When the boat docked in Marseilles we decided we'd had enough. We disembarked and got a room in the city. One night we were looking for a little action and went to a nightclub down by the docks. We both speak French. We entered an amateur striptease contest and won. The rest, as they say, is showbiz history."

"What a story! Any plans?"

"We learned a while back to not look too far down the road. We're enjoying the here and now. We've never been to Germany, and we're looking forward to Munich. After that, who knows? Our motto is just say yes."

"What say we all go out for a nightcap?" I can't think of any better drinking companions.

"Now you're talking," the sisters say in unison.

I had forgotten how well these two can hold their liquor. They steadily nip down the vodka lemonade but remain clearheaded and stimulating. Their stories keep coming. Men half their age want to pay them for sex.

"We like to fuck but we don't do it for money. We're rich. Our standards are pretty high."

"Are you still doing drugs?" I've always liked sex and drug tales.

"That's a long story," the elder sister says. "Marijuana was the first drug, after booze, that made us feel good. We'd done quite a few drugs. Drugs given to us by our doctors. Eventually marijuana was prescribed. We liked it and decided to totally change our treatment. We had cancer. It was to counter the side effects of chemotherapy. We began to suspect their cure was worse than the disease. Marijuana was the catalyst that opened our eyes. We came to realize that healing was a minor byproduct of their operation. Making money was their major concern. Since we had the wherewithal to pay the bills, no one wanted to see us go. One way or the other, so to speak. The unspoken rule is keep them alive and inside as long as the checks continue to clear. We nearly had to fight our way out the door. We're doing alternative medicine now. Holistic stuff. We feel better and the cancer is gone."

"It sounds like you saved your own lives," I say. "I hope you can help save mine." They say they will do their best.

"Thank you. Now I want you to bear with me for a bit. I haven't told this story often because it's a bizarre tale."

I tell my story slowly. It has all been rehashed so many times in my own mind that I easily remember all the subtle details. The three listeners give me their full attention. They occasionally shake their heads but do not say a thing until I have finished.

Monica is the first to respond. "It sounds like a thriller novel."

"I was hoping for a little more insight. That I already know."

The women are all intrigued by Zorro. They think he might be a key to unraveling the puzzle.

"The guy scared the shit out of me," I say.

"My sister and I talked about this earlier, before we knew we'd ever see you again. There was one person on that ship who wasn't who he said he was. The guy was an imposter. No doubt about it."

"Who's that?"

"Your roommate, Karl."

"What? The consummate nerd?"

"Think it over. He looked too old to be a recent college graduate. He acted innocent but his eyes betrayed him. We're not saying he's a murderer, but we know he isn't the naïve kid he portrayed himself to be. We didn't like anything about that guy."

"I'm flying back to London soon," I tell the Cat Sisters. "I've got a charter flight down to Nairobi. I'm on the run but let me know if you're going to be anywhere close. I've been told that Poste Restante at the Nairobi post office works pretty well. If you're near, send me a letter there."

"If we're anywhere close we will. In the meantime, we would be happy to lie down on our bare butts if you asked us to. You could have a sister sandwich." The three women seem to find that thought even funnier than I do.

"I might be in Kenya soon myself," Monica says. "It's a trendy place for Europeans to vacation. Five stars all the way. Some resorts even have German-speaking staff. They're also talking about sending me to South Africa."

"Try to push for Kenya," I reply. "I have good connections on the coast."

The next morning Monica and I are eating a scrumptious room service breakfast in her suite overlooking Luxembourg Garden. She spends most of her time on her typewriter while drinking coffee. I am reading *Le Monde*, enjoying the feast, and counting my blessings when Monica breaks into my thoughts.

"I hope I'm not asking too much, but please do me one big favor before we split up."

"What's that?"

"I have a very good friend in Amsterdam. I'd like you to meet her. Let's take the train this afternoon."

"I'm still on guard, but I'll follow you anywhere."

"You might regret saying that."

"I've never regretted being around you. Why not be around you in Amsterdam? What's up?"

"I enjoy having sex with men," she says earnestly. "But I like having sex with women even more. I want you to watch it. It will be a different perspective for both of us."

"This sounds like it might be real tough on me."

"You can do it."

Veronika, Monica's friend, greets us at the train station in Amsterdam, and we walk to her spacious apartment on Dam Square, the largest tourist zone in the city. She is not what I expected. Beautiful, gracious, and attractive all still apply to my unseen assumptions, but I did not anticipate that she would be nearly old enough to be my mother, and not all that much younger than the Cat Sisters

"Monica and Veronika," I say lightly. "It sounds like they go well together."

"You haven't seen anything yet," Veronika says. "Sometimes we spank each other gently. Only to be naughty." She smirks and winks at me simultaneously.

I use my most charming smile. "Thanks for inviting me."

The enormous steel and glass dining room table is covered with an extensive array of food and alcohol offerings. Veronika opens a bottle of champagne and fills our flutes.

"Here's to continued good health." Monica raises her drink. "And an exciting threesome. I look forward to it all."

Monica stays in the open kitchen while Veronika shows me

Erik Erickson

149

around her apartment. She moves with the fluidity and grace of the professional tennis player she once was, and at the end of the tour she shows me to my room.

"Our room is up above. You're not allowed above this level. All of the action involving you happens down where Monica is." I am curious about what type of action she is referring to, but I bet I'm going to find out all too soon.

We go back downstairs and she opens another bottle of champagne. I make for a window to admire the fabulous views over Dam Square, the historical center of the city. The two women join me and ask if I would like to watch lesbian porn with them while they get warmed up.

"I'd love to. But I've made a commitment to Vanessa. No cheating or lying. I'm sure fondling applies as well."

"That's our proposal," Monica says. "You don't touch us and we won't touch you."

"Do I have any responsibilities?"

"Just watch us for awhile," Veronika says. "We'll ask you later about getting involved. It won't be physical. Our bodies won't touch yours."

"Do you mind if we get naked before we put the movies on?" Monica asks.

"Not at all. Make yourselves at home. I feel like I should join you, just to be social."

"That's part of the plan. But we'll see how it goes. And how you feel."

They kiss and fondle when the movie reaches orgasmic climaxes. The live action show in front of me is much more erotic than the screen in the background. These two deserve top billing on any venue—except maybe with the Cat Sisters. They have sex toys that even I have never seen before. They use them on each other and drink champagne between noisy orgasms. They are both screamers, and neither of them make any effort to muffle the sound. It has always been music to my ears, and duets are even better.

I am pleasantly confused about my role here. Am I destined to be the untouched torture victim with the big blue balls? I reason that it is their show, but I'm having trouble keeping my erection under control. Where is this headed?

"I can see that prominent bulge in your pants." Monica is treating me to a coy smile of invitation. "Why don't you take your clothes off. We promise not to touch, but we would like to take a look at it."

I am tempted to do a slow striptease but think better of it and disrobe quickly. I am under their command, and after a long pause Veronika tells me to turn around, and after a short pause, she tells me to face them again. My erection is as big as it gets.

Veronika smiles. "What do you think of all of this?"

"My hard-on says it all."

"We want you to be our untouchable man. A living sex toy that we use at our pleasure. We want our imaginations fulfilled. Should we all play the game together?"

"Absolutely."

"Our intuition tells us that you are the perfect leading man. Your starring role requires stamina and rapid recovery. There's a pile of perfect powder over there on the table. Silver straws. It's real good stuff. Do enough and it will keep you up all night. Help yourself whenever you think you might need a little more energy."

"What's my job?"

"Your mission, should you choose to accept it, is to masturbate and ejaculate on us throughout the evening. We love the taste of semen, and we want to massage it on our breasts. We will use it on each other and look forward to the next shower. You won't be doing anything different than what most lonely men do in front of a screen. I'm sure you've done that before. Your sacred vow will be unbroken. You'll just have to masturbate a lot. What do you think?"

"I think my hand can handle it. Like you said, I've had plenty of practice."

"Before we get too far into it, is there anything you would like to see us do? Anything. It's up to you. Your wish is our command."

"This doesn't have to happen, and I don't mean to put on any pressure here at all, but I would love to see you strap on the dildo belt and butt fuck each other while using the vibrator in your pussies. It's merely a random thought that just popped into my mind. I don't know where it came from."

"Great request," Monica says. "We'll make it happen. Cum on us when we do. I can tell already that you are going to exceed our expectations. We're glad you're into it. Keep it up, if you don't mind the pun."

The powder on the table helps, and the hookah filled with hashish makes the entire night vibrantly hallucinogenic. I have not masturbated that much since I was a teenager, and it was all for a good cause. Besides, easy pleasure is the best kind, and sometimes it cannot be denied.

The women are in the kitchen when I wake up the next morning. I shower and go down to join them. They cheerily greet me and praise my performance. It is always tough for me to act modest, but I try.

"I may have been the leading man, but I was only a supporting actor in a star-studded cast. You two are too much. I learned a lot. I'll be a better lover from here on out."

"That's why we like you so much," Monica replies. "And you can honestly tell your Vanessa you haven't touched a woman since she saw you last. She can rest assured, because it's the truth. We never grabbed."

"There's a fine line with truth sometimes, but not often." I laugh. "But I'm going to side with you two on this one."

"There is no need for full disclosure when it's not helpful to anyone," Veronika says. The two women kiss and stroke each other's crotches before serving me a large Irish coffee.

"How about a fairly quick session before you have to take off?" Monica asks. "It's entirely up to you."

"Take a look at my pants. One more session is not going to condemn me."

"Orgasms are good medicine," Monica says. "Particularly for women. Most men tend to be a little more piggish about it. Not you. In the meantime…let's get naked."

7

THE STRANGE SAFARI

M Y FLIGHT from Amsterdam to London is a living nightmare. Uncharacteristically, I had mustered my courage and boarded the plane sober. I realize that safe flying statistics do not mean anything, and I don't like statistics in general, because disasters can happen at any time, and therefore I begin to wish I had gotten stinking drunk. Halfway across the English Channel the plane starts shaking violently as if it is preparing to disintegrate. I imagine the side next to me ripping open, and me being sucked out, never to be seen again. The plane makes a sudden drop in altitude. I scream and hope I pass out before impact. When the plane levels out and it gets smooth again, I look around and grin, but my fellow passengers do not find me entertaining. I suspect they think I'm drunk. Even our successful landing at Heathrow does not relieve my anxiety, since I know I have to fly again soon, and that my odds have decreased by a factor of one. I fear I might be about to become the victim of poetic justice. My killer will not have to perform his task, the plane will go down on its own. Either that or there is a bomb on board unrelated to my presence. I come close to becoming religious when we land safely in London.

The international departure lounge at Heathrow is mobbed, and I have never seen such a wide conglomeration of humanity. Unlike me, they all seem confident that they are going to make it to their destinations alive. I want to share their faith but cannot marshal any more bravery without alcohol. Two hours before my flight I have successfully worried myself into an emotional lather, despite getting fairly liquored up. I am terror-stricken about getting aboard a claustrophobic death missile again, and regret so blithely brushing aside the travel agent's vague caveat about the cheap charter. What does she know that I do not? Do they blow up their own planes for the insurance money?

I decide on more drinks, just to take the edge off. I know I do not want to get too smashed before a fourteen-hour flight to Africa, but I break my own pledge. A few becomes quite a few, and the more I drink the better I feel. When boarding is finally announced, I can barely stand, much less ambulate, but most of my fear has been drowned. I stagger to my cramped seat and fall asleep before we get off the ground.

When I awaken I think the plane has crashed. My body feels mangled, my head is pounding, my mouth is parched, and my heart is racing. I open both eyes and see no blood and no wreckage. We are flying through the air just like we are supposed to, and everyone is smoking cigarettes, which is making my throat so dry that I am having trouble swallowing. Once again, I have picked a bad place to have an epic hangover. I summon all my energy, sit up in my seat, and lurch for the call button.

"Yes sir?" The flight attendant does not look friendly.

"May I have a bottle of water, please?" I cannot decide if my voice sounds more like I am begging, or if I have some sort of advanced throat cancer.

"I'm sorry, sir," the pretty young woman says. "We are out of water."

"What?"

"I said we are out of water, sir."

"Is this some type of cruel joke?" My voice is gaining strength. "How can we be out of water? It's one of life's necessities. Are we going to run out of air as well?"

"They forgot to fill our plane before we left London."

"You've got to be kidding me!" I lower my voice. "Did they

remember to put any gas in the tank?"

"Everything else is fine, sir."

"May I have a beer then, please?" My condition makes it difficult but I try to be polite. After all, it's not her fault.

"I am sorry. But we do not serve alcohol."

"No one is allowed to get drunk except the pilot. Is that right? Are there any drinkables on board at all? Or do I have to slice my wrist and drink my own blood?" I am beginning to think that crashing might be better than this.

"We have cola and pineapple juice."

"May I have one of each, please."

"Will that be all?"

"I hope not. But let's start with that and see what happens."

I was under the impression that we made a stop in Khartoum, and then flew on to Nairobi. This proves to be a false assumption. We make an unscheduled stop in Cairo, which lasts three hours. The air conditioning is turned off and only departing passengers are allowed to leave the plane. The cabin becomes stuffy and my body aches all over. When I get up to use the restroom, the attendant blocks my path and tells me no one is allowed in the toilet. I threaten to urinate and defecate in the aisle. She can tell I am not bluffing, and relents. I force a smile and remind her that we need lots of water.

Some of the passengers depart in Cairo, but others board, and every seat is still taken. A middle-aged American is the last to enter the plane. He has thinning red hair and a puffy pink face. His nose and stomach are both wrinkled and engorged. He acts as if he owns the airline, and he has the look of a person no one would ever want to know. The big man barges down the aisle and throws himself into my adjoining seat. It immediately starts to get grim again.

"The name's Henderson. How ya doin'?" I cannot tell if he is slurring his words or not.

"I'm wretched." I did not think my life could get any worse but Henderson's presence has proved me wrong.

"Pleased to meet you, wretched." Henderson laughs too loudly. "Where ya from and where ya headed?"

"New York and Nairobi."

"Goddamn, I sure hope I get to make it down to Kenya before I leave this fucking continent. I've been stuck in Egypt and Sudan for the last six months. To be perfectly honest, just between you and me, I'm sick to death of the desert and all these fucking Arabs. Can't say I like blacks any better but I'd love to see those game parks. Maybe shoot some big game while I'm there. And I don't mean with a camera, if you catch my drift. What'd you say your name is?"

"I didn't... And my sister-in-law is an Arab... And I work for the NAACP."

Henderson doesn't seem to hear me, and he only briefly stops talking. I do not think the flight to Khartoum will ever end. Henderson proves to be the worst human being on the face of the earth. He never stops talking, and he should be banned from the planet by the Geneva Conventions.

"I was in the Marine Corps most of my life," he says proudly.

"It shows."

"What do you mean by that?" Henderson puffs up like a rooster, and I decide to back off.

"I mean you look like a military man." I hate the military and wish Henderson's name was on a cross in Arlington National Cemetery.

"I retired early as a colonel. And then I saw how much money could be made selling weapons, instead of shooting them. What the hell, says I to myself, I'm as smart as those guys are. I can sell weapons too. And I've made a lot of contacts over here. Right now I'm selling stuff to buyers I'm not even sure of. I don't even really know what side they're on. Can you beat that?"

"Can't beat that."

"I'll bet you can't beat this either." Henderson lowers his voice for the first time. "But you have to promise to keep it under your hat. I'm not only selling to the government, but I'm also selling to the rebels down south."

This guy scares me on so many levels, but there is something about his demeanor that does not ring true at all, and I wonder what it is.

Sixteen hours after leaving London we begin our descent

into Khartoum. My physical and mental states have both deteriorated to the point where I hope the plane will crash. It would serve two purposes, put me out of my misery, and take Henderson to the fiery death he so richly deserves. To my ultimate relief, we land safely and Henderson files out. I have seldom been so happy to see someone go. I wonder how a guy like Henderson, doing one dirty deed after another, is able to get through it all unscathed, while I, an innocent babe in the woods comparatively, am threatened with extinction. I decide there is obviously no justice in this world, or I would be allowed to stretch out and sleep right now. It has not been a good flight, and I have another one yet to come, but at least Henderson is gone.

"Ladies and gentlemen," the pilot's voice announces over the intercom. "We are experiencing minor technical problems. To make everyone more comfortable, you are allowed to exit the aircraft and wait inside the terminal. Do not leave the building. We will keep you updated."

I greet this announcement with mixed feelings. I would love to get off the plane, but I would like to be off it for an extended period, and that only happens in Nairobi. Plus, I never like to hear about technical problems when they relate to a plane I soon will have to board. Flying itself is frightening enough. I do notice a decidedly military presence around and inside the terminal. Henderson's business is probably quite profitable here. I find a place at the far corner of the waiting room, stretch out on the floor, and go to sleep.

"Ladies and gentlemen," a loud voice bellows over the intercom, waking me from my fitful nap. "I am very sorry to announce that there is a change of plans. We will have to spend the night in Khartoum. The airline will provide hotel accommodations and pay for your meals during this unavoidable delay. Another aircraft will be here in the morning to fly you on to Nairobi."

This announcement wakes me up completely. I am ecstatic. A free stop with room and board, and I will be able to see the true heart of the Nile. The White and Blue rivers converge in Khartoum. This is a special place. After an hour of customs formalities, we are herded off to the hotel. I relish the sights and smells as we rumble along the road toward the capital of the third largest country in Africa.

The modern six-story hotel is near the river and the city center. It is surrounded by dusty, rutted streets and ramshackle old buildings. An empty lot directly opposite the hotel is filled with trash and weeds, but the interior reminds me of a Holiday Inn, complete with a coffee shop and dining room. When I get to my fifth floor room I lay down and fall asleep.

It is late in the afternoon before I wake up, feeling much better, and determined to do some concentrated sightseeing. No one on earth could possibly find me here, and it makes me feel secure. I will be able to walk around town and not have to worry about being killed at any moment.

I have a quick shower before taking the elevator to the lobby, where I look around for a bar, which is not easy to find in this establishment. Finally, I have to ask directions. There is no one in the bar except the young bartender, who brightens up considerably when I arrive.

"What can I get for you, sir?" he asks in perfect English.

"May I have a beer, please?"

"What kind would you like?"

"Sudanese beer, please."

"There is no such thing." He smiles. "We don't make alcoholic beverages in the Sudan. Not legally anyway."

"What kind of beer do you have?"

"Watneys, Guinness, and Lowenbrau. We usually have a better selection, but we're low right now."

The bartender is friendly and informative. He is obviously happy to have company. His uncle owns part of the hotel, and he has been to Europe. We exchange travel stories over three beers. I have one of each variety and think about having one for the road but decide to cash out.

"Exactly how much are these beers?" I ask when I count my change.

The bartender points to the price list above the small liquor cabinet. It does not take me long to calculate that I have been drinking in the most expensive bar in the world.

"It's kind of pricey, isn't it?"

"Very," the bartender replies.

"About the same all over town?"

"Some places are a little cheaper, but not many."

"How do people get high around here?" I ask.

"There are many ways to get high, my friend."

"You wouldn't happen to know where I could get a little smoke, would you? I'm only here for the night, so I don't need much."

I know I am breaking one of my cardinal rules of travel. Never talk about anything illegal until I have a secure sense of person and location, but I'm feeling my oats on this unforeseen, fortuitous evening, and trust that the bartender is not the one trying to kill me.

"I can help you out." His demeanor and smile bolster my already great mood. "I don't have any on me right now, but I can get some after work. Meet me at the park downtown, by the river, at seven."

I leave an overly generous tip, firmly shake the bartender's hand, and return to the lobby. The beer has made me a new man, and at this moment Khartoum conjures up romantic images of Arabian nights, and of vicious battles between Europeans and the locals. But I also know the political situation here has been a human rights disaster for decades. Ethnic conflicts are ongoing and countless thousands of innocent civilians have been killed. The city has always occupied a strategic location in African history, and as a crossroads of cultural diversity it remains full of mystery and intrigue. I can't wait to get my smoke and tour the town in style.

I charge around the downtrodden streets and try to absorb as much as I can in the time allowed. It does not take long to see that times are tough in the ancient capital. There is an instant reality of Third World poverty, and the overwhelming nature of it is alarming. I find it a much greater shock than when I got off the boat in Casablanca, as the indigence here is much worse. Morocco looks like an economic paradise compared to this. I pay my dues to the beggars as I explore their city, but there are more of them than I can possibly compensate. I also visit some wealthy enclaves, and I can clearly see that this is what an extremely poor, class-stratified, greed-driven society looks like up close and personal.

At six forty five I walk down to the river, toward the park and my rendezvous. It is a very peaceful evening, but transactions of this sort always make me tense, and I become more restive as I stride along. At seven o'clock I see the bartender striding briskly from the opposite direction.

"How's it going tonight?" I ask.

"Fine, thanks. I have your stuff. But just to be careful, let's walk along the river for a while. I'm sure everything is okay, but I have different sources, and I don't want to take any chances."

"I'm with you there." I am not so sure anymore, remembering the irreducible fact that illegality always invites risks.

The bartender seems edgy. I had hoped for a simple deal with no risk, and now I regret the entire transaction. I am contemplating my next move when he thrusts out his arm as if to shake hands, and the exchange is made. I can feel that I have just received a large joint.

"Unfortunately, I can't join you tonight," he says. "My father is expecting me and I'm already late."

"Thanks. How much do I owe you?"

"Your tip took care of it. I'll see you tomorrow morning at breakfast. Have a good time. It's going to be a great moon for sightseeing along the river tonight. I wish I could show you around."

I walk for ten more minutes, further downstream. The recently acquired joint makes me uneasy but I light up anyway. Two inhalations establishes its strength and I snuff it out, putting the remainder in my pocket and deciding to go back to the hotel for my free dinner. I have not gone more than three hundred yards when a heavy, forceful hand grips my left shoulder from behind.

"Where do you think you're going?" I am instantly paralyzed.

The low, gruff voice sends shivers up my spine, and I am frozen in place. We both know where I am going, either straight to jail or straight to hell. I curse myself for being so stupid. I am busted and it is over. I have instant visions of being locked up in a dark, steamy prison. The Black Hole of Calcutta goes through my historical mind, and I know it will look like a picnic compared to what I'm in for. My death will not be a clean, lethal strike, but a slow sexual torture. The bartender obviously befriended me for a reason. His ingratiating smile cleverly concealed his true intent, and now he will be granted sadistic sexual privileges as a reward. My vow to Vanessa will be broken without my consent.

I wonder if suicide will eventually become my only option, or if my real would-be murderer will find out and have me killed inside. Or maybe this *is* the real murderer, and the flight delay was artificially engineered for just this purpose. I will be forced into the river with cement shoes and my bloated body will not be seen again until it reaches Egypt. All of these horrible thoughts instantly race through my mind as I slowly turn around to face my tormentor. At first I do not recognize the face, but the leering smile is unmistakable.

"What's going on, Henderson?" I ask with my best face forward.

"I heard your plane was grounded," Henderson says. "I've been looking for you all afternoon. But goddamn, you're a hard guy to find. Since we're buddies I thought I should buy you a drink and show you around town. I was really looking forward to having an American drinking partner for a change. I know you like your alcohol."

I am so relieved that I could kiss Henderson's fat ass, but my trembling body still makes any action difficult.

"Did I scare you?" Henderson asks. "My military training kicked in. Sorry about that."

"No, no. What a wonderful surprise!" I compliment myself for regaining my composure so quickly. I never thought I would make a statement like that to this person, but I go further and follow it up. "It's great to see you again, my friend."

"Good to see you too, old buddy." Henderson gives me his toothy grin. "I was hoping I'd be able to hunt you down." I do not like his phrase. However, I am almost certain that this idiot does not want to kill me. He could have easily done it here and now; instead, he wants to be my friend.

"What's your plan?" I ask. Thankfully the terror is gone, but I could certainly use some alcohol to settle down, and I've got a sneaking suspicion Henderson is just the guy I'm looking for in this country right now.

"I could tell you're the type of guy who likes his drink." Henderson punches my shoulder a little too hard but I do not object. "And you can't afford to drink well in this country unless you know ole Hendy. I've got an expense account as long as my arm, but not as long as my dick. But then again, not much is, if you know what I mean." His low chuckle is very disturbing. "In any case, let's go suck down a few fingers, just you and me. We're both Americans, for Christ sakes. Let's show them what we're made of."

Less than a minute ago, I was sure I was bound for a Sudanese jail, or worse. My equilibrium has not yet returned, but I could use a few stiff ones even if I have to imbibe with this repulsive dunderhead. It could be much, much worse and I know it. I look Henderson in the eye and feign my most deferential smile, one I have used successfully countless times.

"I'd love to have a few drinks with you." I grin. Henderson pats me on my back. "They're all on me tonight."

There are not many places to legally drink in Khartoum, but Henderson knows them all. From our meeting onward, the city becomes an unreal experience for me. My finer senses fade as we carouse from one establishment to the next, always looking for the elusive better time. Henderson leads the charge because he is the military man, and despite his outward arrogance, he reaffirms friendly contacts along this well-worn route. The people I see seem to like him, and everyone smiles when he approaches. He tells them jokes in Arabic and always leaves them laughing. His language skills amaze me.

"I deal with these people every day," Henderson says.

"You do quite a job."

I can also see that Henderson is not as stupid as he acts, and not what he claims. The jester is camouflaged smartly. The ultimate ugly American is able to disguise himself when he so desires. Everyone Henderson greets sees a different side of him. The two of us drink gin and tonic until three a.m. I wake up the next morning at six. I need eight more hours of sleep, but know I am not going to get them, and I blame it all on Henderson. But I have to admit that it was all well worth it. Henderson is one of a kind.

A new plane has arrived to take us to Nairobi, and we are loaded back onto the busses. Running on three hours sleep, I haven't come close to sleeping last night off. Destiny has decreed that I will always have a horrible hangover when I fly.

I did not have time to shower, and know I look rough; the other passengers stare when they see me get on the plane. I try to keep a low profile, but I vomit violently shortly after takeoff, and everyone within earshot turns to observe my disgusting display. They are appalled when I miss the bag and it sprays all over the floor, and I know my noises make it sound like I might not survive. When they see I am going to live through it, Muslim passengers shake their heads. I want to beg for sympathy but decide to keep my mouth shut. I fall asleep immediately thereafter and do not wake up until we touch down in Nairobi.

Once inside the terminal we are all confronted with lengthy customs procedures. The Kenyan officials are not friendly. While waiting for the crowded action to clear, I make friends with two Australians who have been through this process before, months earlier. They are both dressed like guides on the jungle cruise at Disneyland, turned-up hats and all. They look ridiculous, but I find them friendly and informative. It is early afternoon when the three of us finally clear customs and approach the exit. Dozens of taxi drivers await our arrival outside the terminal.

We make a deal with a young driver and hop into the back of an old Peugeot station wagon. I immediately find the equatorial plain of East Africa exhilarating. Scraggly cattle, oxcarts, and pedestrians clog our approach to the inner city. I have never been in a place like this before. The driver uses his horn incessantly and curses in English. People and animals clamber to get out of the way, and there are near collisions. It is a nerve-racking ride and I make a mental note to look both ways before crossing a road in this country.

"They don't call these taxis flying coffins for nothing," Bill, the older Aussie says.

"It's an ironic turnaround," Bruce, the much younger one chimes in. "Human life is cheap. Wild animals are invaluable. It's a strange paradox that is not improving for either."

Bill and Bruce are staying at the New Stanley Hotel, a landmark from the colonial past that has seen better days. I like it because it houses the Thorn Tree Café, an outdoor watering hole overlooking a busy downtown sidewalk. By the crowd inside, I can see that the restaurant is a popular meeting place for wealthy people. We make multiple winding trips past the sun-drenched tables before finding three empty chairs. It reminds me of the popular bars back in south Florida. The beautiful people are out in force here as well. I am glad I did not buy a safari suit, and I make a vow to stay away from the clothing stores. I have never seen anything quite like this crowd before. Every skin color possible is represented, from lily white to shades of deepest black. Some women wear European clothes and others are entirely clad in African attire. Large parts of India and Asia are stylishly represented. All are dressed well; many are strikingly attractive. I wasn't prepared for this scene, but the real life visuals enhance my appreciation for what people told me is "Jomo Kenyatta's precious Nairobi."

I decide to spend the night at the New Stanley Hotel. I am just too exhausted to look around for another place. Bill and Bruce get me a great rate because "we are special and so are you." It's still not cheap, but I get a good sleep. I want to get closer to the locals and the next morning I get up early determined to find another hotel.

Mousa said to inquire about him at the Iqbal Hotel, so I set off for it. I cross Tom Mboya Street and enter a much poorer section of town. Street signs become hard to find. I walk a crooked line for twenty minutes and finally realize I have walked off the map. I do not know my location and decide to turn back, but now I am not sure of the proper direction.

Everything is out of place. The streets are crowded and dirty.

I become aware of something more ominous than being lost. The people around me are cognizant of my presence. Their eyes follow me as I walk along. I see that they are very poor, and that most of them are barefoot. They wear tattered clothing, and some are handicapped or diseased. All of them are black. Everywhere I look, everyone is black. It is the most remote situation I have ever experienced in my life, and I try to walk like I know where I am going.

A loud voice addresses my from behind. "Jambo bwana. Habari?"

I turn around and see a policeman in a gray cotton shirt and shorts. The cop nearly stands out as much as I do, because he is remarkably clean and well-appointed. I also notice that he is much taller than most of his countrymen.

"I think I'm lost, officer."

"Where are you going?"

"I'm looking for the Iqbal Hotel."

The policeman looks stern and unsmiling. "You had better follow me. I will take you there."

My trepidation had been building, and for the first time in my life I am exceedingly relieved to be walking next to a policeman. We draw a great deal of attention as we stride along. The cop does not acknowledge the stares or say anything to me. I look around and try to smile at everyone I see. The onlookers discuss us as we go past, and I wish I could understand what they are saying. The route we take is off-the-charts visually stimulating, and I know I never would have found it on my own.

"This is the Iqbal Hotel." The cop stops and points to a two-story building.

"Thank you very much, sir."

He never changes expressions. I find him impressive and hope all my engagements with the locals will be this pleasant, most importantly the ones with guys carrying guns.

The Iqbal Hotel sits on a wide street and has a ramshackle taxi stand out front. There is a movie theater next door, advertising exotic East Indian films. Street vendors operate on the sidewalk, selling everything from used books and magazines to grilled corn and meat. It looks like the set from an old John Wayne epic, only much grittier. There are many shades of brown people about, and a few whites. The double-door entrance stays permanently open, and the building looks like it has not been cleaned or painted since independence.

When I enter, I see that the ground floor is a bar and restaurant, and the hotel rooms are up above. Ceiling fans help keep the warm air moving but it is still stuffy. There are people eating; all but four are either African or Asian, nearly an equal number of both. The only two women present are white. They are sitting in the corner, slurping soup with their male companions, also pale-skinned. The ubiquitous flying insects keep them busy while they eat, but they look like they are having a good time with it.

Near the entrance, on my left, is a young Japanese traveler. He is thin, has a Fu Manchu mustache, and sits alone at a small wooden table. There is a bundle of twigs in front of him, and he is slowly chewing his way through it. His expression never changes. He looks straight ahead, strips the tiny bark from the stems with his teeth, and chews it like a cow. His energy is readily apparent despite his serene exterior, and his constantly moving jaw displays steady determination. I pass by his table, and we nod to each other in a friendly fashion.

In the middle of the room, near the kitchen, is a cluttered reception desk. A huge, heavy Sikh oversees the operation from this vantage point. He puts down his newspaper and stops eating when I approach.

"Do you know a guy named Rowalyn Cummings?" I ask. "People call him Mousa."

"Yes, I know him."

"Have you seen him lately?"

"Not in a fortnight. I think he's down on the coast. But you might ask across the street at the Green Bar. A friend of his is sometimes there. His name is Ibrahim, but everyone calls him Ibby."

"I need a place to stay. Do you have a room?"

"Sorry. We're full. Try the Sunset. It's right next door to

the bar."

The Sunset Hotel is also above a restaurant, although it is a much smaller enterprise than the Iqbal. I like the look of it right away. The approach is a narrow alley on the outside of the building, and a long flight of stairs leads up to the second floor where fourteen rooms have been built on the roof. They ring the perimeter and form a small concrete courtyard. Once again, a massive Sikh is in charge.

"Do you have a vacant room?"

"The only thing I have is a double. You can have it if you don't mind paying a little extra."

"How much extra?"

"Please let me show you the room first."

I immediately see that I could not have found a better room in all Nairobi. The price is right and the simple room is clean. Best of all, it overlooks the wide, teeming street, and has a small balcony just big enough for a chair. I have a fabulous view of the ever-changing street scene below and can see the Iqbal Hotel across the wide street. Suddenly, I'm thirsty for a beer. I book the room and head downstairs to where Ibrahim, Mousa's friend, might be.

In the last few months I have been in some strange drinking establishments, but the Green Bar is unique. The music is above any tolerable level, and the voices are even louder. If someone wrote a book about the roughest bars in the world, I'm sure this one would be on the list. There are over forty people in the small room, most of them standing. Two white men are at the far end of the long bar. Their light color stands out prominently. Everyone else is a shade of brown or black. The only women present are young, black, and attractive. Their aggressive and suggestive behavior determines their means of support. I politely push my way to the bar and order a Tusker beer.

"Warm or cold?"

It is the same question I was asked at the Thorn Tree Café, and I hope they are not all in a conspiracy to make fun of me, because I cannot imagine anyone requesting a warm beer, especially in this climate. I stroke my recently grown beard and look at the ceiling fan before responding.

"Cold, please."

"Buy me a beer, bwana!"

One of the young ladies has come over to greet me. She follows her command by putting her arm over my shoulder. She is fetching and appears to be intoxicated. I would find her sexier if she wasn't so intimidating, but her line of work requires many different approaches, and this must be one of her most successful greetings. She is chewing the same twigs the Japanese guy was chewing, but her jaws are moving much more aggressively. I wonder what the attraction to that stuff is, and I resolve to find out soon.

"I'll buy you a beer." I remove her arm from my shoulder. "But only one. And nothing else."

"That's all I ask." She laughs and strokes my genitals. I pull away and ask the bartender about Mousa.

"I have not seen Mousa for several weeks," the bartender says. "He must be down Mombasa side." The bartender pauses and scans the smoky room. "Do you see that Somali guy at the table over there? With the two Goans." He points to three men at a table near the door. "Ask him. He's a good friend of Mousa's."

I have a difficult time saying goodbye to my new girlfriend, and she does not want to let me go. I finally convince her that she has nothing to gain, but I still have to physically extricate myself from her clutches. I work my way over to the table and introduce myself to the three men.

They all stand up to shake my hand. Ibrahim, the Somali who is Mousa's friend, does most of the talking.

"Mousa's down on the coast now," Ibrahim tells me. "He's likely at his mother's, near Malindi. Although he could be anywhere from Mombasa to Lamu. His mother has property on the beach, and she is developing part of it into a resort. When I last talked to him, a couple of weeks ago, he said he was getting things done, and working long hours. He complained about too many officials, too much paperwork, and too many bribes. But as you no doubt know, Mousa is good with people."

I think most Somalis, including Ibrahim, look like

members of a huge extended family. When I compliment his perfect English, he points out that he also speaks German, French, Swahili, Somali, and Kikuyu. His smooth skin is the color of deeply tanned leather. He is slender and firm, and his movements seem effortless. He has a long neck, high cheekbones, and a fine thin nose.

The women in here are beyond compare. All day long, on the streets of Nairobi, the Somali women have stood out, and captured my attention. They are extraordinarily sensuous and attractive, and maybe the most beautiful women I have ever seen. It took me less than a day to understand why Mousa's English father chose a Somali to mother his only child.

"So what do you think of Kenya?" Ibrahim asks.

"I've only been here for a day. But I love it already. If the countryside is as pretty as the women, you will have to deport me, because I'll never want to leave."

"Nothing is as pretty as the women," Ibrahim says.

"There is one thing that I'm dying to know about, though. What is that green stuff people are chewing?" The three locals laugh and raise their beers.

"It's called miraa," Ibrahim says.

"What's it do?"

"One thing it does is keep you awake. Truck drivers use it for long hauls." Ibrahim nods to my girlfriend at the bar. "Whores use it for long nights."

"It's legal I presume?" I have always been intrigued by drugs, legal or not, and I am anxious to give miraa a try. The intensity on the Japanese face, and the energy the hookers display, intrigues me.

"Oh yes," Ibrahim says. "It's legal. For many people it's vital. It only grows up north, near Meru and Mt. Kenya. The Somalis love it. It has to be fresh to be good, and planes fly it in daily. It's frowned upon in some quarters. Regular users tend to end up wanting to do nothing but chew miraa. It can be habit forming, but it's not physically addictive, and like everything else, some people do too much of it."

"What about marijuana?"

"What about it?" Ibrahim asks.

"Is there any around?"

"We can get you anything you want." Ibrahim chuckles. "Watch what you ask for in Kenya. You'll always get it. You're in Africa now. Enjoy yourself. Humanity started here."

"Watch out Ibby, this guy could be setting you up. Maybe he's really from Interpol, looking to nail an international drug dealer."

"Marijuana, or ganja as the authorities call it, is seriously frowned upon by the government," Ibrahim says. "But our people have used it for centuries, primarily for medicinal purposes, and in certain circles it is considered a religious herb." He pauses and gestures to his two countrymen. "But we use it when we want to get real high."

I am very much enjoying their company; the laughs come easily, and I buy more rounds. We drink and tell stories until midnight. The more I drink, the more I like them, but fatigue finally overcomes exhilaration, and I return to my room for much-needed sleep. I learn that the ski mask comes and goes in my dreams no matter where I am.

The street noise below wakes me early the next morning. From my small balcony I watch the busy commercial activity unfold. Miraa is my first order of the day, and I decide to have it for breakfast. I find a salesman around the corner from the Iqbal Hotel. When the transaction is completed, I dash back to my room and begin chewing. I wasn't expecting it, but I like the taste right away.

It does not take long for the drug to take effect. After fifteen minutes I am feeling appreciably jauntier, and after half an hour I feel downright sublime. It is a splendid sensation, more powerful than I had expected, an untapped treasure. The energy penetrates to my core. It is hard to believe that I have never heard of this fabulous plant before. It is a magic amphetamine, straight from mother nature, with no synthetic chemicals involved. I am convinced that there is nothing more healthful than eating fresh produce like this on a regular basis. I wish my old connection in Washington Square Park were here to taste this with me. It makes me feel good all over, and I hurry down the stairs to explore the city.

It also doesn't take long to learn that speeding around Nairobi on miraa is the world's best way to spend the day. I am more thrilled to be here with every twig. It makes me feel friendly and powerful. Everything is going my way. It is a feeling that I know might not be true, but it is strong enough to erase most of my doubts. I cannot remember when I felt this vigorous and vibrant. I thank mother earth for my good fortune, and I hope it goes on forever.

I buy a newspaper and walk to the Norfolk Hotel for coffee and cognac on the famous veranda. The rich and powerful traditionally stayed here, and the entire establishment reeks of empire. The quiet, dignified atmosphere and landscaped grounds are to my liking, but after I finish my coffee I cannot finish the newspaper, because caffeine and cognac work well with miraa, and both mind and body tell me to keep moving.

I have energy to burn. If I have to keep running away from danger much longer, I would like to do it on a full tank of miraa. My high spirits carry me back to the Thorn Tree Café. I want to share this feeling with friends, or anyone capable of loving life, like me. My Australian buddies are not there, and everyone else looks too pretentious to befriend, but this city has a special vitality and an optimistic air. It is dynamic, full of life, and conveys the feeling of endless possibilities. Nairobi surprises me with its delicious diversity. I relish its dynamism. Vanessa should be here for this one. I decide to return to my favorite dive bar back in my part of town, where I really belong.

Ibrahim and Robert are at the same table they were at last night. It is early and the bar is quieter than it was on my previous visit. The same barfly is there, still chewing miraa. She acts as if Jack Nicholson has just arrived when she sees me enter. She throws her arms around my neck and talks me in to buying her a beer. Now I have a better understanding of her energy, because miraa works well with alcohol, it enables the user to drink more.

"Hey, it's great to see you guys," I say to Ibrahim and Robert. "I personally don't think I've ever felt better."

"It looks like you're tried some miraa," Ibrahim says.

"How can you tell?"

"Your eyes are wild and your teeth are green."

The Kenyans order another beer. The miraa has taken hold of me, and so have they, and their country, or what I have been able to see of it.

"I've got some of the other substance you asked about," Ibrahim says, flashing a smile. "I just happened to run into a guy this morning. It's grown up by Lake Victoria. It's the best."

"Let's take some beers up to my room and give it a try. Don't wake me if I'm dreaming."

The Kenyans follow me up to my room. Robert and I sit on the beds and lean against the wall. Ibrahim sits on the hard floor and hands me three fat marijuana cigarettes. It smells pungent and sweet when I put a match to it. I offer it to Ibrahim but the Somali declines. Robert takes it, inhales once, and nods his head. I have four hits and put it down in the ashtray. The familiar rush floods through my body, and I look at my two new friends and smile.

"It's strong all right." My mouth is very dry and I'm very high.

I stand up to get a beer from the table, and barely take a full step before blacking out, and falling over backwards. Ibrahim springs up and catches me on my way down, perhaps preventing my head from cracking on the stone floor.

"Jesus Christ! This stuff might be little too strong." I get back to my feet and grab a beer. The Kenyans slap their legs and howl with amusement.

"Welcome to Africa." Ibrahim pats me on the back.

It does not take long to realize that not only is everything new to me here, but that my senses also feel new, if only from constant exposure to unfamiliar sights, sounds, smells, and tastes. The locals have an avidity that complements it all.

I spend the next five days in and around Nairobi. Each day is filled with adventure, and I am astonished by the Kenyan people. Like everyone, they experience pain and suffering, but their zest for life is infectious. Their viewpoint makes me question my own. Maybe I should start doing something for someone else before it's too late. I am on my balcony drinking beer, smoking dope, and chewing miraa when there is a strong knock on my door.

"Who is it?" I try to sound like a drill sergeant.

"There's a phone call for you," the owner says. "He says to tell you Rowalyn is calling." I scurry out of the room and take the owner's phone.

"Mousa! How are you?"

"Doing well. How about you?"

"Better than I deserve. How did you know I was here?"

"I talked to Ibby. He said you guys have been partying together. I'm jealous. I've been working my tail off down here. My mother's project requires large amounts of time and effort. Why don't you haul your sorry white ass down to the coast? Make sure you take the train. Go first class."

"Is it the Last Train to Clarksville?"

"It's the best train ride on the planet."

Mousa's assessment is correct. From the moment I board I feel as if I have stepped into another time and age. The train is a relic from the colonial past, a slow-moving antique. I settle into my cozy cabin and admire the view, continuing to chew miraa to stay awake and see as much as possible.

The lunar cycle is obviously high because the moon is nearly full, and the central Kenyan plains are flooded with light. I have read that the equatorial moon is larger than other moons, that paradise is both a place and a state of mind, and now I know it's true. After we pull out of the station there are no settlements for extended stretches. The train rolls over the semi-arid landscape without stopping. There is an abundance of wildlife, and it makes me think of the old days, when hunting from this train must have been quite the sport. I imagine that Karen Blixen would feel at home on this journey. Not much has changed on these old tracks. The train rumbles slowly along on the uneven surface, and I see elephants, zebras, giraffes, and antelope from my window. There are also baobab trees and acacia, scrubby brush, and flowering cactus. This is the Africa I have seen in my wildest dreams, and I hope the scenery never changes. I also hope I will be allowed to come back someday, to share this magnificent night with Vanessa, without the terrifying fear that consumes me all the time. I feel safe on the train, but I'm still running, and I'm not getting any closer to a solution.

The dining car is three cars in front of mine. The waiter seats me at a small table meant for two. Old English bone china is set on immaculate white linen tablecloths, and the car is dimly lit by small electric candles. The faint illumination enhances my feelings of timeless romance. The service is perfunctory but not impolite. The hearty meal is delicious, and a bottle of Italian Chianti makes it taste even better. I go back to my room, continue to chew miraa, and take in the wonders outside my windows.

In the early hours of the morning I begin to see and feel the change in topography. The air is warmer and the humidity rises. Thirsty terrain slowly gives way to more tropical vegetation. Palm trees appear, along with thick, broad-leafed undergrowth. There are more bird calls and monkey screams.

The final hour into Mombasa proceeds at a crawl, I could walk faster most of the time. As the land becomes more fertile, I see the human population increase. Countless children play along the tracks and wave at our passing train. Mud huts with thatched roofs provide protection from the elements, and barefoot women wrapped in brightly colored cloth cook over open fires. The train creaks over an old bridge and crosses onto the island. The ancient porter rings his bell and calls Mombasa.

I push my way through the crowd gathered to meet the train. There are dozens of taxis parked on the street, and I engage the oldest driver I can find. The proud driver speaks English like a Lord. He protects his beloved old Rover by moving cautiously around the many potholes.

"It is good to see an American," the driver says. "Yours is a great country."

"So is yours."

"Amen, bwana."

The local population looks different than it did in Nairobi. They seem to move at a slower pace. There are more Muslims here, and some women are veiled and covered entirely in black. There are also more Arabs, Indians and Somalis, and even fewer whites than I had anticipated. The overwhelmingly dominant color is black, and I find myself liking that color more and more.

When I check into the small hotel that Mousa has recommended, the desk clerk tells me that Mousa left an hour earlier and is not expected back until the evening. The sleepless night with miraa has taken its toll, and even a glass of fresh passion fruit juice does not do much to revive me. I turn on the ceiling fan in my room and crawl under the mosquito net. It is late afternoon when I wake up, take an overdue shower, and go down to the lobby.

"Have you seen Mousa?"

"No, but he might be at Mickey's Bar," the desk clerk says. "Sometimes he stops there for a beer. It's on Kilindini, before you get to the tusks."

I find the bar and see Mousa at a table in the back, talking with another man. They are in a private conversation and do not see me enter. I decide not to interrupt and order a beer. At that same moment Mousa leans back in his chair and scans the room, much like he had done at the pub in Glastonbury, when he spotted Kerry and me. My beaming white face is hard to miss in this establishment.

Mousa's handsome smile always lights up my room. "Welcome to Mombasa."

"I'm starting to owe you big time. Thanks for inviting me."

"Nonsense. I owe you for flattering me with a visit. Come meet my friend, Butu. You guys will like each other. You're both funny and horribly self-indulgent. I mean that as a compliment. You two are good friends already. I guarantee it."

The three of us walk around town and watch the sunset from the old harbor. The narrow, winding cobblestone streets remind me of the medinas in Morocco, but this is different, a fascinating blend of African, Asian, and Arab. The amalgamation is mesmerizing. We walk back to the new city and have a spicy meal of chicken tikka at an outdoor restaurant. While we eat, Mousa explains the work he is doing for his mother, and that he and Butu are only in the city to take care of some legal entanglements relating to the proposed water system.

"Bribes help," Mousa says. "Most of my time is spent at the project site, a few miles south of Malindi. We're doing business in Mombasa until the weekend. Then we'll drive back north to my mother's property. Come along. Butu and I could use all the help we can get."

"I'd love to be helpful for a change," I say, "but I can't really do anything but talk."

"Well then, welcome aboard," Mousa says. "Butu and I are sleeping on a large old yacht that's tied up to my mother's pier. You can have one of the cabins. We're trying to convert it into a passenger cruise boat. It needs work, but it's a great ship. Do you know anything about engines?"

"I'm afraid not." For the only time in my life, I wish I did. "But despite my appearance, I've been told by some women that I'm a quick learner."

"You're our type of guy!" Mousa slaps hands with the smiling Butu.

We finish our meal and head for a nearby hotel, an inexpensive place with a small bar that caters to prostitutes and their clients and has cheap beer, always cold. Mousa says the women who work there usually have good smoke. When we arrive the bar is crowded with drunken Korean seamen. The sailors are boisterously making friends with the women who make their living at the hotel. I can see that neither side understands anything of what the other is saying, but body language overcomes all linguistic barriers in the most basic of business deals, the world's oldest profession. Mousa leads the way through the noisy bar area and into the inner courtyard, which is quieter.

Three young women leave the Koreans in the bar and follow us. Mousa and Butu know them well. The five Kenyans exchange jokes and banter in Swahili. I wish I could understood what they are saying, but I like watching the action from afar, and I am content to be the odd man out. I vow to start working on their language soon; unlike French, it appears to be spoken at high volume, which makes it even more engaging.

Much to my delight, the women here are their usual tantalizing selves. They are sensuous and know how to play it up, because their desirable looks are what keep them eating. I wonder if I'll ever mature beyond pretty women who like loud music and strong beer. The women sense my heavily repressed interest, and like other women I have known, they quickly begin to complicate my life.

They all insist on being introduced to Mousa's new friend, and when they shake my hand, they giggle and compliment my good looks.

"My name is Fatima," the youngest one says. "You are a very handsome man."

I look over at Mousa, and then down at my feet, but I do know that shy is not going to work here. Mousa asks Fatima about marijuana for his "wild and crazy American friend." I wish Mousa would not even mention me, particularly with a wild and crazy label.

"This guy loves his smoke," Mousa says. "Pretty women he doesn't want."

"It's true." I look open for an attack and I know it. "I have a girlfriend."

"I have good ganja," Fatima says. "If you want some, you need to smoke it in my room. Everyone come with me."

All six of us march upstairs to Fatima's sparsely furnished small room. She lights two joints and passes them in opposite directions. The men speak English while the women speak Swahili. I settle in on the floor and am beginning to relax and get comfortable when I am stunned by Fatima's surprisingly loud voice. She has switched to English, and I have a sneaking suspicion it is directed my way.

"I am sick of black, brown, and yellow. I want to fuck a white man for a change!" Her loud, strong statement silences the room. I know this is nothing but trouble; no one has to look too far to see the only white man in this group. The spectators all stare in my direction. I squirm and say nothing. Fatima comes over and stands in front of me.

"What do you say, white man?" I'm aware that no one is going to win this one, and I can see that despite her occupation, she is young and fragile.

"I'm terribly sorry," I stammer. "But I will have to decline. I'm engaged to be married. We have made vows and promises to each other." I'm trying to act like a contemptible hapless wimp, but I can tell I'm not pulling it off. Fatima responds accordingly by sneering derisively.

"I don't care about that shit. I'm going to fuck you, white boy. I want to fuck you bad. I want to fuck you hard."

"Come on man, give her a break." Butu offers me very poor advice. "If you can impress her, you might be able to make a career out of this kind of work." I do not think Butu is amusing at all, but everyone else seems to have a different perspective, and I'm afraid they are beginning to side with Fatima.

"I'll tell you what, white boy," Fatima says, patting my head. "I'll let you do it for free."

"You can't beat an offer like that!" Butu chuckles. "It's a good deal at twice the price!" I find Butu very unhelpful at this moment. "If he won't do it Fatima, count me in on that free stuff."

"You have to pay!" she shouts at Butu with a snarl.

"I'm sorry, I just can't accept." My anxiety has made me sound even worse, and I feel blood rushing to my face. "You are a lovely woman. And if circumstances were different…"

"Poor excuse," Butu reprimands me. "Just this once, man. She's talking free. No one here is going to tell anybody. Isn't that right, ladies?" I wish Butu would shut the fuck up.

"Maybe he's embarrassed by what he has," the oldest woman says, joining the fray. "Or by what he doesn't have. Can you make it hard, white boy? Does your dick work?"

The nature of these questions prevents me from formulating a clever response. Besides, I do not think cleverness is appropriate just now. I want to stand up for my dick, but I can sense that the tide is turning against me.

"I'm sure it's long and hard." Fatima continues to stroke my head. "And I know how to make it work."

Fatima chases everyone else out of her room. I try to leave with them but she will not allow it. Her physical strength surprises me, and I realize my weak struggle looks ridiculous.

She locks the inside of the door with her key and puts it down her pants.

"Now you have to go through me." She throws her head back and looks me in the eyes. "You don't leave until I make you cum."

"I'm sorry. I just can't." I do not know what to say or do.

She takes off her blouse and exposes her breasts. They are small, firm, and high, with nipples that taper upwards. Her rounded stomach is lean and tight. She has muscular arms and strong, delicate shoulders. She is the epitome of a Somali woman, beautiful like no other. I am upset for a number of reasons, but primarily because I am beginning to get a better understanding of our predicament. She is a businesswoman offering her product for free, and I am a desirable customer turning her down. In any money-making endeavor, that is the ultimate insult. I know there is not much time to work this out, because everything about Fatima is demanding and immediate.

"You are an absolutely amazing woman. You are very beautiful. And you have one of the prettiest bodies I have ever seen."

"I will pay you to do it." Before I can respond she takes off the rest of her clothes and lies down on the bed.

"I can't, Fatima. Under any circumstances. I have made a promise I have to keep. She would never understand."

"She will never know. Please. I will lose face."

Her hardened exterior begins to soften, I can see that pride is at stake here, and it breaks my heart. She interrupts my thinking about my predicament with a shocking question.

"Have you ever fucked a woman who has been circumcised?"

Before I can formulate a response, or even fully understand her question, she has spread her legs and pulled back her labia. I am appalled by the mutilation she displays.

"Who did that?"

"It was done when I was a young girl. After my father died. My uncle had it done."

A massive sadness engulfs me. I feel horribly ashamed. I want to scream and cry, but all I can do is clench my jaw and fight back tears.

"Let's just tell everyone we had sex," I say quietly. "Only you and I will ever know we didn't."

"You lie," she says. "You will laugh at me with your friends."

"No! I would never laugh at you. One woman trusts me. You can trust me too. Look what I'm giving up, the most beautiful woman in Kenya. I promise you I'll tell Mousa and Butu that you are the best I have ever had. I'll act like I'm a big shot."

She modestly puts her clothes on with her back turned and says she would like to meet my woman someday. I look away with tears in my eyes, and silently curse the cruel conditions that I have never had to endure. I give her more than her asking price and we walk downstairs together. Fatima returns to the bar area. I swagger over to the courtyard and join Mousa and Butu.

Early Saturday morning the three of us drive north in Mousa's Volkswagen van. We stop at the Nyali Beach Hotel, one of the oldest resorts on the coast. Mousa and Butu discuss design options while I admire the grounds. There are a handful of bikini-clad bathers on the beach. Almost all of them are white. We have lunch and drive north to the large Cummings compound south of Malindi, a splendid spot with miles of pristine white sand beaches. The main two-story house dates from the colonial era, and there are also old outbuildings. Mousa's mother hugs her son and Butu before extending her hand to me. I can see that Mousa's magic comes from his mother's side.

"It is a pleasure to meet you," she says with a slight English accent. "You are always welcome here."

"Thank you very much," I say. "This is a heavenly place."

"We are fortunate," she says. "Let me show you around."

The three of us spend the next month working on the old ship that is tied to the pier. It is a massive undertaking. There are twenty guest rooms that need to be rehabilitated, and no small detail can be overlooked. Since I have no building skills, I become their gofer and enjoy delivering what they ask for.

"When we're finally finished with this," Mousa says, "it will be the finest tourist yacht in East Africa. But it's time for a break. Let's go up to Lamu and relax."

"Let's make sure we get plenty of miraa for the road," I say. "I don't want to miss a thing."

Lamu is an island that was initially approached and settled from the sea, but now most international visitors come in by air. Though the ocean is still the best route, going overland is more scenic. It is late in the afternoon when we drive into a cleared area opposite Lamu Island, the staging ground for the ferry and the buses and lorries that supply the island. A small settlement here handles the business end of the operation. Mousa recognizes two teenaged boys. He arranges for them to watch the Volkswagen while we are in Lamu. We leave the van there and get on an old barge that serves as a passenger ferry. After the short crossing we make our way up from the water and into the center of town.

Our progress is interrupted frequently by friends who want to chat with Mousa. The only white man present is me, and I wish I could understand what is being said. I can see that Mousa is fluent in their dialect, and that everyone perks up when he talks. Greetings are exchanged and invitations extended. Mousa has once again returned to one of his ancestral homes, his beloved Lamu. Butu points out to me that there is a distinct advantage to being a member of Mousa's entourage. People assume anyone who passes muster with Mousa is to be trusted, and the spirit affects the retinue as well as the star. Butu and I exchange knowing glances while Mousa works the crowd. We know who the main attraction is, and feel lucky to be members of the supporting cast.

Lamu is an ancient trading port and Kenya's oldest continually inhabited town. Mousa has made reservations at Petleys, which is on the waterfront, and is the oldest hotel in town. Since the island has no motorized vehicles, most of the transportation depends on over three thousand donkeys. Much of the small town makes me feel like I have stepped back into an earlier time. Little has changed since the seventeenth century.

The next morning Mousa borrows a catamaran from his

Erik Erickson

181

uncle. It is high tide when we set sail, and there are four dhows anchored in the small harbor. Mousa explains that the little ships are secured to the sand below by long poles attached to their sides. When our catamaran sails past them the first time, Lamu's main exports, mangrove and mangoes, highly prized by northern desert neighbors, are being loaded aboard the dhows.

Mousa makes a few passes and demonstrates his sailing skills while the tide recedes. When it does I see that the poles prevent the little ships from falling over onto their sides. The dhows rest on their keels and sit high and dry on the sandy beach. We sail north along the island coast and stop at an old colonial hotel for lunch. It is very exclusive and expensive. The small establishment is near what Mousa maintains are the most stunning beaches in the world. The bartender is enthused to see Mousa and behaves accordingly. He pours strong gin and tonic while preparing cucumber sandwiches. We sit on the outside veranda overlooking the water. The three of us recognize our separate worlds but marvel at the immediateness that unites us all. It is as if we have settled here by ourselves for eternity. Three drinks and a few tokes later our much jollier crew is convinced that life cannot get much better than this. We rejoin our small craft and continue to sail north along the coastline.

We spend the next five days sailing around the island. I have never seen water this clear, and we stop often to swim with our snorkels and goggles. The profusion of sea creatures around us astounds me. We ride the surf into isolated beaches and race each other in pure white sand that is so fine it squeaks beneath our feet. I would like to stay longer, but Mousa insists on getting back to what he calls "the real world of work."

Our return trip to his mother's place is faster because the dirt roads are much drier. Mick and Steve, who are filmmakers from England, are waiting for us. They have come earlier than expected, driving down from Nairobi with Ibrahim. The two Englishmen have set up camp in a picturesque flat near the beach. I am glad to see Ibrahim and greet him effusively. I like to be around people who are smarter than I am, and Ibrahim is. We all spend our first night around their campfire, chewing miraa, and telling stories. Every joke is better than the last one, and it is always time for another beer.

I like the two Englishmen right away. Mick is forty-eight and has been involved with cinematography his entire adult life. Mick says he prefers to work alone, but this project is well funded, mostly by Steve, and the ready availability of money has helped him compromise.

"I've worked with Steve before. We're a fairly decent team," Mick tells me around the campfire. "He's an elitist asshole but he doesn't know it, and he's deluded to the point where he thinks he's open-minded. And all joking aside, he's a great guy, and we're good friends. This is a big project. It's important research."

Steve is ten years younger than Mick. He lives with his wife and two children on his father's estate in Berkshire. Inherited wealth provided him with expensive toys at an early age, and he has been making films since he was a teenager. Steve's father brought the family to East Africa several times while he was growing up, and Steve is familiar with the areas they plan to visit. The bulk of the money for the venture came from Steve's family and he considers himself to be the final authority. Steve is the producer and Mick is the director. Their camp is like a movie set and I enjoy hanging out with them.

All their equipment except the vehicles has been sent down from Europe. They have an incredible amount of gear. A multitude of compact conveniences and gadgets are spread out around their encampment. Swedish stoves and lanterns are examined and tested. Tents are set up and mosquito nets are examined. Steve tells me that this photographic expedition has been planned for over a year. When I approach the camp late one afternoon, Mick is busy taking another inventory and checking his master list. I have been planning to make an appeal to him and have even rehearsed my plea.

"It looks to me like you've got everything in the world you could ever need," I say to Mick. "And you appear to be the most organized person I've ever met."

"I divorced my first wife because I didn't like the way she kept house," Mick says. "Things were moved constantly and inconsistently. I could never find shit and it drove me crazy.

I'm obsessive and compulsive. It serves me well, particularly on expeditions."

"I'm lucky to find my shoes in the morning," I say.

"If I drank like you do, I'd be lucky to wake up in the morning," Mick replies.

Their equipment and all the material has to fit into a Toyota van and a Land Cruiser. Mick experiments with the most effective way of storing the goods while practicing loading and unloading. They plan on spending six weeks traveling through Tanzania. Cities and population centers are going to be avoided. They are looking for rural scenes and want to concentrate on the areas that surround the game parks and reserves.

"The adjacent areas are part of the ecosystem," Mick tells me. "They are being severely trampled by human hooves. It threatens the parks themselves. It's all so small anymore. There are indicator species here, and the entire region is an indicator area. We're all interrelated. All of us, human and otherwise. If it fails here we all fail. It will mean that mankind has failed. All of this is really life or death for the planet."

"I know this is a bad thing to ask," I say to Mick. "Shut me up if you know where I'm going and don't want to hear it, but I've heard you and Steve talking to Ibrahim about your occasional need for extra labor. I'd do anything to be able to go along with you. I'll pay my own way and carry twice my weight."

"We all talked about you last night," Mick says. "At length. After you passed out. Do you remember the tale you told?"

"I wish I couldn't remember."

"Is it true? I mean really true."

"I wish it wasn't," I say.

"What a story!" Mick says. "I liked the guy in the ski mask. Steve and I wished we'd had our cameras rolling. Everyone but Mousa thought you were bullshitting. It's too much! I can see it being one of the reasons you want to come along. There's nothing safer than being on an expedition in the wilds. Unless one of us is in on the plot. We could be the killers who will put you away forever."

"I'm betting you're not," I say.

"It's a safe bet." Mick laughs. "Who really gives a shit about you anyway? Did you steal someone's girlfriend?"

"That's anybody's guess. Can I come along?"

"You're invited, but only if you're willing to help out. Like you said, we were planning to hire local labor. We expected to pay them. More than what we'll pay you. Which is nothing. Not only are you cheaper, you're easier. But always keep in mind that we make the rules. Abide by them or you're out."

"I'm eternally grateful. I hope I live long enough to tell another good story."

"Don't be so fucking heavy. We did agree with another point you made last night. You're too insignificant to deserve that type of deadly attention. It sounds worse than a bad mystery novel. Nobody thinks you give anyone that much shit. You're only looking for a laugh."

"Who wants to be the dead victim in his own story?"

"Steve thinks your alternative theory is the accurate one. That you're suffering from coincidence, and paranoid, drug-induced delusions. You do consume a lot of everything. You chew more miraa than the locals, you drink like there's no tomorrow, and you smoke dope all the time."

"So I'm either losing my life or losing my mind?"

"You got it."

An atmosphere of excitement pervades the camp and the surrounding area. Modern technology captures everyone's attention. The local people think the machines are fantastic magic. They all shriek when they see themselves on the small screens. The two energetic Englishmen curry everyone's favor. They study maps and talk over their proposed route with Mousa, who has traveled extensively in Tanzania.

"Tanzania's Nyerere is better than Kenya's Kenyatta. He's not so greedy," Mousa says. "Go see for yourselves. It's a fabulous country. The people are friendly and welcoming."

Monday morning Mick, Steve, Ibrahim and I say goodbye to our friends and drive south through Mombasa. It is a clear, crisp day, and we stop often to shoot footage of birds and beaches. Everything goes well until we reach the Tanzanian border. Mick and Steve have made sure that special permission has been granted to use this point of entry, but the surly Tanzanian officials play dumb. All our material has to be removed from the vehicles, and even the cans of petrol are inspected. The border guards go home at the posted closing time. "They just wanted a fucking bribe," Ibrahim tells me. "Steve refused to pay it." We have to camp in the bush, on the Kenyan side of the line.

Our clearance comes early the next morning, and we are allowed entry shortly thereafter. We reach Tanga at noon and drive around the crowded, dusty streets before continuing south, toward the Zanzibar ferry. It is late in the afternoon when we set up camp in a small clearing, just back from the beach, only a half mile from the dock and the ferry.

Mick, Steve, and Ibrahim have already received prior permission to visit the old slave and spice island. I had been told earlier that part of my job was to stay on the mainland and watch the camp while they are gone. Now I'm not so sure I'm cut out for this responsibility. I feign a hearty smile and wish them well when they take off. This part of the world has become much wilder than I had expected, and although I know no one on earth could find me here, I feel uneasy and unsure of myself after they leave.

Camping by myself in the bush makes me consider the old racist days of African travel, when big game rifles were an integral part of the white man's equipment, and everyone had pistols on their hips. I think I might have felt safer back then, when renowned explorers were in charge, but I know it does not matter now. It is not so bad during the daylight hours, since there is always activity in the neighborhood. Barefoot village kids hang around the periphery of the camp. They stare at me and all my possessions. I feel safer with the young ones ringing the camp. They are my first line of defense against encroaching carnivores. They're all cute, but I know they are also tasty little morsels, and certainly a predator's first dining choice. I also know that their plaintive screams would probably allow me enough time to scramble back into the relative safety of the vehicles. Survival of the fittest, be it economic or otherwise, continues to plague me, and I wonder where my vulnerability fits into the grand life and death scheme of things. Somebody might want to kill me for an altogether different reason.

My daylight hours are agreeable, but the nights are an entirely different situation. There is no moon and I cannot see beyond the light of my lanterns. The sounds from the bush are louder after dark. The not so distant rustlings make me realize that anything or anyone could be out there. I worry about machete-wielding locals as much as I do about big cats, or even homicidal westerners. People have been killed for a lot less than the expensive equipment I am watching over.

I can also easily see that the local people are dirt poor. Europeans have been taking advantage of them for centuries. They can see a defenseless white man sitting on a pile of wealth, sleeping nearby. Everyone knows the frightened paleface is an easy target; there have been worse rationalizations in this world. I rearrange everything and sleep in the van, not the tent, the second night. If nothing else, it will keep the animals at bay and allow me to honk the horn if a weapon comes calling.

Three days in camp alone gives me time to think over my ever-changing situation. I come to the conclusion that filmmaking is not as glamorous as I had expected, and that making pornographic movies might be more to my liking. I drink plenty of the local hooch but always keep my guard up, because I know I do not want to lose control.

A constant throng of curious children visit the camp. They are all well-behaved, shy, and easily amused. Older folk stop by regularly to investigate. Unlike the children, some of them speak English passably, and most are considerably bolder. Everyone I meet is friendly, but I worry that they covet all this miraculous equipment. If they decide to take it, I hope they will spare my life. I act polite and reserved, but cultural isolation and solitary obligation combine to produce paranoia. I begin to realize that the belongings are weighing me down, and I am sorely tempted to leave it all behind and get a cheap room in Dar es Salaam. But before I have to make that ultimate decision my three traveling companions return from what they say was a very successful side trip.

I can see that Ibrahim is becoming indispensable. For one thing, he speaks everyone's language. Mick and Steve depend on his translations. Although he has never been to many of our locations, Ibby is the most knowledgeable person on safari.

"Thanks for staying here and watching all the stuff," Steve says to me.

"There's nothing I like more than stark terror and being surrounded by hungry animals and hungry people at the same time. It would put anyone at ease. I couldn't sleep but who cares? Who needs sleep?"

"At least you're sober," Steve says. "We made sure we didn't leave you anything to drink."

"I noticed that and I cursed you for it. But the locals had strong stuff, and it did the job. It's organic. It wouldn't be my first choice, unless you're bulimic or looking for a laxative. But it did the job."

The road west takes us through shifting countryside, and this turns out to be one of the most remarkable features about East Africa—how quickly and dramatically the topography changes within a short distance. Level agricultural ground gives way to steep hills and thick undergrowth. Sharp, narrow canyons are covered with lush forests, and then a few miles down the road it opens up again, into a flat fertile valley that is heavily farmed. We stop near the town of Morogoro for lunch. Steve and Mick are enticed by the lovely vale and the surrounding steep, green mountains. They decide we'll stay a few days and do some filming.

"After all," Mick says, "we're halfway between the sea and the tallest mountain in Africa. Let's slow down and digest what we've seen so far."

"It's too bad about what's happening," Steve joins in. "Nyerere's brand of socialism chased most of the short-sighted capitalists out of this country. Indian shopkeepers left with them. That's the big difference between Kenya and Tanzania. Western entrepreneurs look for instant profits, but community health care centers don't convert into big bucks like expensive tourist resorts. The tragedy is that both countries are part of the same magnificent ecosystem. But all the attention and money pours into Kenya, while Tanzania has practically had to go it alone."

We drive northwest toward Mount Kilimanjaro, and set up camp near Moshi, near the base of the mountain. We film around the back roads and trails for four days. Most of the time the top of the great mountain is covered with clouds, and we only get one glimpse of the peak before breaking camp and moving on to Arusha.

Arusha is the center of the Tanzanian tourist trade, and most of the wildlife safaris originate here. We set up camp at a small park near the center of town. There are Europeans on the streets, and although it is much smaller than Nairobi, it has a similar air of safari excitement. We film in and around the city for three days, and despite a great hamburger stand across from our camp we've had our fill of city life and prepare to move on.

We leave Arusha before dawn and drive toward Lake Manyara. The sun is rising when the tarmac ends and we turn onto a narrow dirt road. There is no traffic, and the only people are occasional groups of Masai crossing the road from the bush. The Masai are singular, even by African standards. Their finely chiseled features are held regally erect. The warrior's plaited hair is smeared with ochre. They carry spears and look striking in their colorful clothing. They stride with a purposeful movement that makes me wonder where they are going and where on earth they came from. The group ignores us.

"They are the most noble of all African tribes," Mick says. "They've always lived in harmony with their surroundings, and they don't compromise with outside values or imported customs. In ways they are like your Native Americans. Members of this tribe die when they are put in jail for any length of time, because they will not eat when they are confined."

"We all love the Masai," Ibrahim says. "Look at them. We know species are becoming extinct at an alarming rate. It threatens them and they know it too. The animals in this region are an essential part of their lives. And like the animals, the Masai numbers are decreasing; our so-called progress is destroying their habitat. They are too proud and honorable to adjust to the encroaching money-driven reality. Those who know them best respect them the most. If it comes down to it, I hope they are the last surviving human ethnic group on earth, since they understand real harmony better than the rest of us."

"Andreas." Steve looks over at me. "That's why we're paying Ibby a lot, and you nothing."

We enter Lake Manyara National Park before noon and reconnoiter the area before setting up camp. I marvel at the diversity of the landscape. Some regions of the Park are covered by thick, impenetrable undergrowth, while others are open, treeless grasslands. The large lake and surrounding territory are home to most every species of East African wildlife. We stop often to film, because Steve and Mick are afraid we will never get this close again. Twice we approach docile rhinos on foot, and after sensing massive belligerence, we are sent scurrying back to the vehicles.

We stop in a lush grove of large acacia trees for a late lunch. While sitting in the shade of the trees we pass around the food and start eating. Just then, a tour bus arrives. The African driver and his six passengers are the first humans we have seen since entering the park.

"Jambo," Ibrahim says. "Habari?"

"Jambo. Musori sana, bwana," the driver answers and keeps smiling while rubbing his chin. "Are you guys blind or just plain stupid?" he asks loudly in English.

Up until now our group has tried to act like veteran filmmakers, casual and confident, well above the tourist fray. But the driver's question is difficult to answer, because no one wants to admit to being either. We know we are not blind, and we do not like the implications of the alternative. We look at each other but no one says anything. The driver is still smiling when he points up to the branches above us, and all our eyes move upward.

"You'd better do your homework," the driver laughs. "Or hire a good guide. Can't you see? The lions sleep in the trees in Manyara."

Sure enough. There are seven big cats directly above us. Their legs are dangling down, and they are all sleeping. The driver laughs while one of his American passengers howls like a hyena.

"I guess you dudes are pretty lucky we came along," the American says. "If we'd been much later I might have had some front page photos for the newspapers. You boys can write us a check right now for saving your sorry asses—or come over here and kiss our butts instead."

"Where are you from in the States?" I ask him.

"I'm a Montana man." He throws back his shoulders and takes a deep breath. "Where men are men and sheep are nervous. You dudes are looking a little sheepish yourselves."

The American is still laughing when the tour bus pulls away. We do not say anything until it is out of sight.

"There is nothing worse than being made sport of by a stupid, fat American," Mick says. "I hope a buffalo charges that van and fatally horns him through the door."

"What about me?" Ibrahim moans. "Think how I feel. I'm the only native guide we've got. You're the white guys. You're *supposed* to look stupid. I guess you've learned you're going to have to look out for yourselves from now on. Please try to keep an eye out for me as well. I like all the animals but I'm not fluent in all of their dialects."

The lions in the trees have barely budged. They stretch and yawn occasionally but pay no attention to the observers below. The king of beasts finds it easy to relax. Mick and Steve film an hour of very little action. We are all thankful that the cats had full stomachs when ours were empty. Man, the most dangerous predator on earth, has survived, but only because the cats were full, whereas humans often kill when they are completely satiated, and I'll bet that the Montana man would have taken one of those cats if he could have.

We return to the campground near where we entered the park. One outhouse and two picnic tables are the only amenities. The aggressive baboons are even thicker than the mosquitoes.

"I've had trouble with baboons before," Steve says. "It's not worth the hassle. When they're not harassing us for food, they'll be stealing our things. These bastards are used to people who don't use guns. It makes for a bad baboon. Let's find another place to camp."

We are busy reloading our gear when the same tour van turns into the campground and stops next to us. The driver gets out and shakes hands with Ibrahim. His Montana client stands up through the roof and looks us over.

"What are you guys doing?" the driver asks Ibrahim.

"We're looking for a place to set up camp."

"What's wrong with this campground? You have it all to yourselves."

"Not quite. Too many monkeys."

"Still a little jittery, eh?" The Montanan jeers from a distance. "You dudes had better follow us back to our hotel. That way we can keep an eye on you. I hate to see greenhorns get into trouble."

The Montanan laughs derisively. I seldom feel like this, but now that I'm not drinking I want to leap across the van, rip my countryman's tongue out, and strangle him with it. The driver rolls his eyes, shakes his head, exhales through his pursed lips, and gives Ibrahim much needed advice.

"There is a great place to camp near the far end of the lake. It's not on the map but you can drive in if you're careful. There's fresh water, not many mosquitoes, and no monkeys."

He shows us the location on our map and explains how to get there. We take the wrong track three times, but our persistence is finally rewarded at dusk. It is a perfect spot and the filming opportunities from the camp itself are plentiful.

Every morning for a week we get up before sunrise, eat a quick breakfast, and scout locations, always filming when the light is best. The filmmakers are pleased with the progress of their work, and Ibrahim and I make our contributions. We work well together, do most of the physical labor, and after the strenuous days, I feel relaxed and renewed. Ibrahim maintains that porter status is good for me, and that I would likely learn more about life if I stayed a porter forever.

"Honest labor is its own reward," Ibrahim tells me. "Despite your desire to believe otherwise, you're made for it. And also because you're not really as smart as you think."

There is mutual satisfaction, and unanimous excitement, when we break camp in Manyara, and drive west toward the Ngorongoro Crater. Steve tells us to brace ourselves because we are in for the sight of our lives. The mist has still not lifted from the crater when we reach the rim, and the visibility is less than fifty feet.

Everyone going to the floor of the crater has to be accompanied by a Tanzanian official. "They won't be ready for us this early," Steve says. "Therefore, I suggest we go to the lodge and have a Bloody Mary on the deck. You are going to need two, Andreas. We can set up the cameras and watch the view unfold from there."

We sip our drinks on the edge of the veranda as the sun begins to burn through the clouds. It starts slowly, but all of a sudden the moisture lifts and exposes the huge basin below us. It is much grander than I had envisioned, and it is the most awe-inspiring unveiling I have ever seen, even the Grand Canyon cannot compete.

"Look how steep the sides are, and the limited access," Steve says. "The floor has everything. Lakes, forests, and grassland. It has the highest concentration of big game anywhere on earth. Gluttony on a grand scale for the wildlife gourmet. The ultimate safari package."

We learn we will not be allowed to stay on the crater floor, so we set up camp several miles from the tourist lodge, adjacent to the road that leads down into the crater. The Tanzanian authorities assign us a guide, Salim, who must escort us on all of our trips into the cone. He is a sixty-year-old nonstop talker who knows every inch of the crater. He refers to the animals by the names he has given them and points out the subtleties of their behavior with philosophical panache and eloquence.

"The crater is a great example, maybe the best visible example on earth, of the interdependence of all life forms." I can tell that he is well rehearsed. "The animals live in close proximity at all times. They depend on each other for life and balance. Predators and prey. We all share the same fate. The scavengers, like all scavengers, prefer to have someone else do their dirty work. Only the elephants are above it all."

193

Salim explains that most kills are made in the early morning or late evening. We film three fierce, gruesome lion kills. Young wildebeests and zebra die thrashing for life in pools of blood. I cannot take my eyes off the battlefield.

Later that night I feel sick to my stomach and have to leave the tent. The stench of the latrine makes me feel worse. I decide to dump my bowels away from the camp, and walk a few hundred feet into the bush. My flashlight points the way because there is no moon and it is pitch black. I am squatting in the grass when I hear heavy movement from the nearby trees, which throws me into an immediate panic. Before I can pull my shorts up, I am surrounded by elephants. They are surprisingly quiet as they walk through the open grassland, and except for an occasional grunt, I hear very little. I turn my flashlight toward them in an effort to be a human lighthouse. I am rewarded by sporadic glimmers from their large, high orbs, and I realize I can practically reach out and touch them. The brief contact is both mesmerizing and terrifying. I count fifteen but I am sure there are more. It is my nose that provides the strongest sensations. I can smell the elephants all around me, and I fully expect to be trampled at any moment. Before I work myself into a complete frenzy, I sense that the herd is past me, but the smell lingers.

"They literally scared the shit right out of me. My bowels have never been this clean."

"You are stupid but lucky," Salim says. "I've seen entire villages destroyed by migrating elephants. They don't run amok as much as they just plow through everything in their path."

"I suspect they got the first whiff of his farts and steered clear," Mick says.

We leave the crater after four days and camp for a week in the Serengeti. Most of our time is spent trying to film cheetahs making a kill. We see different cheetahs, but we never get closer than a hundred yards, and are never able to film the world's fastest mammal on a dead run. No one complains. The weather is cooperative and the scenery is unspoiled. The solitude and isolation of the last great plains is ours alone to fathom.

Our outlook changes when we cross back into Kenya and enter the Masai Mara. The contrast between the two countries is startling. Much of the northern section of this migratory route has fallen victim to overuse and encroaching development. Tour buses and other vehicles crisscross the landscape frequently. The old roads are deeply rutted and new ones scar the once pristine terrain.

"The government is more intent on promoting tourism than protecting what the tourists come to see," Mick says. "The British were worse. They encouraged tribalism. So that the white man could stay in control and haul in profits, short-sighted ones."

"For the average Kenyan," Ibrahim says, "the only thing that's really changed since independence is the color of their landlord. Greed is greed. It took over the world when the hunter gatherers disappeared. The Masai aren't greedy."

Tourists become the focus of our filming efforts in the Masai Mara. Mick and Steve are intent upon making them look as bad as they possibly can. It becomes an easy script to follow, because the entitled assholes act their roles well. Our crew conducts extensive interviews with the tourists who stay near us. Whenever someone starts sounding particularly arrogant we begin filming and encourage them to talk at length. Steve asks leading questions and always agrees with their answers, only to keep them spouting more of their narcissistic nonsense.

"I'm going to have a field day editing some of these sequences," Steve says. "I can't believe what these people are saying."

Four days of filming tourists proves to be exhausting. We finish packing our gear and drive toward Nairobi. Mick stops to film a couple of areas just outside the city. While we are setting up, a familiar vehicle pulls in next to us. At first it does not register with me, because everything is so out of context, but on a second look I recognize three of my erstwhile shipmates from the Atlantic crossing. They look comical and ridiculous, but since they were all on the boat, I have to wonder if they've been tracking me all along. Is a coincidence, or an orchestrated threat?

Mr. and Mrs. World Traveler are dressed identically. They are wearing tan polyester leisure suits. The red leather fringe on their sleeves matches their wide belts. They are also wearing red cowboy boots and hats. They look like halfwits who have been cruelly attired as twins by their abusive parents. I cannot imagine anyone in their right mind wanting to look like this. They appear as if they are ready to audition for parts in a satirical, pornographic jungle movie. Where did all of this come from?

The Persian is with them. He looks even more ludicrous than they do. No one should ever dress like this unless it's Halloween and everyone is on LSD. Apparently, the Persian has stormed out of the closet in a big way; the turtle necks and casual slacks have gone bye-bye, his old wardrobe replaced by an outfit that makes him look like a cross between a geisha and Sinbad the Sailor. The purple pajama pants are tied off below his knees. He has a wide, brightly colored sash knotted on his hip, and the loose ends dangle down his thigh. His billowy pink blouse is rolled up to his elbows and is strategically buttoned to expose most of his hairy chest. He is wearing heavy makeup, and an abundance of gold jewelry. I already like them better than when we were all together on the boat. They look happy together. Good for them. Who cares what people think.

The Persian is the first to recognize me. He smiles sweetly when I approach. Mick, Steve, and Ibrahim hustle for the cameras. I try to shake hands with the Persian but my offered hand is delicately kissed instead.

"Your eye shadow makes you look sinister," I say honestly. "But I love it!"

"How grand to see you again." Mrs. World Traveler rushes over and gives me a slight hug.

She looks even more resolved than before, despite the outlandish outfit, and that her husband must be a psychopath to go along with this charade. These people are on the cusp of being deranged. Perhaps they are all in cahoots, and anyone who does not respond to having their genitals fondled by Mrs. World Traveler is automatically sentenced to death.

"How was your trip across the Sahara?" I ask.

"It was a gruesome trip across the desert."

The Persian, who spoke eloquently before, has affected a lisp that is difficult to understand. Mick, Steve, and Ibrahim act as if he is the cutest guy they have ever seen. They dote on his every word while filming the entire stilted conversation. I walk up to the theatrical threesome and look them all in the eye.

"You people aren't trying to kill me, are you?"

"My heavens," Mrs. World Traveler says. "What on earth do you mean?"

This does not reassure me, but I didn't really expect her to confess. The Persian, on the other hand, seems determined to kill me with kindness, and Mr. World Traveler offers me a beer.

Erik Erickson

8

APARTHEID AND THE
RECKONING

W E STOP for two hours at Ibrahim's family home, outside the sprawl of suburban Nairobi. Ibrahim unloads his gear while everyone else sips tea and talks about the success of the safari. Ibrahim's parents tell us that Mousa has come up from the coast and is staying with friends in Karen.

"He came to meet a friend who just flew in," Ibrahim's mother says to me. "His friend's name is Dris. Mousa says you and Dris are old friends." Both of Ibrahim's parents look at me and wait for a response, but I do not know what to say, because I don't know anyone named Dris. I think they must mean Cris, but I cannot understand how the connection was ever made.

"Do you mean Cris? A blond guy from California?"

"No." Ibrahim's mother seems puzzled. "This Dris looks more like Mousa than you. He is not an American."

"Where is he from?"

"We did not ask."

"How does he know me?"

"We presumed you knew." I'm puzzled by this exchange but figure Mousa will explain it when I see him.

I consider returning to my old room at the Sunset Hotel,

Erik Erickson

but Mick and Steve convince me to stay with them temporarily. They have expatriate friends who own an estate within the foreign section of Nairobi, and they maintain the security is almost as tight as at an embassy.

"This guy is more uptight about assassinations than you are," Steve says as we approach the heavy iron gate. "This is one of the safest places in the city."

The owners are not at home, but arrangements have been made. We enter the property through a large courtyard that is lush with roses in bloom. The two-story colonial house is immaculate, and the spacious grounds and guest houses are more lavish than most resorts. We are greeted by staff in the foyer. The house is invitingly cool and pleasant with an Olympic-size swimming pool that beckons with crystal blue sparkles. We deposit our belonging in adjoining rooms and immediately take a swim. I feel more physically fit than I have been in my entire life, and I don't want this to end.

"First things first," I say while drying off. "I'm going to go downtown and check my mail. Plus I'm dying for some miraa."

"Do you want a ride?" Mick asks.

"No thanks. I'll take the bus, for the experience."

When I clamor out of the crowded bus near the central post office, I head for Poste Restante, wait in line for ten minutes, and get letters from Vanessa, Cris, and Monica.

Vanessa's first letter is quite long. She chronicles her career movements and brings me up to date on the latest gossip. She still loves me and misses me horribly! A much shorter second letter nullifies all the good news of the first. She says that unspecified big changes might occur, although nothing has been decided yet, but there is a chance she will return to Canada. She says she will keep me up to date.

The letter from Cris is a bad news, good news story. I discover that I missed a Nairobi meeting with him by one week; he was in Kenya while I was in Tanzania. I know Cris likes to travel fast, and I decide to rendezvous and join him on his journey.

"I hear the smoke in Malawi is the best on the continent. That's where I'm headed. Meet me there," Cris writes.

"Although I hate to say goodbye to miraa, I'm headed south. I met a guy with great freighter connections out of Durban. Let's make another crossing together. Africa to India."

The news from Monica determines my future course, if for no other reason than it is so auspicious. She writes that her "two great loves in life, radical left wing politics and capitalist travel will collide next month in South Africa. "See it firsthand. I'm on tourist business. Join me there. I have a car and hotel reservations. It will cost you nothing to be my companion and chauffeur. Remember our earlier jokes? I promise not to force sex on you again."

A year ago I might have had trouble finding Malawi on a map, but now it beckons. Malawi will be my next destination, and after that South Africa, and then on to India. I am moving erratically and on the spur of the moment, which I like because it makes me more difficult to trace.

I walk down to the Iqbal Hotel and buy a few bundles of miraa. It feels good to have the familiar stimulant rush through my body. This is my all-time favorite drug, and like that local drink near Zanzibar, it's organic. I keep rationalizing that it's practically like being on a health food diet. I have three quick beers at the Green Bar before engaging a taxi for the ride back. As always, the miraa makes me feel on top of the world, and it mixes so well with alcohol. I ring myself in at the security gate and Mousa greets me at the front door.

"We were hoping you wouldn't get killed downtown," Mousa says with his smile. "It would have completely ruined the party. I've brought an old friend of yours with me." We walk through the house and join the others on the patio, near the pool. Mick and Steve are talking to someone I do not recognize, but their conversation ceases abruptly when Mousa and I appear. Everyone stops and stares in my direction.

"Do you remember Dris?" Mousa asks me.

"I'm afraid not," I reply.

I shake the newcomer's outstretched hand and look into his eyes. There is a faint glimmer of familiarity, but nothing with any certainty. I wish I wasn't the only odd man out here, and I look over at Mousa, who stares back at me.

"Do you need a hint?" Mousa asks.

"I need more than a hint. Maybe a drink." They crack up. "Thanks, but I know the joke is on me. If I may be so presumptuous I would like one question answered... Who the fuck is this guy?"

"Do you want a big hint or a small one?"

"Big. Please."

"Zorro."

"That's too big!"

I dive into the pool with my clothes on and swim two laps. Everyone is still laughing when I get out, walk over to Mousa and grab his shoulders.

"You're kidding me! What's the fucking story?"

"When I heard your drunken ramblings down on the coast I knew two things. Number one, someone *was* trying to kill you, or so I, like you, believed. Number two, more of a certainty, my old friend Dris was your mystic Zorro. It took a bit of effort, but here he is. Unfortunately, and I mean no offense to this Zorro, but the man behind the now nonexistent mustache does not know as much as we'd like. Zorro was just fucking with you that night."

"Sad but true," Dris says. "I'm as mystified as you. It's a strange case for sure. The only reason I met you at all is because I heard someone wanted you dead. The contract had one stipulation. Your demise had to look like an accident, or no one would get paid. I'm always curious why someone would pay to have someone killed. It might happen every day, but there are as many motives as there are people. And since I had noticed your fetching traveling companion earlier in the day, I decided to don an oft-used disguise and investigate the proposed victim. You. Once I met you, I decided it didn't make any sense. I didn't stay up nights thinking about what might have happened to you until our mutual friend here contacted me a few weeks ago. Mousa's story fascinated me. I was curious and overdue for a journey anyway. Here we all are. Talking about you. And you're still alive."

"How did you find out about it in the first place?"

"My family has lived in Tangier forever, we have connections.

I heard rumors about a large shipment of contraband weapons coming in to the port, and that you were involved. None of my contacts knew anything beyond that. To this day they don't. That's why you were kicked out of the casino that night. The people who run the joint had heard the same rumors. They didn't want any trouble. Nobody knows who wanted the hit. But reliable sources said it was real."

I have trouble digesting this information. Everything is moving too fast. I cannot seem to get a grip on his words, or their context. I chew the miraa even faster but think miraa might not be the drug I need at this moment. A triple gin with a beer back would be just the ticket.

Dris becomes Zorro again. "I'll bet you could use a drink right now. You don't really need one, but you'd like one all the same. And I know like you know, everything goes better with miraa."

"Let's have a drink to our continued good health," Mousa says raising his glass. "You guys kick back and relax. Get to know each other. I'll bring the liquor and we'll have a feast."

"How were you able to do what you did that night?" I ask Dris after Mousa has left. "Nothing like that has ever happened to me before, or since. There hasn't been a day since that I didn't think about you. How you saw through me. What you said. How you said it. What do you think I should do now?"

"It's the same as I told you then. Keep your wits about you. I think you're moving toward a resolution, but I can't foretell the future. Someone has an explanation."

"At least I finally know the threat is real. I'm not a paranoid alcoholic."

"You're not paranoid," Dris says. "But from what I've heard the alcoholic accusations are on solid footing."

"Am I going to get killed?"

"I hope not."

"That's the best you can do?"

Dris shrugs. I am so overwhelmed that I can't think straight. The mystery has been confirmed, and I am vindicated.

My last three days in Kenya are spent chewing miraa, smoking dope, and drinking beer by the pool. I manage to get a visa for Malawi and buy a ticket for my upcoming flight to Blantyre. The morning of my flight we all jump into Steve's van and head for the airport. I have been chewing miraa all night. The power of the plant kept me awake and makes me confident. However, I board the plane with trembling knees. But the takeoff is smooth, and it's is a clear day, and I am able to appreciate my lofty perspective. Mighty Kilimanjaro drifts by beneath us, and the soft landing in Malawi makes me even more grateful.

I am mildly disappointed by the topography around the Blantyre airport. It is not what I expected. The travel brochures advertised a country dominated by the third largest lake in Africa. I had visualized lots of water and hanging vines. Instead, the land looks like Utah: rocky, dry and dusty. Unlike Nairobi, the taxi drivers are indifferent and I decide to take the local bus into town.

Blantyre is rife with charm. Large shade trees, neat sidewalks, pedestrian areas. Hotels are scarce, and I check into the least expensive one I can find, and then continue to see the town. The vistas are not hindered by tall buildings, and there are inviting, green mountains in the near vicinity. All in all an undiscovered jewel. I am once again in an off the map paradise and look forward to seeing the lake.

The occasional hostile glances and cold stares I encounter are quickly understood. Everyone I meet assumes I am from South Africa. Most of the white tourists here are from there. It is the only African country they are allowed to enter, except their own. No other country on the continent will let them in. I learn to reveal my nationality immediately. Doing so raises my esteem with the locals. I make a point of trying to sound as American as I can at all times and tell people I'm friends with Michael Jackson. Their English is good and I'm pleased to be here.

"This must be the only place on earth Americans are so well thought of," I cheerfully say to my bartender. I always try to cultivate people who serve me drinks. It makes for a better pour.

"It's probably because we don't see so many of you," the bartender replies. "Except on TV or in the movies. America is a long way away." He points to three drunken South Africans on the patio. "Plus, we usually only see that type of white folk. Even when they're sober they're a pain. Racists. They come here to hide from themselves. What about you?"

"I'm hiding, but not from myself," I say as I finish another drink. "I've met doctors, lawyers, and diplomats. But the smartest people I've ever known are bartenders."

"That's only because you drink so much." The bartender pours me another. "This one's on me."

The next morning I am on the veranda of the Ryals Hotel in downtown Blantyre, midway into my second cup of coffee when I am tapped on my shoulder from behind. I swing around and see Cris.

"I thought I might find you here," he says as we hug. "You always know the best place for a morning caffeine fix. We've both made it to Malawi and the great smoke."

"Fuck! I'm lucky to be alive," I say. "I've got a great story to tell you. You're part of the plot. One of the suspects."

"What's the story?"

"It's a long one. Just let me say that the crack on the head I got on the boat was no accident. There was a murderer aboard. And a boatload of possibilities. Whoever it is will more than likely keep trying." I make quick work of the whole sad story.

"Maybe whoever it is realizes now that he was chasing the wrong guy," Cris suggests. "At least there haven't been any recent attempts."

"I've been hard to catch up to. I feel like I'm on the run for my life."

"I think we ought to keep it that way for awhile. There's no better place to disappear than India. Let's keep moving and keep a low profile. I'll watch your back. But first things first. Let's check out Lake Malawi. We'll rent a vehicle under my name. The car will give us much more flexibility," Cris says. "Better odds if we keep your sleeping location unknown and move frequently. Hitler always did it."

"You're putting me in that category?"

"Not really, but I can't imagine anyone caring that much about you. No offense. I mean, what the fuck have you ever done? Given someone a bad grade? Made a few insulting jokes? It has to be a mistake, but we've got to be very careful all the same."

After three days of driving around Lake Malawi and sleeping in small guesthouses, we drop the rental car in Lilongwe, where we board a South African Airways flight to Johannesburg. There are no black people aboard the airplane. Mainly, the passengers are South Africans returning from holiday. After everyone is seated, and just prior to takeoff, the flight attendants march up and down the aisle spraying the entire cabin with aerosol cans. Several people start coughing and choking, but the spraying continues until the cans are empty. Cris stands up when one of the sprayers moves near him.

"What the fuck is going on here?" Cris shouts.

"It's a disinfectant, sir," the homely attendant answers. "We don't want to risk having any black germs enter the country."

"Oh my god!" Cris exclaims. "We haven't even left the ground yet and you are already living up to your well-deserved reputation."

"What reputation is that, sir?"

"I'm afraid to talk about it now."

Jan Smuts International is the largest airport I have seen since I left London. All of the world's major airlines are represented here, and American enterprises are conspicuous, with the Marriott Corporation being the most visible.

"Mormons have always had a thing against blacks," I say. "They own Marriott. It doesn't look like there has been much of an international effort to isolate the present regime. Economic sanctions certainly appear to be nonexistent around the airport."

Security is tight but the customs people are very friendly. Cris calls a hotel while I check out the information center.

"The desk clerk sounds like she's brain damaged," Cris says. "But she says she'll hold the room for an hour. Let's grab a cab and check in. It's cheap, just the spot for us. We'll save money and disappear in a dump. I always sleep better in shitty rooms."

A major expressway connects the airport to the city. It makes me feel like I am back in the States. Modern shopping malls and tall apartment buildings line the route. I can see that this part of Africa is very distinct, and like America, white wealth rules the roadways.

"It looks like they've adopted L.A. as a role model," Cris observes. "I haven't seen this many cars since we left New York."

"These white people look like they're doing better than they let on," I say. " Everyone we've seen so far looks loaded."

"It's weird all right," Cris says. "Where are all the Africans?"

At the hotel, Cris's mentally handicapped desk clerk is actually a middle-aged Afrikaner woman who owns the joint. Her obese, pockmarked teenaged daughter helps run the place. An old black man leads us up to our room. Guilt by association starts to creep into my mind. I overtip in a big way to compensate, just like a good slave owner should, and I begin to wonder if I have made a major mistake by coming here.

"Race relations don't look all that good," Cris says. "Let's investigate the city and scout the drinking holes. Have a few and think it over."

We wander the streets of Johannesburg for over three hours. The vast majority of the people we see are white. I have to keep reminding myself that I am in Africa, and that 90 percent of the population in this country is not white. How can they hide the others so well?

"I guess this is what abundant resources and slave labor will do for you," Cris says as we enter through the downtown area.

"At least we haven't seen any black people being beaten to death."

"Maybe they're saving that for right after happy hour."

"Why are the few black men we do see all wearing blue overalls?"

"It must be the required fashion for the disenfranchised. Wear blue overalls or die."

We walk by the Hilton Hotel and I stop to use the telephone to call New York. I have tried to reach Vanessa more than once since Nairobi but have not had any success making connections. The information people at the airport told me the best chance of making a call to New York was from the desk at the Hilton. It takes the better part of an hour but I finally get it done. An unfamiliar voice answers after ten rings, and I ask to speak to Vanessa.

"She doesn't live here anymore," the woman says. I nearly drop the phone.

"Where is she?"

"Who's asking?"

"Andreas."

"She's moved back to Banff."

"Do you know her very well?" I thought I had run out of surprises. This is the biggest one of all.

"Vanessa is a good friend."

"I hate to use these terms, but what the fuck is going on? Why is she back in Banff?"

"She told me not to say anything. She wants to tell you herself. That's all I can say."

I repeat the process at the desk and place a call to Canada. It rings thirty times without a response. The Hilton people get fed up with me and I back off. I cannot understand why Vanessa would leave New York on the verge of her big break in theater. She seemed so intent upon pursuing her flourishing career. Is the fact that she insists on telling me herself tantamount to the obligation of notifying the next of kin? I think it should be fairly easy for her to say, "Get lost, asshole, I'm sick of your bullshit." Is it such an ugly job that she feels she has to do it herself? I imagine other possible scenarios. Maybe something bad has happened to her family, or worse, to her.

I continue to try to reach her the next morning, and into the afternoon, up until Cris and I have to go back to the airport to meet Monica, who is flying in from Vienna. She is in high spirits and I am hopeful that both of us have put the splendiferous threesome with Veronika in our forgettable past.

We accompany Monica to her luxury suite at the Hilton, of all places. She unpacks while Cris provides her with the highlights of his travels since Morocco. Cris is a winning storyteller, particularly when he wants to impress his listeners, and he is at his charming best with Monica. This is the first time he has seen her thin, and it is an unabashed flirtation, mutually engaged in by both participants. The chemistry is there, and it appears to be just a matter of time before they consummate it. I leave them talking in the room and take the elevator to the luxurious lobby. I call Canada and finally get an answer.

"Hello."

"It's me."

"I was wondering when you'd call. Did you get my letters?"

"I got two in Nairobi. What's up?"

"Where are you calling from?" she asks.

"A hotel lobby in Johannesburg. What difference does that make, Vanessa? What's going on? Why are you in Banff?"

"Are you sitting down?"

"Hell no I'm not sitting down! There's no place to sit! Why do people always say that?"

"I'm pregnant," she says quietly. "I'm going to have a baby. You're the father, of course. Congratulations. You did a great job. I hope it's not going to be a one of a kind performance."

"Are you joking?"

"If you saw my stomach you would know it is no laughing matter."

"My god! How did this happen?"

"The same way it usually does. In our case it was that last night in the Lake District. Or don't you even remember?" I know she is making fun of me, because she has done it since I've known her.

"Of course I remember it."

She sounds remarkably calm and cheerful. "This is for the best. It's meant to be. After the baby is born, and we are well settled, I'm going to stay here and teach. I just can't raise a child in New York. This is my home. My parents have a fair amount of property, and I can help them manage it. And go horseback riding at the same time! The big city is not for me. I tried it. I enjoyed it. But the best thing about it was you. And now you're gone. I want you back!"

"What about your dancing? And fame and fortune? What do you want me to do?"

"Grow up, Andreas. Be happy for us. Or maybe I want you to continue gallivanting around the globe while I sit here lonely, fat, and miserable. So that my mother will have to drive me to the hospital when the time comes. And so I can tell everyone I know that I'm not sure where the father is. Last time I saw him was nine months ago in England. My first child a fatherless bastard. Isn't that what all mothers want?"

"When do you want me there?"

"Now. But you can make up your own mind. You should be here for the birth classes. We have to prepare. And as you can see, I'm cashing in on your promise. Don't forget, we made a deal."

"I'll be there at least three months before your due date."

"Also. Don't forget that babies are sometimes born early."

I cannot believe how chipper she sounds, because I feel exactly the opposite. We talk for another forty minutes. Vanessa tells me about the quality of life in the Canadian Rockies. I have trouble concentrating on anything other than her pregnancy, and I dwell on the fact that I should have been more careful during our last wild night in England. Once again my emotions have been turned upside down. The whole concept of fatherhood is too hard to grasp. I definitely do not feel like bragging to the boys and buying another round for the house. On the contrary, I feel like running and hiding from everything. This is just about as bad as it can get. Then I remember Dr. Peterson's exhortation: "Things can always get worse."

"I'll try to call you again next week," I say. "The phones don't work that well around here. Plus it will take at least that long for the news to sink in anyway. But I want you to know that I keep my promises. And that I love you."

"You know I love you too." I can hear her start to cry and it makes me start to do the same. "This wasn't planned at all. But I'm counting on you now. You'll be the best father ever. I know it."

We say our tearful goodbyes and I walk directly to the hotel bar. There are too many conflicting thoughts careening through my brain and I can't organize any of them. If there was ever a time I truly needed a drink, this is it. I deserve it. In a certain way it was better news than I had expected. At least Vanessa is still with me; she's practically stuck with me now. While I have been questioning my ability to even stay alive during this whole trip, now I feel I owe it to more people than myself. Now I've got to stay alive; it's not all about me anymore.

What will I do in Canada? It might be worse than death, although I do like their healthcare system. But am I destined to wear plaid shirts and take hikes? Will I have to learn how to speak Canadian? At least my French is impeccable, but they don't speak it out west. What will happen if the kid's father is murdered? A range of depressing possibilities come to mind. The forthcoming blessed event has thrown my life into even more turmoil. Parenthood evades evaluation for me. I have always hated bad kids and bad dogs. Will I have to get a dog for the kid? I decide to keep the news to myself until I have made some definite decisions. I quickly drink another double gin and brace myself before returning to Monica's room. She and Cris are acting like teenagers who can't wait to get their hands on each other.

"Did you get a hold of her?" Cris asks.

"Yeah." I try to act casual.

"How is she doing?"

"Fine."

"What's she doing in Banff?" Monica has never met Vanessa, but feels like she knows her, because I talk about her all the time.

"She decided to take some time off."

"You don't look good," Monica says. "Is anything wrong?"

"I'm too sober for my own good, for starters." I try to throw them off the scent with a jaunty riposte.

"Monica wants to take a tour of Soweto tomorrow," Cris says. "The government runs the show, and it's all staged, but it's the only legal way to get in. They want to make sure that we only see what they want us to see. I think we're complicit by just being here, but I don't know if we're making it even worse by going along with their game. Monica thinks any look is better than no look. I'm going. What about you?"

"Why not?" My mind is far away. I do not know what to

think or say. There is too much to consider, and no rhyme nor reason to any of it. I am confused by my confrontation with fatherhood, but I suspect touring the terrible township will take my mind off that for a while. I have talked to other travelers who think this country could all blow up at any time. I don't want to be around when it does, but I might as well take a look before it actually happens. But I wonder if my presence will mean I am basically supporting a slave auction.

The expensive tour of the huge black township is a major propaganda effort by the government. Despite the fact that there are over a million people living in the sprawling township, we are not allowed to see very many of them. We only visit small, isolated areas that are clean and affluent. Our guide continually makes comparisons to black slums in the United States, and all the information we are given is totally self-serving. Race riots in Los Angeles and elsewhere are prominently mentioned. There are negative implications, and references to similar situations in "supposedly open societies" are strongly expressed. I find much of it difficult to deny, because I do know how African Americans are treated in my own country, but I also know it is not even close to as bad as here. This is on another demonic level that defies description unless you are here.

I am struck by the complete physical separation of the two cities. A large, uninhabited buffer zone provides a false sense of security for the whites in Johannesburg. The two worlds are connected by a wide, modern expressway that knifes through the open plain. Blacks commute to white man's land during the day and return to poverty at night. Whites only visit Soweto to exercise control over the populace. They return to their exclusive enclaves after darkness falls. It is by far the worst artificially contrived symbiotic relationship I have ever seen. Neither city can survive without the other, but both are pitched in opposite directions that will never merge.

The tour is fascinating, but mostly horrifying. Our guide doubles down on the not so subtle U.S. bashing. "Most of our blacks live as well, or better, than blacks in other countries. Look at the real world around us. White-governed countries are doing better everywhere. That basic fact cannot be denied."

Monica becomes more outspoken and sarcastic as the tour progresses. She asks insulting questions and ridicules the rehearsed responses. "Get real yourself, Adolph." She says in her usual loud fashion. "And give us a break, for Christ sakes. I'm not saying America isn't a racist shithole. It is! But it's a black man's paradise compared to this depravity, and every black person on earth knows it. You people are out of your fucking minds!" I agree with everything she says.

One of our fellow passengers is a Dutch pediatrician. He is even more vocal and acerbic than Monica. "I took a tour of Dachau recently," the Dutchman says. "But in a way this is worse. Even the Nazis did not have the insolence to give guided tours of their death camps. Like them, your days are numbered."

Most of the inhabitants of Soweto ignore our tour bus. They are used to whites patrolling their streets, and tourists are better than tanks. I notice that many of the policemen are black, and I think it must be the worst job on earth. Occasionally I see a menacing, murderous stare through my wide window. My presence makes me feel guilty, and I do not want to be here when the thought behind his look manifests action.

No one is converted on the tour. If anything, the sides are more polarized than ever. The driver and the guide have become sullen and quiet. Monica and the Dutch doctor rail against apartheid and discuss European political options and sanctions. The tour ends back in Johannesburg, an hour earlier than advertised. Monica objects to the brevity and demands a partial refund. They return it all and tell her she is going to be reported to the authorities.

"We'll see that you never get into South Africa again!" the driver nearly shouts.

"Oh, I'll come again," Monica says calmly. "But when I do, I won't have to listen to this racist bullshit from the likes of you. You'll be long gone by then."

Monica needs to rent a car and drive to Sun City. Her agency wants her to evaluate the amenities offered there. She has appointments to meet with officials from the Department of Tourism, and she wants Cris and me to come along. We both look forward to an outing on Monica's extravagant expense account, but I'm afraid Sun City and Soweto in the same week might not be the dichotomy I'm looking for.

When we get there I learn that Sun City is fundamentally a concentrated version of Las Vegas, only much worse. Its main attractions are gambling, drinking, and pleasures of the flesh. It is garish and gaudy beyond compare; hordes of South Africans flood in on the weekends to shed their customary restraints. All the service people are black, and most of the revelers white. The only intermingling between the races involves older white men and younger black women. It's always the same old story.

"This is really an ugly place," Cris says while surveying the scene.

"That's why we're here," Monica replies. "This is where Sodom and Gomorrah get together. It's just what we're looking for."

Monica and Cris prefer playing craps. They gravitate toward that table. I wander away, meander for a while, and eventually sit down at the roulette wheel, where I buy fifty rands worth of chips. After five spins I have doubled my money, and it reminds me of Kerry's winnings back in Tangier. I haven't had much luck lately, and for a few more spins of the wheel I am lost in the flush of winning. However, that giddy moment is short-lived. While I am spreading out my next bets, I glance up from the table, and see a smiling face looking down at me, a face I recognize but do not want to see, quite possibly the most evil face I have ever seen in my awake world. Even if this person wore a ski mask, I don't think things could look any worse.

"Henderson! What are you doing here?" I'm apprehensive to hear his answer.

"Call me Hendy. I was going to ask you the same thing. I'm still doing the same old shit."

"You sell weapons in Sun City?"

"No, no." Henderson looks around, puts his index finger to his lips, and lowers his always loud voice. "I'm just up here for some R and R. I've been in Cape Town and Pretoria doing business. It's been a tough one too. You know what it's like doing business with a bunch of Jews."

"I don't think I do. Which bunch of Jews?" I know from the past that Henderson can slander entire groups of people in a single sentence, and I am curious to hear his response.

"Israelis mostly, but there are a lot of Jews down here as well. Try working the middle of a Jewish money deal sometime. Believe me, they squeeze till it hurts. But when you think about it, both countries have similar needs, and a lot in common. They have to be masters of suppression! It gets more difficult all the time. It's all pretty hush-hush from my end, but solid business. Some of this crap is getting out of control. It's a complicated insider deal. I hope I can trust you on this one."

I briefly consider sliding out of my chair and laughing hysterically underneath the table, but something tells me there is nothing to laugh about here, and that this blackguard is someone to fear. I did not think my terror level could get any higher, but it just did.

"Sure Hendy, you can trust me." Trust me to have you killed, if I could. Most of all, I'm convinced this chance meeting is not by chance at all, and I wonder what Henderson is really up to here. This development defies definition, and I worry that I might be running out of these culpable coincidences.

"Boy, I wish we could party together again." Henderson says. "But I've got to head off to Durban tonight. I've got a big deal going on down there."

Henderson buys drinks for the two of us, finishes his quickly, and says goodbye. It is a great relief to see him go, but I am horrified by my encounter with the omnipresent arms merchant, and think this worthless bastard is beginning to smell like the stench of death.

Cris and Monica did not see Henderson but agree that his presence in Sun City is not a good sign. We are all particularly troubled by the fact that Durban is our next destination as well. Monica is scheduled to evaluate the beach resorts for her company, and Cris's freighter connection to India leaves from Durban. I've always thought dangerous people are much more effective when they are likable. Henderson can summon up enough of that quality when he needs to, and I wonder where it leads for him and me.

The next morning we pack up early and drive toward Natal Province. Whenever possible we avoid the major highways and stay on the smaller roads. The scenery is green and sparkling, and I begin to understand the attraction to this land. We stop for a late lunch in a small farming community, where a bountiful meal is served in an old brick hotel. The black people in the area are nearly invisible. The only evidence that we're in Africa is the woman who cleans our table. Most of the locals look like farmers in Iowa. They have white, sunburned faces, wear old blue jeans, and are universally friendly, undoubtedly pleased to see a few more white faces around town, though they must know their days are numbered, and that major reparations might be on their horizon, or even worse.

The vegetation becomes thick and lush as we approach the coast. I have not seen the ocean since Tanzania and look forward to swimming in the salt water. We join the major coastal highway north of Durban and approach the city. Large, extravagant homes overlook rugged coastline and stunning beaches. It is a subtropical paradise; the invigorating salty breezes lift our spirits, and I can see that this is a magical part of the continent.

By the time Monica checks us in to her luxury hotel it is late in the afternoon. Her itinerary includes a recommended restaurant nearby, and a short walk takes us to a major intersection. It's closing time for many businesses, and there is considerable traffic on the streets. We round a corner on a busy thoroughfare and see an old Tamil man squatting on the sidewalk selling flowers. There have been other flower vendors along the route, but this fellow catches my eye. There is something about him that stands out. A large cloth is spread out in front of the old man, and he has a display of bright flowers. Monica breaks stride and moves in closer to get a better look. Cris and I are not interested in the flowers and we back off down the street. At the same time, a group of four young Afrikaner men approach from the opposite direction. They are all carrying big bottles of beer in paper sacks, and they are both burly and boisterous as they amble down the sidewalk. When they see the old man and Monica, they swerve over in that direction.

"How are you doing, baby?"

One of the toughs leers over at Monica and tries to capture her attention. She ignores him and bends down to have a closer look at the flowers.

"I asked how you are, baby. Are you deaf?" Like most women of the world Monica has dealt with drunken men like this before. She looks at him briefly, does not say anything, and directs her attention back to the flowers.

"Do you like flowers? Do you, baby? Well here, have some flowers, beautiful lady." His massive hands snatch up and thrust a bouquet of flowers at Monica. "Do you like these?" He sneers drunkenly. "Take them. They're on me."

"Please put those back," Monica says calmly. I never know what she might say or do.

"Don't you like them, baby? Well then, fuck you." He starts kicking the old man's remaining collection around the sidewalk. I consider intervening but decide that Monica can handle herself, and I know she'll call us if she needs help. Cris looks on and inches closer. Monica takes off down the street and yells back over her shoulder, "I'm getting a policeman." Cris and I maintain our position off to the side and watch her go.

The old man slowly tries to retrieve his possessions, which are now widely scattered around the area. It is a pathetic sight and it makes me sad and angry. The old man manages to gather a small bundle. Then he is once again accosted by the young thug.

"If you like these flowers so much, I think you should eat them. What do you say, guys? Don't you think this old man should have flowers for dinner?" His friends hold the passive old man against the wall while flowers are shoved in his face.

"Eat! Eat or I'll break your face!"

They wrench his head back and force flowers into his mouth, in full view of the dozens of people who are passing the scene. Onlookers pause briefly to see what is happening, but then they proceed. No one says a word to the attackers and the old man does not resist or make a sound. It is one of the cruelest public displays I have ever witnessed, and I cannot understand why no one objects. Everyone walking by basically ignores the spectacle.

"I wonder what they do when no one is looking," I say to Cris.

"I wish I wasn't looking," Cris says. "But I can't stand it any longer." Cris walks over to the perpetrators.

"That's enough!" he says firmly.

"Who the fuck are you?"

"I'm the guy who just said that's enough. You've had your fun. Now let him go and leave him alone."

At that moment Monica arrives back on the scene with a white policeman. I am happy to see reinforcements and silently compliment her good timing.

"What's going on here?" the policeman asks.

Cris clearly explains the situation, from the time we first saw the old man. He pretends he does not know Monica and gives an accurate description of the recent events. He is respectful to the officer, and presents himself as a calm objective observer, albeit with an American accent.

The Afrikaner attacker interrupts often and quickly proves himself to be a drunken, aggressive imbecile. He justifies his actions by expressing racial slurs. Monica, Cris, and I stand back and watch him make a fool of himself. The policeman listens to the two white sides of the story. He ignores the old man completely and tells the drunken foursome to go home. They laughingly protest their innocence and stagger off down the street. After they have turned the corner, the cop turns and addresses us.

"In the future," he says, "I think it would be wise if you minded your own business. This isn't your country."

"What?" Monica screams. "Mind our own business? Four bullies are terrorizing an old man on a public street and we're supposed to mind our own business?"

"The old man should not have been here," the cop says. "He's lucky I didn't arrest him."

The policeman walks away and leaves us surrounded by a small group of white spectators. Monica looks around and tells them they should all be ashamed of themselves. They say nothing and drift away. She helps the old man retrieve the few flowers that can be salvaged, keeps a couple for herself, and hands the old man a hundred rand bill.

"I am very sorry," she says to him. "From what I can see, most white people in this country are assholes. I apologize on behalf of my race. We're not all that bad."

"God bless you," the old man replies. "They are not all bad either." It is the first sound the old man has made throughout the entire affair. He smiles at us and limps tiredly into the night.

"You showed up just in time," Cris says to Monica. "I was afraid that guy was going to flatten my nose. What about the cop? This fucking place is too much! Let's find a bar."

"You took the words right out of my mouth," I say. "But I don't like things around here at all. Something is very wrong. I can sense it."

We are finishing our second drink when the same policeman enters the bar, accompanied by two men in business suits. They walk over and identify themselves as members of the federal police.

"You are all under arrest," one of the plainclothesmen announces.

"You've got to be kidding," Cris says. "What's the charge?"

"Espionage." These guys look very dangerous to me.

"Oh my god!" Monica shouts. "You people are out of your fucking minds."

"Will you come peacefully or do we have to handcuff you?"

"What choices do we have?" Cris asks.

"None."

We are led out onto the street and loaded into the back of an unmarked van driven by a young white man. The policeman wearing the uniform and one of the plainclothesmen stay behind. The van heads toward the harbor.

"Hey, this isn't the way to the police station," Cris says. I always marvel at Cris's geographical awareness, but I am not prepared for the response it elicits.

"Is that right?" the man riding shotgun says. "You're a pretty smart guy, aren't you?" He draws an automatic pistol and points it at the three of us. If there was any doubt in my mind about the severity of our situation, looking at the pistol in my face removes it all.

"We're not going to any station. We've got something else in mind for you."

I think maybe this is it. That same old premonition tells me my mystery is about to be solved. I hope I receive the solution before I die. I know my death is a given, but the answers are not forthcoming, and I want to know why.

We enter the harbor area, stop at a warehouse near the dark docks, and are led inside a cavernous metal building. There is a lighted office at the far end of the warehouse, and I can see two men moving around inside. Most of the building is dimly lit and empty, except for a few shipping containers off to the sides. It is a long walk for the three of us, particularly because the people with the weapons do not talk, they point our way with their guns. Whenever any of us start to say something, a barrel is pointed at the offending head.

We enter a small room and I nearly faint. Vanessa's Canadian suitor, Dr. Peter Wilson, and my roommate on the freighter, Karl, look at us but say nothing. Glancing over at Cris and Monica, I can see they also recognize Karl.

"Peter! I wish I could say it's good to see you. I should have known all along. No one knows better than me that Vanessa is worth killing for. But you should know that you're not her knight in shining armor. You're just not her type."

"Shut up," Peter snaps. I wish Vanessa could see her childhood friend right now, and that we could argue the finer points of his furtive behavior.

"What now, Peter?" I ask, but I already know the answer to that question.

"Now you finally disappear for good. Unfortunately for them," Peter nods toward Cris and Monica, "your friends will be collateral damage."

"Why didn't you do this months ago? And why bring them into it?"

"I made a series of mistakes," Peter replies. "I wanted it to look like an accident. I knew if it was an obvious murder, Vanessa would spend the rest of her life trying to track down the perpetrator. When I discovered you were going to be on the same freighter as Karl, that was my big break. Karl and I go way back. He could kill two birds with one stone. It was like it was meant to be. He could keep an eye on one of our weapon shipments and eliminate you in the process."

"You were lucky those sailors came along when they did," Karl says. "You were about to be tossed overboard."

"You're going out on a ship tonight," Peter smiles. "Never to be seen again. Everyone knows that disappearances like this happen all the time in Africa. Most murders are never solved down here."

"You know something, Karl?" Monica shouts. "Everyone on that boat thought you were a fucking loser. You are. I'm sure you've been an insignificant little shit your entire life. This madman will probably kill *you* before it's all over. Good fucking riddance. Hell is too cold for the likes of you two!"

Once again, I agree with everything Monica says, but I question her timing. Provoking psychotics at this juncture can serve no useful purpose, but nothing is going to make any difference anyway. Our fate is sealed within a warehouse on the waterfront. Where is Brando when I need him? Or Sir Harry Flashman, for that matter.

"She's never going to have anything to do with you, Peter," I say. "At one time I thought you were a competitor. But she feels sorry for you, Peter. If you were the last man on earth, she would never let you touch her. She made me promise to never say this to you, but these are special circumstances. She finds you repulsive on more levels than I can count, starting with your body odor."

"You're the one who is getting out of her life." Peter opens the top drawer of the desk, extracts a stainless steel revolver, and places it on the surface in front of him. "I've only let you live this long so you could see me. I win. You lose."

"I want you to know that she is pregnant with my child. But humor me. Do you ever wear a ski mask?"

"Mostly when I ski," Peter says, laughing.

"What color?"

"Only black. It's always been my color."

"What about back in New York?"

"What about it?"

"The push in front of the train? The car that tried to run me down?"

"Hired thugs. Overpaid flunkies. Failures. I'm the boss. I'll get the job done this time."

Suddenly a side door of the warehouse opens off to my right. Everyone turns as Henderson stride into the room. I consider this to be the final nail in my coffin. Who could be worse than Henderson? I am amazed at the width of the conspiracy and wonder how I've lived as long as I have. After all, these people are real killers. I am just a pathetically good-looking unemployed school teacher who drinks too much. I have always heard that it is better to be killed for love and not money. Now I know it's a toss-up, because the ending is the same.

"What's going on, Hendy?" Peter asks. "What are you doing here?"

"I came here to ask you the same thing," Henderson says. "I was dining downtown when I saw your employees loading these fine people into a van. What's up?"

"This is personal," Peter says. "No offense, but it's none of your business. Our deal is over. Get out now or you might be in the same boat they're going to be in."

Henderson takes a deep breath, puts his hands on his hips, and straightens up with automatic pistols in both hands. He points one at Karl, the other one at Peter, and then he looks over at me.

"I was led to believe you were important. It turns out that you're not important at all. I'm pissed off at my mistake. In reality, you're the nobody you deserve to be. But here I am. Saving your fucking life."

"What are you talking about?" Peter shrieks, and briefly jerks his head toward Karl.

"I'm talking about you being under arrest, Peter. The game's over. I had hoped to burrow a little deeper, but you're right here in front of me. A gun-running bloodthirsty Canadian doctor—now I've seen everything."

"May I interrupt, please?" I shout my loudest and look

at Henderson. " Is this true? Right out of the movies! You're really a good guy?"

"I'm the best!" Henderson says, with a thunderous guffaw. "Too good for you. I've spent a long time cultivating this connection. Now you and your buddies blow my whole scene. I work with Interpol. Wilson here has been a target for a long time. Not the big fish I was headed for, but big enough."

"You?" I am incredulous. "Of all people. How could you ever be a good guy? You're the worst person I've ever met. The ugliest man on earth."

"I love you too, Andreas. You're my secret favorite." Henderson's crazy laugh gets even more outlandish. "Actually, you were a world-class drinking buddy. We had quite a time in Khartoum. But why I felt an obligation to come over here and rescue your sorry ass, I don't know. Don't push it."

"What the fuck?" My world is upside down. I look over at Peter.

At that moment Karl executes a quick hand movement toward his midsection. A bullet from one of Henderson's guns takes the top of Karl's head off. Blood and brains are splattered against the wall, and small pieces of flesh dribble down to the floor.

The sheer volume of the weapon stuns me, but the crumpled bleeding body both sickens me and helps clear my mind. I realize that the impossible has happened. We have been saved by none other than the hated Henderson, and I find the rapid change of fortune impossible to comprehend. I look at Henderson and then over at Peter.

"I don't want to be too dramatic here, Peter," Henderson says with his toothy smile. "And I hate to sound like Clint Eastwood, but you would be doing the world a favor by trying the same move as Karl."

"You lying, double-crossing son of a bitch," Peter says.

"That's exactly what I am. Andreas here learned that in the Sudan. Now he wants to come over here and kiss my fat ass."

"You're wrong there, Hendy," I say evenly, having regained my composure by avoiding looking at what's left of Karl. "Right now I'm willing to suck your fat dick if that's what you want.

It's up to you. Anything you want."

"I should have followed my first impulse," Henderson retorts, obviously in his element. "I should have waited until they killed you before I made the bust. There is nothing more effective in a court of law than innocent dead bodies as evidence. Plus, I wouldn't have to be putting up with you right now. Oddly enough, you owe your lives to a flower vendor. I didn't know anything about what was coming down here tonight. Our deal was done. I got interrupted during dinner by this old Tamil man who wouldn't take no for an answer. He insisted I take a look down the street. I got there just in time to see you guys being loaded in the van."

"What happens now?" I ask. I know it cannot get much better than this.

"We'll need you around town. Only for a couple of days. A lot of legal shit has to be straightened out. After that you're free to go. What are your plans? Go back and do stand-up comedy in New York?"

"I'm flying to Canada as soon as I can."

"What for?"

"Long story. Chasing a woman I guess. I'm going to be a father. She's the reason this guy wanted to kill me."

"Don't tell me you're in love? Not you?"

"You got it. I'm at her command. When she says come I do. That's a double entendre."

While I am still looking at Henderson, Peter Wilson, Vanessa's old family friend, the respected Canadian doctor, does the unthinkable, and makes Henderson's taunt come true. Wilson grabs the gun from his desk. Before he can even raise it, Henderson pulls both triggers on both guns. Blood drips down between Wilson's eyes and there is a hole on the left side of his chest. He manages a crooked smile as he slides down the wall. There is no guilt on his face, only jealousy and resentment.

"Are we having fun yet, Hendy?" I am shaking so violently that I have to grab the back of the chair in front of me just to steady myself.

"I hate this shit." Henderson can hardly be heard. "But I sure cleaned up your life, didn't I? He shouldn't have tried that.

It was stupid."

"You saved my life. You saved their lives too." I nod toward Cris and Monica. "You're an unbelievable fucking hero. Someone should write a book about you. Make a movie. The truth is stranger than fiction."

I look over at Cris and Monica. Neither has moved since Henderson entered the room. Tears are streaming down Monica's cheeks but she does not say a word. Cris stares stoically straight ahead. He looks like a condemned prisoner calmly awaiting the firing squad. That is what we all expected. Death was certain and we all knew it.

Henderson finally ushers us out of the building and into a waiting unmarked car. We are herded into the back seat while Henderson lumbers into the front and shakes hands with the driver.

"Where do you guys want to go?" the African driver asks Henderson while continuing to shake his hand and smile.

"Ask them," Henderson says.

"Who's buying?" I ask. "I need a drink."

Henderson pokes the driver with his elbow. He turns all the way around and looks at the three of us in the back seat, before zeroing in on me.

"Your next forty-eight hours are on me, buddy. I can write it off as security. The sky's the limit. I'll bet you can't beat an offer like that, can you?"

"I think you'll regret it when you see my bar tab," I say.

"We owe you our lives," Monica says, still trembling. "If I ever have a child, I'm going to name it Henderson."

"Try not to brag too much about me being the father." Henderson has the best white man laugh I have ever heard.

EPILOGUE
Five Years Later

THINGS WERE NOT always perfect during the early days in my new adopted country. I learned that Canada is actually a foreign country, in more ways than one. The final weeks of Vanessa's pregnancy were hard, mostly for her. When I told her I felt her pain, she made it clear that I didn't really have any idea. As usual, I stood corrected. Living with my in-laws after the hasty civil ceremony was difficult. Her parents viewed me with suspicion and behaved with formal reserve at all times. I was so ecstatic to still be alive, and living with their only child, that I did my best to ingratiate myself to them, with mixed success.

"Vanessa, your parents get nervous when I have four cups of coffee. They can't believe anyone could be so weak and self-indulgent. Four cups in one day! What's wrong with me? Your father has never been drunk. Not once in his life, for god's sake. What's wrong with him? No curiosity? Do they ever do it doggy style? Just to make the canines feel more comfortable. How can you possibly be related to these people? I don't think I have anything in common with them. Their definition of recreation is working hard, reading a periodical, and going to bed early."

"I told you they would take some getting used to."

"Getting used to? They're obsessed. I hate to make an accusation like this, because they *are* your parents, and I know you love them, but they're worse than Mormons. That's a horrible thing to say about anyone. I apologize."

" At least they're not religious."

"It's their only saving grace. That and the fact that they put up with me, the son-in-law from hell."

"Don't be silly, Andreas," she laughs. "They like you. They think you're funny."

"Oh sure, every father likes the guy who knocks up his daughter and takes off."

"Believe me, you two are already friends."

"I feel like I've entered a monastery, the whole thing is based on clean living and self- discipline. Tell me it's not true."

"I can't tell a lie," she jokes. "But your perceptions are not accurate. They are welcoming you with open arms."

"This is how they treat people they like?"

"Give it time."

The time I gave it passed like the blink of my eye. I learned to admire her family and friends, but sometimes wished they were not all so pale and polite. But that is the world as it is, and I acknowledge that I am one of the luckiest guys who ever lived. It all began by being born a white male. That was certainly a big leg up for me right away, and there was just nothing I could do about it.

One thing I had to do right away was find a job and make a living. I enjoyed teaching in New York and decided to pursue the same vocation in Banff. Citizenship and a credential took time and money. Thankfully, my parents became more generous, their grandchildren increasingly became the center of their lives, and they spent accordingly. They got two grandkids at the same time. Our daughter, Malika, was born twenty minutes before her brother, Karston.

We have been lucky to live where we do. Banff is an attractive place to visit for people from all over the world. Subsequently, old friends have come to visit over the years. Cris has stayed with us on three different occasions. He loves hiking in the Northern Rockies, and we have done horse trips on the trails in Jasper National Park.

Kerry is happily married to a wealthy gynecologist and lives on the beach in Santa Monica. They've flown up to Calgary three times in his twin engine airplane and laugh about high altitude blowjobs. They always rent the largest suites in the grandest hotels and frequently have the four of us over for dinner.

Monica married Veronika. They appear quite content "living life to its fullest." Shivering when I think about what that might imply, I hope I'm the only one who remembers that night in Amsterdam. Monica is still working for her agency and the two of them travel extensively. They really like children and stop in Alberta occasionally. Our children think they are the funniest people on the planet.

Mousa and Ingrid split their time between Europe and East Africa. They spend most of their working time on environmental issues. We stay in contact and hear they are planning a family.

Henderson is the mystery I have not been able to solve. And never will. After Durban he dropped off the face of the earth. There is no record of him anywhere. In fact, there is no record of me as well, or Cris and Monica. The three of us have investigated extensively. No one has ever heard of him. The South African authorities I contact deny everything I say.

"Daddy, daddy! Come look. Look what we've done."

"Oh man, give me a break," I groan. "I've been following you two around all day."

"Mommy, come look what we've done. It's the best."

"I'm sure it is, but I've got work to do. My concert is this weekend and I'm behind schedule. Andreas, would you please entertain these two urchins while I make some calls. I promise that once this concert is over I'll be your love interest once again."

I take the twins on a hike we have done many times. The three of us pack a lunch and have a favorite picnic spot along the trail, near the creek. Both little Malika and little Karston caught their first fish here. It has always been a very special place for all of us.

"Daddy, who really rides horses better? You or mom?"

"Your mother is actually much better than me at everything. But promise not to tell her I told you."